# The View
# From Who I Was

Heather Sappenfield

Woodbury, Minnesota

First Edition
First Printing, 2015

Book design by Bob Gaul
Cover design by Lisa Novak
Cover image: iStockphoto.com/8220664/©Milous

Viktor Schauberger quotes taken from *Living Energies* by Callum Coats, 2nd edition, published by Gill & Macmillan, Dublin, Ireland © 2001. Used by Permission.

Quotations on divider pages from Emily Dickinson, "To learn the transport by the pain." All Dickinson quotations from *Poems* by Emily Dickinson, First and Second Series, edited by Mabel Loomis Todd and Thomas Wentworth Higginson.

Flux, an imprint of Llewellyn Worldwide Ltd.

This is a work of fiction. Names, characters, places, and incidents are either the product of the author's imagination or are used fictitiously, and any resemblance to actual persons living or dead, business establishments, events, or locales is entirely coincidental.

**Library of Congress Cataloging-in-Publication Data**
Sappenfield, Heather.
 The view from who I was/Heather Sappenfield.—First edition.
    pages cm
 Summary: As part of herself observes, eighteen-year-old Oona Antunes attempts suicide, tries to pull her family and her life back together, and begins to understand her own problems and those of her parents before finally becoming one with herself again.
 ISBN 978-0-7387-4174-1
[1. Suicide—Fiction. 2. Family problems—Fiction. 3. Depression, Mental —Fiction. 4. Dating (Social customs)—Fiction. 5. Portuguese Americans —Fiction. 6. High schools—Fiction. 7. Schools—Fiction. 8. Colorado— Fiction.] I. Title.
 PZ7.S27Vie 2015
 [Fic]—dc23
                                                              2014031276

Flux
Llewellyn Worldwide Ltd.
2143 Wooddale Drive
Woodbury, MN 55125-2989
www.fluxnow.com

Printed in the United States of America

*For all the teens I've known.*
*The ones who chose death, most of all.*

*Killing yourself seems like an end
when you're doing it,
but really,
for everyone else,
it's a beginning.
Especially if you don't die.*
—Oona Antunes

# Part One

*As Blind Men Learn the Sun*

# One

FROM OONA'S JOURNAL:

*Water must be treated as something alive.*

—Viktor Schauberger

I finally split in two when I was on the dance floor. Gabe held my hand, grooving like crazy, his bow tie gone, his white shirt wide open at the neck as he mouthed the words to the song with Ashley. Ash, with her up-do and gauzy blue dress, was Cinderella's look-alike except for her plunging cleavage. Her date, Kyle, heaved over with laughter.

A great knife of honesty swooped in and sliced me down the center. There wasn't blood. Instead, *I* escaped, rushing out of that pink satin bag and darting into the silver and blue balloons crowding the ceiling. I stretched out like a genie released from a lamp and watched my body flinch back in stunned surprise. *I* became *we* and *she*.

It was a kick up there, luxuriating in freedom, watching myself try to dance, try to act like I was having as good a time as everyone else in the dim light under that flashing disco ball. The whole room seemed to writhe like the amoebas we'd studied in AP Bio, gathered from Crystal Creek behind school and pressed between slides under a microscope. But it grew more sad, really. Sad to watch my drunk body keep faking it, acting like it was fun and it meant something. I named her Corpse.

My body survived that one song. As they weaved back to our table, Corpse told Gabe she needed to use the bathroom, and I knew she was finally going to do it. With that shell-pink, spaghetti-strap gown against her olive skin and her brown hair cascading down her back, she was gorgeous. I'd never seen myself from this perspective, and for the first time I understood why people made such a big deal about our looks. But it no longer mattered.

On her head rode a rhinestone crown. Ashley had been voted Snow Queen of the winter formal, but it didn't fit around Ash's up-do, so the minute she'd come off the stage, she'd slipped that glittering crown right on our head, saying, "I want this back." For some reason, we liked it there. It kept making everybody crack up, but we didn't do it for laughs.

Corpse leaked a tear, but I didn't, and I realized this was the way it had always been: her wanting to cry, love, whatever, and me not allowing it. She shocked me, then, by lunging and grabbing Gabe's arm as he was pulling out his chair. She spun him to her and kissed him. Really kissed him, like never before. His arms slid around her, and I almost came down, almost shot back within her to feel that kiss.

"What was that for?" He spoke over the music.

Her gaze roamed his face. She touched that one left dimple, loved his lopsided look with those shining dark eyes. Lips to his ear, she said, "You're so good. So good a person. Thank you."

His grin faded.

She kissed his cheek and strode past the ice sculpture swan on the dessert table, under the blue-and-silver heart-arch, and out the door. As she strolled by the bathroom and down the hotel hall, it was the first time in as long as I could remember that she hadn't had to force one foot in front of the other. We were flowing. Free. A maiden liberated from her tower of confusion. She swerved out a side door marked *Emergency Exit*, threw back her head, and laughed. I laughed with her. Rapunzel headed for a date with Rip Van Winkle.

We'd been considering this for weeks. In English class we were studying poetry, which had become our oxygen. But before that, we'd read this book, *Into Thin Air*. A really good book about climbing Mount Everest, but sad. Really sad, because in the end, eight of twenty-three people freeze to death. Yet overall, as a means of death, it seemed a pretty sweet exit. You just relax in the cold, staring at the stars until you get sleepy. Sign us up.

Corpse strolled through Crystal Village—trees coated with lights, lampposts with garlands. She passed ski shops, fur shops, T-shirt shops, a heated fountain shooting arcs of water, art galleries, jewelry stores, fireplaces with decorative iron logs that tourists milled about, laughing, talking. A toy store, two candy stores, a coffee shop, restaurants.

She moved toward the bus station, not feeling the cold, just smiling in the mountain air with freezing teeth. Like Miss America in a parade.

People stared, but she didn't care. She started to feel things were really going her way when the red and amber lights of the bus to our house were right there, preparing to pull out, the click and hiss of the brakes releasing and steamy exhaust rising from underneath, a wreath wired to the front. That late at night, the bus didn't come often.

It was just me and Corpse, four loud drunk guys in the back, and the driver. He kept looking in his rearview mirror at her. His round, brown spectacles made him seem like an owl. I couldn't blame him really. I mean, it wasn't every day a princess got on his bus. He was probably concerned that the drunk guys were going to harass her, but he didn't know they couldn't hurt her. That she wasn't in the same place. It was weird, floating against the ceiling with the ads, watching myself gaze out the window with that serene smile. I realized I knew everything Corpse experienced, yet all she knew of me was a hollowness from her toes to that crown, as if she'd lost her shadow from the inside out.

She stepped off the bus at the stop near our house, but instead of walking toward home, she turned right and headed up the trail where we'd hiked with Gabe last fall. Where, surrounded by yellowed aspens and grasses cast velvety orange by a setting sun, he'd said, "I love you," and given us the heart-pendant necklace, the replacement heart that had nursed us along. Now she could feel its refrigerated outline against her chest, touched it. She wished we'd said *I love you* right back. But it had been so long since we'd felt anything but numb, and though we'd lied plenty, we could never lie to Gabe.

She found the first real use for spike heels as she forged up the snow-packed trail. She wore these strappy numbers, shell-pink of course, and she lifted her skirt like a curtain and dug in those ice-pick heels. That, combined with grabbing the aspens lining the trail, made the climb easy despite her dress dragging along the snow corridor.

After about fifty steps, the trail turned right, leveled out, and snaked toward the ski mountain. She walked about a hundred yards to this spot we loved in summer and fall because of all the wildflowers and the brook that bubbled by. We'd watch that new water flow past for hours as if it held an answer. That night, it lay beneath three feet of snow.

Corpse felt lucky again when she found that the wide, flat rock where we'd hoped to sit had been wiped clear by snowshoers. She climbed onto it and scooched back till she was at its center. She wrapped her bare arms round her satin legs and gazed at the stars. I darted up and perched in a tree. A white-plate moon spotlighted her smile, her crown, and her little veils of breath.

Her ears had pounded with the bass beat from the dance, but now it was wearing off, and in its place was ringing, which matched her shaking. After a while both stopped, and she heard just mute winter night and the distant highway. Through the aspen trunks, headlights zinged by. We'd never have to beeline toward anything ever again.

A fluty sound seemed to seep from below. The brook, Corpse guessed.

Her thoughts, her movements, grew syrupy, and she sensed Sugeidi hovering over her like a ghost in the stupid maid dress Mom insisted she wear. That's "Sue-hay-dee," by the way. Mexican. It took us forever to say it right, but after, it rolled off our tongue way easier than "Mom." Sugeidi's wise face and mouth pressed to lines, but Corpse swatted away the image, noticed that the numbness in her fingers had crept up her arms. She thought *This will kill Mom*, and pictured her at our memorial service in a black designer dress, clingy of course, dabbing Kleenex to her perfect face. Thinking of how she'd resent us for the rest of her life was better than any fairy tale. We banished thoughts of Dad.

I recited this poem we'd first heard in English class. Ms. Summers was an Emily Dickinson fanatic, and she viewed it as her duty to teach us the poet's lesser-known poems. She read it great from a page-yellowed edition published by Dickinson's actual friends after she died. Ms. Summers said those friends stomped all over Dickinson's punctuation to make it conform with the times. That our class would compare this version with the original—an archived photo of it written in Dickinson's own hand—so we'd understand the real poet.

As Ms. Summers read, we stared out the window, transfixed on the autumn mountainside, awed at finally realizing what we needed to do. Later, we copied both versions into our journal and memorized it, so its lines could course through our head like a song. My genie voice was soft as a breeze rustling leaves. I couldn't discern if Corpse could hear me while I talked, but her head tilted as if she strained to listen.

*To learn the transport by the pain,*
*As blind men learn the sun;*
*To die of thirst, suspecting*
*That brooks in meadows run;*

*To stay the homesick, homesick feet*
*Upon a foreign shore*
*Haunted by native lands, the while,*
*And blue, beloved air—*

*This is the sovereign anguish,*
*This the signal woe! ...*

Signal? Precisely. Poor Ms. Summers had no clue she'd plotted our map.

After a while Corpse slumped to her side, bare shoulder against snow-crusted rock, crown nudging up. When her chest settled into a steady rise and fall, I took one last look at this alpine world I loved. At the ridges, sharp silhouettes in the moonlight that turned jagged as they curved to the valley's end.

My gaze dropped to where our house would lie. I pictured the pond bordering our yard, Crystal Creek feeding it, the golf course fairway beyond, how evening made it all glow. Mom probably lay asleep. Sugeidi was with her grown kids at the trailer park down the valley. Dad, somewhere in the sky, raced toward us in his private jet.

*Goodbye*, I said. Crystal Creek fed the pond and continued flowing to our left, a vein through our life that passed the ski mountain, town, school, Gabe and Ash dancing at the winter formal. It flowed past the stretch of homes till the trailer park, and then the airport thirty miles beyond. *Goodbye.* I took in my audience of stars, the inky space between them. *See you soon.* I drifted down and curled against Corpse. I wrapped my arm on her arm, matched my breath to her breath, and lost myself in slumber.

# Two

FROM OONA'S JOURNAL:

*Water exists in the natural environment in all three of*
*matter's physical states: solid, liquid, and gas. It is the*
*only common substance to do so.*

—Biology: Life's Course

As we lay there, body transforming to ice, we had this
dream. Actually, more like reliving a day from three
months back. Like we were right there again.

I'd better rewind beyond that, so all this makes sense.

Our name's Oona Antunes. Yes, it's weird. That's "An-
tune-ayes," accent on the "ayes." Dad's Portuguese, lived
there as a kid. Everyone at school thought it sounded like
a rock star's name. Oona came from Mom's mom, who's a
nightmare. Her dad's a jerk too. Dad's parents? They died
when he was ten. He never talked about it. As if he talked
about anything.

Loads of people at school called us Tunes. Even some

teachers. "Hey, Tunes," people used to say in the hall. Music was our soul. Always it surrounded us. But then our favorite songs started landing in the wrong places in our ears, and words became our music, especially poetry. Especially Emily Dickinson.

Once, Ms. Summers kept us after class and told us we could be a writer, that some of our phrases made her sit back in her chair and roll them around her mouth. We didn't have the heart to tell her science was our true love. Anyway, with our looks, our grades, our name, we were sort of a phenomenon. Oh yes, and we'd been one of the stars of the soccer team. A killer defender.

As a desperate effort to get Tunes back on track, Mr. Handler, our school counselor, invited us to represent Crystal High at the annual leadership conference in Denver. Mr. Handler had always called us Oona, and even though he wore golf shirts every day with little logos on the fronts, he was smart as a fox. Instead of inviting us into his office, like the year before, he called home during the day and left a message.

Mom loved things that made her look golden, plus she'd known Mr. Handler for years from sitting next to him at Crystal Village Foundation board meetings, so despite us saying no, we rode down in a school van with two juniors and Clark Millhouse, Senior Class President. Sophomore and junior years, we'd been Clark's vice-president. We wondered how Mr. Handler had gotten Paul Thomas, Clark's VP this year, to stay home.

We sat next to Clark, straining not to lean against him

as the highway curved over passes and descended through valleys. So awkward. Clark didn't say anything. He understood we were miserable. Clark had always been cool that way. You'd never notice Clark in a crowd. Built like a chestnut-haired flagpole, 6'2" or so, his claim to fame was a creamy complexion I envied. He also never treated us like we were some goddess, so we respected him.

The two juniors up front jabbered non-stop, making Mr. Handler nod like one of those bobble-head dolls you see in windshields, but his eyes were steady on us in the rear-view mirror. Clark seemed not to notice, but we glared back.

The conference center brimmed with kids from across the region. At the registration table, the five of us snagged our bulletins, agreed to meet back for lunch, and went our separate ways. They strolled around the hall's corner, Mr. Handler glancing back, but we bolted out the front doors to Starbucks, where we spent most of the morning.

There was a fountain out front, and we sketched a picture of it in our journal. It shot timed arcs of water that reminded us of ballet. There was a fountain like this back home in Crystal Village, but we'd never stopped to watch it. Now we got lost in how those opaque tubes bent through the air like live things.

Afterward, we window-shopped on the Sixteenth Street Mall, not interested in anything. We bought a pricey shirt on the credit card our parents gave us, though. We'd make sure Mom saw it, so she'd know we'd ditched.

This isn't the stuff we dreamed, by the way. What we dreamed started with lunch.

The five of us ended up in an Indian restaurant's round booth, colorful, distracting Bollywood music videos on a TV above and the waiters practically running. It was that busy. Everyone else's babble about their morning and Mr. Handler's expression when we had nothing to say made us feel guilty, so as everyone thumbed through their bulletins to plan their afternoons, we tried not to watch the videos, to look interested instead. Mr. Handler announced he was going to a session titled "Native American Perspectives."

"In March, I'm going to be a guest counselor at a Native American school in Utah," he said. "These folks presenting are from there." He wore a sky blue golf shirt, our favorite color.

"You're not leaving, are you?" Clark said.

"No. I'll just be gone a week. Remember? I go every year, first week of March." Mr. Handler glanced at us. He was handsome for an older guy. Gray streaked through his blond hair in that good way. But the concern in his face made us study his shirt's logo of a curling wave and wish he'd stop trying to save us. We hated disappointing people.

Then we pictured our house. It was filled it with priceless Native American artifacts. Stuff that should be in museums, stuff in glass, stuff you couldn't touch. As if our family hadn't transplanted from Chicago just before we started kindergarten. Mom couldn't care less about Native Americans. She just thought it was cool to decorate her Colorado mountain home like that. The peace pipe over the fireplace, the kachinas on the built-in shelves, the beaded moccasins hanging above; all emitted this energy that whispered *bullshit, bullshit, bullshit,* and it creeped us out.

"I'll go with you," we said, planning to gather facts to toss in Mom's face.

Mr. Handler beamed. "Excellent!" His eyes matched his shirt.

Lunch took forever, so we arrived at the session minutes before it started. People spilled out the doorway, obviously planning to watch from there.

"Great," we said, like *this sucks.*

Mr. Handler peered in, between the folks in the door. "There's space on the floor," he said.

We rolled our eyes.

"Come on," he said and disappeared into the room.

The people in the doorway parted and gawked at us. What could we do? We weaved between standing bodies along the room's wall, squeezed between three rows of chairs arranged in a big circle, and stepped over laps on the floor to where Mr. Handler was settling in. As usual, eyes bored into us.

Time was, mirrors reflected the slight up-curve of our nose, our high cheekbones, our big chocolate eyes, how these features played off each other like singing voices melding in a harmony worth sighs. Anymore, though, our reflection was metal screeching against metal, and everywhere we went, eyes seemed to cringe.

Just as we sat down, a stocky guy with a crew-cut stepped to the microphone. He nodded to Mr. Handler, and Mr. Handler nodded back.

"Dr. Myron Benson teaches at Sego Ridge School and is our flute master," the crew-cut guy said. He sat back down and bowed his head.

Okay, we thought, that's different. Usually some windbag introduced the sessions. The lights dimmed, and Dr. Benson rose in front of his chair but did not go to the mic. With his hair drawn into a long braid, limbs sinewy even through his clothes, he hunched forward and lifted a wooden flute to his lips, but he held it like a clarinet.

A reedy note leaked out that reached across the room and yanked up goose bumps on our flesh. The flute rose to a higher note, then a lower one. Graceful. Simple. It moved into a tune like nothing we'd ever heard, like a conversation with the dirt beneath this concrete city. Every note demanded our attention and reached into a place so deep we felt drunk. I know this sounds weird, but it took us to the aspens and pines around our house, while at the same time sending a sparking charge out our limbs. It was sound-wave honesty, and we felt we'd crumble to pieces.

As Dr. Benson sat down, we realized we'd pulled our knees to our chin like a little kid, so we lowered our legs in the sliver of space. The room was body-heat steamy and pin-drop silent.

"Wow!" Mr. Handler whispered.

The crew-cut guy stepped to the mic again, and we noticed a row of Native American students seated behind him. "Our students will now read for you," he said and sat down.

One of two long-haired girls stood and held out a

piece of paper, brilliant white in the low light. Her eyebrows were vivid arches. The natural curve of her mouth matched her eyebrows. Energy rippled through the room. We felt our listening heart.

The girl spoke in a foreign language, her voice soft, lilting. "I am Angel Davis of the Fort Defiance Navajo," she translated. "I will read an essay." She cleared her throat. "I hold in my hand four feathers." She held up her hand, and out the sides of her fist were the ends of long feathers. "Gifts from my grandfather. Each feather for a good thing I've done." Angel read about how her grandfather was Lakota Sioux while her grandmother was Navajo. She described each of those good things: graduating middle school, attending the Sego Ridge School far from home, completing a summer writing program even farther away, and reading at this conference. She didn't candy-coat things; she just described each challenge she didn't want to do at first, and how after, her grandfather walked with her to a sacred place behind their house where he gave her a feather. Her sentences filled our body till we smashed a tear like a mosquito and smeared it away.

The feathers had belonged to her grandfather's father, his father before that. "I must respect these feathers and treat them with care. Through them the spirits of these birds live on. Through me the traditions of my grandfather's people live on." Angel sat down, and the crowd went wild.

We closed our eyes, crossed our arms, and traced our ribs' structure, willing them not to crack wide.

"We are people who survive in two worlds." It was

the crew-cut guy's voice. "We are of our tribe, yet we are of the United States." He said "United States" like he was careful to enunciate each letter.

His voice blurred as we pictured the self Mom expected us to be: beautiful, brilliant daughter, never veering from the beeline of her future at Yale. When had we stopped wanting that? And why? Who did we want to be? We knew who we'd become, knew every morning we pried ourself out of bed from beneath that heavy thing pressing our chest. We couldn't try in school, in soccer, with friends. Nothing.

Mom said it was rebellion against her. She was so wrong. Emptiness had swallowed us. The only thing that mattered was Gabe, but we weren't honest enough with ourself to admit it.

We remembered last Christmas, when our grandparents, Mom's parents, bickered with Dad and bullied Mom over presents, over dinner, mean air filling the house till it felt like we breathed bullets. No feathers handed out there, just a Kindle, a cashmere sweater, and some new skis. We scanned around the conference room; it would be embarrassing to leave.

A hulking, broad-faced guy was speaking of his grandmother, who for months sewed his dance "regalia." We gulped his words as he spoke of traveling to pow-wows, of how when he danced, he danced for his grand-mother, and for his ancestors. *Ancestors?* Was he kidding? The guy wore a white Oxford shirt with short sleeves and a tie. Dorky by any standard, yet when he finished, the applause and shouts were wild. We considered *our* ancestors, and everything stretched to slow motion. We stared straight down a screeching well.

The self we pictured split to thirds: the view of who our family wanted us to be, the view of who we thought we were, the view of us right then.

We couldn't breathe. We shot up, lurched over bodies, squeezed between chairs, and plunged like a drunk through the people in the doorway. In the bright hall, we staggered to the bathroom, found an empty stall, and locked the door. Our palms pushed back the skin at our temples and our mouth stretched in a silent wail, gasping at the air like a fish. We wished for Mom to cradle us, rock us, but we blinked it away. And Dad hug us? What a laugh. He was always working. In Chicago. Our family lived in a seven-million-dollar house, had a maid, Range Rovers, a Porsche, a private jet. We had everything, yet nothing. Oona Antunes: nothing. From nothing.

When we emerged from the bathroom, Mr. Handler was leaning against the wall. Our eyes were puffy, our nose still running.

"Pretty intense, that session," he said.

We looked away.

"Oona," he said, making us look at him, "I'm always here to listen."

We snorted and wiped our nose with our sleeve.

"Really. Keeping whatever it is bottled inside won't help."

"I'm okay." We shrugged.

"No, you're not. Anyone can see that."

"Please," we said, "not now."

"Soon?"

We nodded to get him off our back. Each day since then, we'd spiraled toward that frosty trail.

# Three

FROM OONA'S JOURNAL:

*For water to exist, two hydrogen and one oxygen atom
desire to congregate, cooperate, to be together. What
makes them come together? Could it be love?*

—Viktor Schauberger

Angels. That's what I'd hoped we'd wake up to. Heavenly
chiming all around with pastel light and clouds cradling
us. Instead Mom's harpy face glared down. The bones
under her pale jaw sharp as an arrow. I fled to the ceiling,
felt sorry for Corpse, who had to face her.

Corpse lifted her hand, dangling a tube and a wire. A
heart monitor whined *bleep-bleep-bleep.* A plastic bracelet
circled her wrist that read *Oona Antunes.* Still us. In hell.

Her other hand, her right one, felt weird. The first and
second fingers and thumb were normal, but the rest were
wrapped in gauze, and where her pinkie and ring finger
should have been was air. She gaped at her hand, could

feel those two missing fingers wiggle. Her right shoulder and arm were wrapped in gauze too. She threw back the thin blanket and sheet over her legs, and where pinkie toes should have been were empty spaces. Below her blue hospital gown, gauze patchworked her legs.

Her face itched, and she realized a cottony, metal smell. She brought her hand to it, trailing the wire and tube, which led to a clear bag of liquid hanging from a pole behind her. Bandages covered her nose. She reached up. Of course, the crown was long gone. I pictured her arriving on a stretcher with that pink dress flowing over the sides and that crown twinkling on her head. A nurse stomped into my image and called out in a New York accent, "Wheredaya want the princess?" Corpse swallowed back bile.

"At least they could fix your nose," Mom said. "A graft from your rear. Seems fitting, somehow."

Mom had this clear, ringing voice that had developed a little scrape in it over the last few years, and her words hung in the air. She seemed to hear her words and sort of barked. A laugh, I guess. An unrefined sound that must have appalled her, and she walked to the window and stood like a stone. I studied her blonde hair's silky side-part, the way its ends collapsed against the soft place before her shoulders. She didn't seem so tall, so ominous, from up against the white ceiling panels. Her temples resembled blue-veined granite.

Corpse saw Dad, then; Mom had been blocking him. Perched on a metal chair in the corner, he wore khaki pants and a bulky sweater instead of a suit, and that drove home more than anything else how long we must have been unconscious. Dad's plane wasn't supposed to even land till we got home from the dance.

He inched to Corpse's side. He pressed his forehead to the bed and shuddered. Corpse gaped at him. Usually Dad was all edges, making your eyes skim off him.

"I'm sorry, Dad." Corpse's normal deep voice was so high, so like a kid, that it jolted me. "I didn't mean to hurt you."

Mom spun from the window. "And what about me?"

Corpse shook her head like she'd lost control of it. The drugs pumping through that tube blurred things, and even without them, we had only a vague sense of why we'd tried to kill ourself. Figuring it out was like peering for a needle through ice.

"Don't!" Mom said. She stood there like she'd shatter if you tapped her in the right spot.

Dad faced her. "Don't what, Muriel?"

I felt sick for him. For her. They stood, not moving, like gladiators preparing to hack away at each other. Dad's hair along the back of his head was a perfect line above a thread of pale skin, and Corpse imagined him in a barber's chair as a razor buzzed along his neck, his sideburns. Such an ordinary thing, yet we could count the ordinary things we knew about Dad on one hand. Make that our right.

Mom and Dad kept glaring, and the width of his back, though he'd turned fifty, was narrower than Gabe's. Then Mom sagged, her hand covered her mouth, and she rushed out the door.

Dad turned to Corpse, almost soft again. His eyes had always seemed black; now they were chocolate. Matched hers. It was freaky, those puddle eyes, yet they seared every inch of her face.

"Things are going to get better, princess." He lifted his palm over her hair, but that hand just hovered. He returned it, carefully, to the bed. Never had he even come close to petting us. He'd called us "princess" all our life, though. A hollow word. As if saying it when he was home one day a week made up for the wide stretches of time he missed. As if it were some sort of replacement for holding us in a blue moment, or listening to us complain about something dumb.

"Don't, Dad," Corpse said. "Just don't, okay?"

Mom's "don't" still hung in the air, and Dad's and Corpse's eyes met.

"I mean it, Oona," he said. "No more Chicago. I'm working remote from now on. I'm a new man."

"Don't." That child's voice again.

"You'll see," he said, like she hadn't spoken.

Her invisible fingers and toes screamed. She gnawed her bottom lip and rocked a little.

"How did you fi—" she said.

"My plane had just landed. Gabe phoned your mother in a panic, had been searching for you for nearly two hours. She phoned the police, thinking you'd been abducted—you've always been so pretty. We've always worried about that. But never this." Dad buried his face in the blanket then, and we felt about as low-down as a person could feel. Finally he sat up, eyes raw but dry, and said, "The bus driver heard about it on his radio, and he called in that you'd ridden to our stop."

We remembered the driver's owl eyes in that wide rearview mirror.

"Your heel marks on the trail were a dead giveaway," Dad said. At "dead," his eyes flickered with something that made Corpse look closer. The machine's translation of her heart sped up: *bleep-bleep-bleep.*

"Oona, that was the worst night of my life. Never do that again."

That was saying a lot, since his parents had died when he was ten. Dad kept mum about it like it was a national secret, like everything to do with his life. Anyway, that's how he'd come from Portugal to live with his uncle in America.

Corpse stared at her bandaged hand. These were the most words we'd ever heard from him at once, and we needed to let them seep in.

"Oona." He made her look at him. "Promise?"

She didn't respond.

"Please, princess."

"Don't call me princess anymore," she said. I couldn't believe she'd said that. Especially since Dad was trying.

His mouth sagged open, a little to the left. He straightened. "Okay. If you promise."

I willed her not to make that promise, not to offer anything to anyone.

"Okay, *princess.*" He rose. "Gabe and Ashley are in the waiting room."

"No! Dad!"

He studied her.

"I can't see them yet. I just can't. Not here. Not for a while."

"Oona, it's been ten days."

"Ten?" She shook her head. "I just can't."

I was with her on that. We hadn't planned to still be alive, and witnessing how much we'd damaged everyone else hurt worse than our wailing fingers and toes. Ash had been our best friend since kindergarten, though anymore, she was exactly the kind of person we'd killed ourself not to be.

And good, honest Gabe. How would we ever face Gabe? We'd only allowed him into our life after we'd started to lose track of ourself. Otherwise, we'd have always known we weren't worthy. Corpse pressed her head into the pillow and wondered how she would live without him. She inhaled the rusty smell trapped in her nose. Who would want the monster she'd become?

"I'll go tell them, then," Dad said, and as he walked to the door, his shoulders, steely as a rule, stooped like the guys' at school when they sucker-punched each other in the halls. I could almost hear lockers slamming.

"Dad?" Corpse said.

He paused, hand on the knob.

"I promise."

Our first promise to Dad. Our first anything with him. Ever.

# Four

FROM OONA'S JOURNAL:

*Birds do not fly, they are flown,*
*fish do not swim, they are swum.*

—Viktor Schauberger

When Corpse asked what happened after Dad, Gabe, and the police found us snoozing under the moon, the doctor popped his stethoscope from his ears, stepped back, and handed his clipboard to his nurse. He looked at Corpse with stern gray eyes that matched his hair and told her she'd had no pulse.

Yet the paramedics had wrapped her in blankets, strapped her to a stretcher, and rushed her along that narrow trail to an ambulance. The hospital was five minutes away, and on the trip there, and after she arrived, her heart said *Nope.* So the ER doc and nurses performed "cardiopulmonary bypass for re-warming." Basically, they'd cut slits in her groin and slid tubes into her that pumped warm saline every ninety seconds. For seven minutes, no heart-beat. Then they detected a pulse. Guess her heart wouldn't beat unless her body warmed up. He estimated she was dead for twenty minutes.

Gangrene had set in "uncannily fast," he said, so they amputated her fingers and toes. Mom insisted they reconstruct her nose and cheek right away, which, from the doc's expression, was also unusual, but I guess since the hospital's largest financial donor was asking, they did it. All this lay in murky, painkiller memory.

He told Corpse she might feel uncoordinated for life. He told her she might have brain damage. He told her she'd probably get pneumonia. He said her temperature when she was rescued was 74 degrees. He said it was a miracle she'd lived. He didn't mention the crown.

Live? She wasn't sure how to do that, so she just endured each breath.

We finally rode home in Dad's Porsche, to our Tuscan villa filled with Native American artifacts on a golf course in the Colorado Rockies. Go figure. But I guess the White House was modeled after ancient Greece, so whatever. Except weren't they going for that democracy theme? What were our parents going for? *Look how rich we are*? *Look at our castle in the mountains*? All we knew was it felt like a swanky hotel. Home? No way.

Chateau Antunes was constructed of stucco and stone and had a turret on one end, an observatory with a copper roof on the other. Part of that roof rolled back to glass beneath. On that one night a week when Dad was home, we could usually find him in there, leather recliner stretched out, gazing at the sea of stars, a highball glass balanced on his stomach, its amber liquid rocking on his breaths. And always, drifting down from the speakers, this same CD of a woman singing mournful songs in a foreign language.

Star charts hung on the walls. A huge telescope stood in the room's center. But Dad usually just lay back and gazed up. I guess he was fascinated by the atmosphere and the universe. Once, as we built a sandcastle on the beach in the Bahamas, one of our few memories with Dad, he said the sky was actually one big ocean, the universe beyond, too. Ocean upon ocean upon ocean.

"What do you mean?" We were only nine but excited at this rare moment with him. We were the one building that sand castle, and Dad just knelt next to us. We squatted, gripping a red plastic shovel. Down the beach, three seagulls squawked to flight and hovered, wailing. Dad glanced at them and scanned the sky. We craned over our shoulder to look at the loud birds and tried to imagine them swimming through the air.

"It starts with the sun," Dad said. "Its energy strikes the earth's atmosphere. That atmosphere moves and rushes in response. It becomes currents, which swell and thin, creating weather. This weather blows across the ocean, making waves. The waves roll onto the shore, finally depositing the sun's energy as ripples in the sand. It's a long, long journey."

His eyes slid across our cheek to the sea and then to someplace far away. We imagined it was to himself as a kid in Portugal. He would have been only a year older.

The grown-up kneeling next to us transformed to a boy. He nodded, kept nodding, so lost and sad. We looked at the sun, then back at him, and he was Dad again.

"Will you help me build my castle?" we said.

He smiled so sadly.

"Dad?"

He rose, brushed sand from his knees, and walked away.

A sort of shiver passed through us, a sensation like sound buckling air, and *I* was born. I watched him move away from us through her eyes, reasoning, doubting, judging what we'd done to make him leave.

Now, at eighteen, we'd wander soundlessly down the long, plank-floored hallway from our bedroom, unable to sleep, and yearn to crawl into that recliner beside Dad. But he was made of sharp edges, so we'd just hover in the doorway, silent, and watch him scan that abyss. We imagined him drifting on that singer's sad words, searching for an anchor.

Sometimes we'd picture Mom, snoozing like a rock in their turret bedroom at the house's other end, the fake fireplace that passes through to their bathroom blazing away. Usually, though, she'd be downstairs in the theater, curled in a recliner of her own, watching a movie, sleepless too.

Now Corpse lay propped up in pillows, me hovering at her shoulder. Against her leg leaned our bible: the Schauberger book. Open in her lap rested the leather journal Gabe gave us last September, for our eighteenth birthday. On its tooled-leather cover, a giant oak stretched across a hillside. For four months we'd been scrimping on homework and writing in that journal instead. Like I said, we'd been a whiz in school, especially science. Lately we'd been fascinated by water, so most of the pages were about that. We'd also copied our favorite Dickinson poems into it: first from an online reproduction of those socially acceptable versions her friends had published, then, beside each, line-for-line, their original archived versions. We'd even tried to mirror Dickinson's handwriting—her narrow dashes, her forward slant, her round loop for capital letters. Corpse ran her finger down the margins between those first published poems and their real selves, wondering.

She turned to a blank page and scrawled *orbits* and *breathe*, below. Below that, *home.*

Writing in our journal used to help, but now it hurt. Her pencil and the two fingers holding it were suspended over air. Her thumb tired fast. Typing would be nigh impossible.

I'd been trying to puzzle out what I was. I'd always been our thinker, reasoner, doubter, but now I was out here. A spirit? A soul? That didn't seem right. Was this permanent? She was nothing without me. I considered whether I was like Aladdin's genie, released from the lamp of our body. Yet I was tethered to Corpse's flesh, had found that when she slept, I could stay alert for only minutes after her. I wondered if I had the power to grant her wishes. What would those wishes be? Death was off-limits after her promise to Dad.

Sugeidi trod in, took the half-full glass of water from our nightstand, filled it at our bathroom sink, and set it back down.

"Drink," she said.

"Sugeidi, I can't," Corpse said. "It makes me pee, and my feet are killing me."

"Drink."

Arguing with Sugeidi was like telling a tree to step aside. But the slow, steady way she moved around the house had always comforted us. Corpse took the glass, and for a minute there was only the sound of liquid rolling down her throat. Sugeidi folded back the blanket, once, twice, and unwrapped the gauze covering Corpse's feet. Bloody blisters had formed on the soles, and the rest was patched purplish-blue. They, along with her hands, issued a monotonous ache. A croak caught in Sugeidi's throat.

Sugeidi had lived in Crystal Village for thirteen years. All four of her kids had moved to this tourist valley from Mexico for the high wages unavailable in Monterrey. She'd followed them. Her husband came too, but he was killed a year later in a hotel construction accident. I had a faint memory of finding her crying at the kitchen sink, our six-year-old self hugging her leg to comfort her.

When we were little, she'd been our nanny too. I supposed she still was. Mom gave Sugeidi weekends off, and she stayed with Jesus, her oldest, in their double-wide at the trailer park. She was never much of a talker, we could always feel what Sugeidi was thinking. When she did talk, it was worth listening. English came hard for her, and she selected her words like she selected apples at City Market. Sometimes she'd say a thing, and we'd think *That's not right,* but then we'd consider what the word really meant, see why she'd used it, and realize the many ways of moving through this world.

That one croak she'd just made at the sight of Corpse's feet was an entire lecture.

In our bathroom she ran the tap. Corpse studied the pink beaded purse on our dresser. The one we'd left at the winter formal. Who had delivered it here? In it was our dead cell phone. She blinked at all the texts it must harbor.

Sugeidi carried out the shallow plastic pan that the hospital had sent home with us, sudsy with baby shampoo. Corpse scooched up in the bed. Sugeidi set the pan next to her feet. Corpse lifted her feet, and Sugeidi laid flat a towel, then eased the pan on top. Corpse lowered her feet into the water, sucking air through her teeth. With a soft cloth, Sugeidi washed them while Corpse rocked back and forth, gnawing her lip. Then Corpse set her feet on the towel and Sugeidi dried them as gently as possible. Her gray-streaked hair was pulled into a ponytail at her neck's base, and sweat beaded her brow.

"Do we have to keep the house so hot?" Corpse said.

"You need stay warm."

"But you're sweating."

Sugeidi waved dismissal and set to rewrapping Corpse's feet, careful of the sutures where her pinkie toes had been. I remembered her saying *This little piggy go market*, remembered one of her rare smiles as she said *Wee, wee, wee, all way home*. Those missing toes just about killed her, and before I knew it, Corpse, head tilted with listening, had reached out and petted her hair.

Sugeidi froze. Corpse froze. Sugeidi brought the back of her hand to her mouth. After a minute, she resumed wrapping the gauze.

She put things away in the bathroom. She stood in its doorway, rested her big knuckles on her stern hips, and gave Corpse a look. "Drink."

Corpse lay back. "Okay."

Us giving in like that was rare, and Sugeidi almost smiled.

"Sugeidi," Corpse said, "where's Dad?"

Early each morning he'd come in and watched Corpse sleep, or at least he thought she was asleep. But we'd wake the minute he entered the room and she'd lie frozen, eyes closed, to keep him there. Coffee cup in hand, he'd lean against the wall and stare at her for half an hour, those chocolate eyes from the hospital gone. I'd hover near his shoulders, close as I dared, feeling Corpse longing to make him stay while I dreaded it. After dinner he'd stop in for maybe five minutes. He'd start fidgeting, rise, and say good night.

"In he office," Sugeidi said.

Corpse pictured Dad at his wide, shiny desk, working away, financial news murmuring from the TV mounted on the adjacent wall. He'd gaze at our photograph, maybe miss us when we were right here.

"Sugeidi, where's home to you?" Corpse said.

Sugeidi pressed her lips. She unfolded the blankets over Corpse's legs and smoothed them flat.

"Sugeidi?"

She straightened. "Mexico *es mi sangre, mi* blood. But home *es mi* children. *Y* you."

"Sugeidi." That child's voice. I hated it. Corpse held out her arms, her one bandaged hand.

Sugeidi hugged Corpse in her slow way, a thing she hadn't done since we were in third grade. I drifted to the ceiling. Corpse smelled coffee and eggs in the gray cotton of Sugeidi's stupid maid dress. I thought how we all knew she'd wanted to come help us dress for the winter formal, a thing Mom would never allow. It had been a Saturday, after all. I realized how she would not even have known the horrible thing we'd done until she'd showed up to work Monday morning. Corpse squeezed shut her eyes against how awful that must have been.

"I'm sorry," Corpse said. Sugeidi rocked her carefully.

*She's our real mom*, she thought, and it came to me why Mom had insisted, all these years, that Sugeidi keep wearing that dress. Why it made us so mad.

Corpse whispered, "You're my real mom."

Sugeidi held her at arm's length. She shook her head. "You have one mother, and she die inside."

Corpse snorted. Mom was probably skiing with her girlfriends at that moment. No point asking where she was.

"Oona." We loved how Sugeidi drew out the *Oo* part of our name, made it sound like it could roll across oceans. "You heal her."

"What?"

"Oona. *Es* time. Promise. Heal her. *Y* him. For you." Sugeidi's eyes darted to where I hovered.

Corpse scowled and looked at the lumps in the blanket

made by her feet. Weren't people supposed to be worrying about us?

"*Me lo prometes*," Sugeidi said. "You are wise, strong." She made a fist.

Corpse laughed. "*Promise you*? I'm not wise! I just tried to kill myself!"

"*Sí*. You know now."

"Know what?"

Sugeidi looked out the tall window over our nightstand. "I watch birds ... " She seemed to search for words. "*Se vuelan*."

"What?"

"Birds no fly. Birds adjust the air."

But Corpse had understood the Spanish. We'd read this same idea in our water bible. Had recorded it in our journal, and considered it long and hard because it had brought back that day on the beach with Dad. Had Sugeidi snooped in our journal? Corpse studied Sugeidi, knew she always underestimated her. She pictured Sugeidi sitting in front of her son's trailer, rocking in a chair, head tilted back to study wings overhead. Maybe Sugeidi longed, just once, to soar.

"Use you air. Promise, *querida*."

Sugeidi had called us "loved one" only once before, when we'd broken our leg six years back. Corpse heard a seagull's squawk and felt a weird sort of dawning as she looked across ripples in long-ago sand. "All right," she murmured.

Sugeidi beamed and tucked Corpse's hair behind her ear, a thing she had not done for years. She stood. "Drink."

# Five

FROM OONA'S JOURNAL:

*At 4 °C, water is at its healthiest, most productive, most dense, most life-giving. Water is the only liquid that stops getting more dense as it gets colder.*

—Viktor Schauberger

Gabe arrived in Crystal Village in sixth grade. From Truckee, California. Another ski town. There weren't that many students in our grade, but enough that he and we only passed each other in the flowing halls. Maybe said "hey" once or twice. I remember him being new, more athletic-looking than the other boys, with intensity about his eyes. I remember hearing he was amazing at soccer, that he could juggle the ball a thousand times in a row. No kidding: a thousand. But that's it. Nothing else. We played soccer too, but back then popularity was our culture.

One day in mid-May of our junior year, we'd forgotten our Chemistry book. Again. Mr. Shaw, shaking his head, sent us back to our locker for it. We couldn't seem to get organized, felt we were spiraling off in different directions and couldn't gather ourself, couldn't fathom what was happening. Four tries, it took, to open our locker. We pressed our forehead against the cool metal of its frame to keep from cracking. Glad that we were at the back of the school, in a hall leading only to Calculus.

"Are you okay?" Gabe said.

We flinched.

"Sorry. I didn't mean to scare you." He looked at us with such honest concern. Our brows pinched so close it hurt, and we sensed that craving exactly this was key to our problem, except we had no idea how to accept kindness. The Corpse part of us longed for Dad, then Mom, and I almost gagged. We were seventeen and that was so uncool. We tried to pry our eyebrows apart but couldn't, and then burst into tears. Gabe drew us to him, awkwardly at first, but within minutes we melted. Or she did; I squirmed. Our forehead rested against his shoulder as if we'd been doing that for years. We actually shuddered as we cried. His T-shirt got soaked.

After we cried ourself out, he stroked our hair. Ash came around the corner and gasped. Gabe and we pulled apart.

"Mr. Shaw is pissed," Ash said, and she lingered there, watching. So Ash.

"Thanks," we said over Gabe's shoulder, still looking at him, and wiped our nose with the back of our hand.

"You gonna be okay?" Gabe's voice was so tender, we

bit our lip. We nodded and sniffed. He touched our arm, smiled a little, that one cheek dimpling. "See you," he said.

We watched him walk down the short hall to the classroom, the letters *CAL* on the wooden hall pass poking out of his back jeans pocket. We'd only noticed him on the soccer field, where he scored or assisted goals so remarkable they launched entire stands of fans out of their seats and into cheers.

Ash was beside us in a second. "What was that?"

We glanced where Gabe had gone. "Nothing."

"Right," she said. "Better hope Tanesha doesn't find out.

"Tanesha?"

"Are you blind? She's loved him for years. You look like hell."

We retrieved our Chemistry book, ran our thumb over the print where we'd pressed our forehead against the locker, and closed the door.

After that, we and Gabe would see each other in the halls or the Student Union, and he'd nod to us and we'd nod back. Ash would elbow us in the ribs and we'd say "stop." Usually Tanesha and her sidekick Brandy were somewhere nearby, watching.

He and we didn't run in the same circles. We were popular, and Gabe was, well, Mexican. Not an immigrant like Sugeidi; that was a whole different social group. He was part of the Hernandez family, who'd lived in the area since before the U.S. stole it from Mexico. *Chicano*, I guess, since Gabe's best friend Manny wore a T-shirt that said "Chicano Power" a lot. At Crystal High, Chicanos and Mexicans usually ignored each other, sometimes clashed. Gabe's family owned a respected stone masonry business. When we asked later, he joked there was probably some Ute Indian in his blood too.

His dad had torn his family apart by falling in love with his mom and leaving Crystal Village, following her to Truckee. Gabe's parents fought mostly. One day, he and his dad returned from work and school to find nothing but a note on the kitchen table and an echo when they called her name. Gabe said moving back to Crystal Village just about killed his dad. He kept hoping his wife would return, but he didn't want Gabe to be raised by just him, alone. He wanted Gabe to understand family.

After a while, Ash's elbow stopped jabbing us when we saw Gabe, but we and he still watched for each other, and we couldn't forget how our body had fit against his.

Believe it or not, we'd never had a boyfriend. A couple dates, sure, but dating always seemed pointless. Everyone said Oona Antunes was stuck-up, but there just wasn't anyone we were interested in.

With two days of school left, we and Ash had walked out the building's front doors after the dismissal bell, everyone rowdy with end-of-year frenzy, and there was Gabe, just ahead, with his friends. Tanesha moved in a swarm of girls several paces in front of us. Gabe and his buddies were walking slower, so we caught up to them as we passed into bright sunlight.

We studied the spread of his gray T-shirt over his powerful shoulders, his black hair curled just at the ends, halfway down his neck, the swale where that T-shirt wrinkled as it met his jeans, and we thought how we would not see him again until August.

"Gabe?" we said.

He turned. "Hey."

"Hey," we said.

We realized we were like a rock in a stream and moved out of the way. Ash had been whisked along and waited a few steps down. Ahead of her, Tanesha scowled at us.

"I'll see you later," we called to Ash.

She scowled too, but she headed to her Audi.

"Gabe," Manny Martinez yelled. "You coming or what?"

Gabe looked at him and then at us. "Or what," he yelled.

Manny flung out his arm and walked toward the lot.

We stood there, so awkward. Everybody noticing and staring. It was bright and Gabe squinted as he said, "Want to go for a walk?"

I fought her, but she nodded. "I live about twenty minutes away."

"Yes, I know," he said. "My dad repaired some of the stone on your house. I worked with him a little."

Our mind reeled back two winters to when a car slid off the road into the wall surrounding our yard. That spring, two men had worked out there for a week—the scrape of chinking off a board, the high ring of chisel against stone. We'd never noticed a boy with them. We hadn't given those laborers a second thought.

We strolled along the recreation path that led past town and eventually near our house, moving aside for bikers, walkers, joggers, or roller bladers. We talked about our summer plans. Right after school let out, we would vacation in New York. In July, we were going to a month-long sailing camp in St. Lucia. Gabe planned to work full-time laying stone for his uncle. We kept seeing Gabe's hands, the beautiful pink crescents beneath his fingernails, and wishing they would reach out and draw us close. Not for romance, but for that sense of rightness we'd found nowhere else.

About halfway home, in a spot where the path bent around a huge spruce tree with Crystal Creek beside it, crashing and frothy with snowmelt, he stopped and turned to us. "How's things?" he said. His thumb was hitched in his backpack's strap to keep it tight on his shoulder.

Our eyes slid off him to the water. It eddied in little splashes under the spruce's exposed roots. We looked to the far bank. On the road a hundred yards behind us, a car rolled slowly past. Our cheeks drew tight, our brows pinched close.

"That bad," he said. "Man!"

We started walking again. After a minute, he took our hand. We sighed and he glanced at us. Though I squirmed, we leaned our head against his shoulder for a few steps, and he glanced down again, this time with a sad smile.

At our house, we crossed the street and stopped at the wall, near where it had been repaired. Gabe studied our clasped hands. Down the street the sounds of hammers pounding on a remodel grew suddenly loud. Every summer, our street endured the leveling of at least one perfectly good mansion and the construction of a new monstrosity in its place. Gabe eyed the wall's stonework, scanned Chateau Antunes with its curving drive and greening lawn.

"I should go home," he said.

Our phone issued a muffled beep from inside our backpack. We rolled our eyes.

"That's Ash," we said. "She freaks when she's not in control of my life."

We let go of his hand reluctantly and grew aware that from the chateau our heads would be visible above the shoulder-high wall. Mom would flip, see him as one more rebellion, but she couldn't be farther from the truth.

"That must suck," he said, and it felt so good to be around someone who wasn't Ash's slave. He traced his fingers along his father's work, following a line we couldn't discern, one shoulder cocked back, holding his backpack in place. We noticed a white sock peeking out of a hole in the side of his sneaker. "Not bad," he said. "See you."

"Bye," we said, crossing our arms, hunching a little.

He nodded and started back along the more direct road. We wondered if he'd take the bus when he reached town. We'd never seen him in a car of his own. When he was at the end of our wall, I tried to stop her, but we still said, "Gabe?"

He turned.

Our heartbeat drowned out the hammers. "Would you like my phone number?"

He glanced at the chateau. "You sure?"

We felt his lingering warmth in our palm, pressed it tighter against our ribs.

# Six

FROM OONA'S JOURNAL:

*When water's temperature drops to 0°C, each
hydrogen molecule locks to a maximum of four others.
The hydrogen creates elongated bonds in a lattice that
has 10% less density than water at 4°C.*

—Biology: Life's Course

Mom flung back the curtains in our room, and blinding sunlight screamed in. Corpse blocked it with her palm, squinting.

"Up!" Mom said. "Up. Life goes on."

She took the glass from Corpse's nightstand, walked to the bathroom, and filled it. Corpse sat up.

"Gabe's coming in a bit." Mom set the glass back on the nightstand.

"Mom—"

She held up her hand like a traffic cop. "I saw him in City Market yesterday, and ... " She dropped her arm and took a breath that used half the room's air. "I told him to come by." She glanced at our alarm clock. "He'll be here in half an hour."

Corpse looked at the clock: 9:32.

Sugeidi did the grocery shopping, so I wondered why Mom had even been in City Market.

"Since when are you a Gabe fan?" Corpse said.

Mom studied the three soccer trophies on our dresser, the tournament medals hanging from a hook above, the two framed pictures on the wall beside them, portraits we'd drawn in kindergarten. One was of just us, a big-headed stick figure with hands the same size as the head, sunrays for fingers. A pink triangle for a dress. The other drawing was of our family, standing, not touching, kid in the middle. Dad's head was as big as ours, but square. His hands were tiny. Mom was mostly big yellow hair. Big red lips. Her hands were tiny too. Behind us beamed the sun, yet a spray of stars arced above Dad. We had no feet because we stood in blue, knee-high grass.

"He's a nice boy," Mom said, and her gaze glued to Corpse. One of her eyes squinted, so slight I wouldn't have noticed if I wasn't studying her.

"Gabe loves you," she said as if hypnotized, looking right through Corpse. "If you're lucky enough to have someone actually love you, cherish it."

"Mom?" Corpse said.

She resumed the bearing of a marble statue. "Get dressed." She left.

Corpse's sigh replaced the air Mom had taken. It wasn't

45

that she didn't want to see Gabe, she just couldn't face what we'd done to him.

She threw back the blankets and limped to the bathroom sink. You wouldn't think pinkie toes would make much difference, but her balance was all wrong. Walking hurt, and she could still feel those missing digits. She hunched over from the hollow space I'd left.

In the mirror, a monster stared back. Gauze hid her nose and cheek. The rest of her face was as splotched as a fetid pool. I wondered what Mom had told Gabe, what the rumor mill had spread about us at school. The winter formal had happened over two weeks ago, and I pictured Ash, furious that we hadn't talked to her yet, gushing the details Dad must have told her and Gabe in the hospital. Embellishing them in her frustration.

One morning, chin lifted against humiliation, Mom had announced there was an article about us in *The Daily Crystal* that had caused quite a stir. Since we were eighteen, they'd mentioned our name. I pictured the headline: *DEAD GIRL LIVES.* The following week, there'd been a string of articles on avoiding not only teen suicide but depression too. Apparently, one suicide can trigger an epidemic.

Corpse ran water in the sink and dropped in a yellow washcloth. She spread her newly important left hand on the washcloth, watched the warm water move in rivulets along its bones. Gingerly and awkwardly, using that hand, she cleaned the unbandaged parts of her face and neck. That screeching, so long present when we braved mirrors, was a distant echo. She applied a special cream the doctors had sent home with us and, halfway to her bed, decided to change out of pajamas for the first time since leaving the hospital. She slid into her favorite jeans, watching her feet disappear into the legs and then poke out the ends.

"The last time I wore these, I was whole," she said. She tugged her favorite forest-green sweater over her head. At the mirror, she brushed her hair and studied its lustrous waves. This, at least, was unchanged. I saw a wig on carrion.

Corpse made her bed, planning to sit there, but found herself hobbling beneath the hall's arched timbers to the kitchen, hand pressed against the wall for balance. Our first journey from our room. She felt her skin pass through the warm air.

Sugeidi was running water in the sink. Corpse wobbled across open space to a bar that stretched beneath a big rock arch. On the bar's other side was countertop and the stove. When designing Chateau Antunes, Dad had insisted the stove be right there, so he could flip pancakes from the pan onto our plates, but he'd never actually done it. Never even cooked pancakes. He'd never once kicked the soccer ball with us either, though he watched games most Saturday evenings in the theater, and I played my heart out, hoping one day he'd watch me. Sometimes we'd join him in the theater, but he'd just become angles and stare at the game like we were invisible. Usually, we went out with Ash.

Sugeidi shut off the water, looked out the window over the sink, and turned. Her hand flew to her heart. "*Dios mio!*"

"You really should turn down the heat."

"No sneak!" she said.

They stared at each other, and Sugeidi burst into a smile.

"What I make for you?" She always asked this way about what she could cook for our breakfast, lunch, or dinner if Mom and Dad were gone, which was mostly.

We'd always loved the rock arch over the bar, one of the few cozy places in Chateau Antunes. Now it blocked my view, from either side. I decided to roam around the kitchen's plaster ceiling.

"Gabe's coming," Corpse said.

"*Sí*," she said. "*Esta bien.*"

"*That's good*? Since when?"

Sugeidi had flipped out the first time Gabe showed up at the house, had given us a month-long silent lecture. Mom and Dad were right there with her. I'd hurled silence back. We'd waged a silent war over prejudice.

"Omelet?" Sugeidi said. Gabe's favorite.

"Sure," Corpse said.

It was trippy, seeing the kitchen from up there. The chandelier, the tops of the cupboards, were spotless.

Sugeidi opened the elevator-sized, stainless steel fridge, plucked out eggs and cheese, and ferried them to the counter. She took down her favorite frying pan from its hook and set it on the burner, lit the gas. As she cracked eggs into a bowl and started to whisk them, Corpse said, "What do I say? I'm hideous." She cupped her face in her hands. I had to agree.

The doorbell rang. Sugeidi started toward it, but Mom answered. Sugeidi and Corpse looked at each other in surprise. Voices carried down the hall, Mom's formal yet laced with that scratch, Gabe's low but strong. Corpse turned shivery, listened for but could not hear their steps on the strip of carpet that ran down the hardwood, so she imagined them moving along, the last seconds of the old Oona still alive in Gabe's mind. I drifted to the ceiling's farthest corner. They entered the kitchen.

Corpse braced for his revulsion and turned on her stool toward him.

Gabe took in her nose and cheek, moved down her body, pausing at her hand, and on to her bandaged feet before returning to her face, his own face so tense. Corpse looked at the floor's wide stones.

"I'm sorry," she said. That little-girl voice. She didn't move, but she heard Sugeidi flip the sizzling omelet in the pan, smelled melting cheese. Gabe's sneaker appeared in Corpse's view of the floor, and she looked up as he climbed onto the stool beside her.

"Orange juice, Gabe?" Mom said.

"Yes, please," he said, and as she opened the fridge, a look passed between Sugeidi, Gabe, and Corpse because Mom never waited on anyone, especially not Gabe. Mom poured two tall glasses and set them on the counter before them.

Dad entered the kitchen, in chinos and a cardigan sweater, coffee cup in hand. We all tensed. Especially him.

"Well, look at this," he said. "Oona, you're up. And hello, Gabe."

"Mr. Antunes," Gabe said. Brave, considering how Dad had treated him in the past, despite our defending him, telling Dad he might even be valedictorian and how much courage that took because all his friends made fun of him. What happened in that hospital waiting room the night I died?

Dad dumped his cup in the sink and filled it with fresh coffee at the machine. He took a sip and surveyed us over the rim. His eyes lingered on Mom, and her chin lifted like a challenge.

"Well." Dad nodded. Nodded like he didn't realize he was doing it as he looked at each of us in turn except Sugeidi, whose back was to him. His phone rang. He answered it like a lifeline, and left. Mom stared after him, her face a stone. We all listened to his voice move down the hall.

That nodding was new. That nodding was weird. It conjured that day at the ocean.

Sugeidi cut the omelet with a spatula and put the halves on separate plates. Usually Gabe and Corpse shared a whole omelet on one plate. Sugeidi looked straight at Gabe as she set his half before him, and they had an entire conversation with their eyes that went like this:

Sugeidi: I've never liked you, but I accept you now.
Gabe: It's about time.
Sugeidi: I feel bad for you, but don't you hurt her.
Gabe: Who do you think I am?
Sugeidi: Sorry.
Gabe: No problem.

Mom watched too, with an expression like she'd tasted

something delicious but didn't want to like it. Sugeidi put the egg bowl in the sink and the cheese back in the fridge.

Mom said, "Sugeidi, I need you to help me with those boxes in the library. I'm sure these two have plenty to talk about."

Corpse practically fell off her stool. Gabe froze with a bite poised on his fork, cheese strings hanging long.

Alone, they just ate. Corpse had hardly eaten anything since we'd come home, but right then, there was nothing else but to eat. Gabe finished, laid his fork on his plate and scooted it forward, then turned and pushed everything but Corpse out of focus. I slunk from my corner to the chandelier.

"Remember that day in the hall, when we first met for real?" he said.

Corpse nodded but could not meet his gaze. She thought how he must be seeing the gauze on her cheek, her right hand.

"I knew what I was getting into, and I watched you sink, deeper and deeper. It sucked. You know this."

She nodded, felt like she'd swallowed sand.

"Oona," he said, "I never cared how you looked. Sure, it helped, I'm not going to lie. But in the beginning, you being so popular, so pretty—it was something I had to overcome. I got a lot of shit about it. You know that."

She nodded and thought of Tanesha's gang and Manny.

Quiet settled over them.

"My mom was white. And very pretty. I never told you. But even Dad gave me a hard time about you."

I slunk closer to them.

Corpse rolled her lips tight and stared at the fraying on the knees of Gabe's jeans. He wore the sneakers she'd given him for his eighteenth birthday, only a week after our own birthday.

"I love you," he said. "Do you get that?"

Corpse's bandaged hand drifted to her heart necklace, pressed it hard against her skin.

"I walked away from you in the hall that first time," Gabe said, "and I could hardly see straight, I was so in love with you already. I can handle all the crap from my family, my friends." He looked down the hall. "Your family. I could handle you being so sad over whatever was eating you."

Corpse couldn't nod, couldn't fathom how someone could love a person who was so screwed up.

"What I don't know if I can handle is how you looked me right in the eye and walked away to kill yourself."

"I'm sorry," Corpse said, little voice. I felt about that small too.

"I don't know if I can handle it. Do you get it?" Gabe said.

She nodded. I wished we could explain why we'd done it. Yet even if I was in there helping, giving her that hard edge, there are some things without words. Our actions would have to talk now.

Gabe wiped his cheek, and that just about killed us. Corpse imagined a tear pooling in his dimple. She swallowed against the hollowness inside her. She straightened.

"I know now," she said.

"Know what?"

I sensed what was coming and braced. We weren't qualified for love.

"That I ..." She looked down.

Gabe slumped back on his stool, and his hands fell to his lap. Corpse studied the pink crescents beneath his fingernails. After a minute, he reached out and turned her to him fully, a gentle motion. At her collarbone, he traced the necklace's imprint. He put his other hand on her other leg.

"Does this hurt?" he said.

Corpse shook her head. I realized she was lifting her chin just like Mom. Understood, then, that it was love's plea.

Corpse and Gabe leaned forward, pressed their fore-heads together, and that did hurt, but Corpse didn't care. I couldn't stop myself. I curled into the arch of their bodies.

# Seven

FROM OONA'S JOURNAL:

*As two substances with different temperatures are put together, the cooler substance increases the kinetic energy of the warmer one. This makes heat move from the warmer to the cooler substance until the substances are the same temperature. An ice cube, for example, absorbs a drink's heat rather than cools it.*

—Biology: Life's Course

Gabe, Ash, and Corpse played LIFE in Chateau Antunes's museum living room—the board laid out, the money and cards in neat piles on the coffee table next to a beach-ball-sized silver saucer mounded with pistachios. Two Christmases ago we'd asked for the game, picturing us and Mom and Dad seated around it, actually laughing like the family in the commercial. After unwrapping it, we'd set the game on this coffee table, in plain sight for the whole day.

No one said a word about it, though, and we never worked up the courage to ask them to play. Pathetic. And

Corpse played it now? After Ash had shown up at the door, Gabe had said "Do you have any games?" and gotten it out to ease the tension. As if. Funny how things work.

Corpse slouched on the velvety couch, Ash in the leather chair adjacent, a dancing kachina doll under glass on the end table at their elbows. Gabe sat on the floor, a Turkish carpet beneath him, the wide gas fireplace flaming over his shoulder. Above its carved wooden mantel hung the peace pipe, a carved-stone eagle's head for its bowl and three feathers draping from its stem by rawhide laces. I floated around the room, inspecting Mom's higher-placed artifacts up close.

"I still can't believe Gabe saw you first," Ash said, joking but also not. "Honestly, Oona, we've been best friends forever."

Corpse's eyes met Gabe's. Over the last week, he'd visited every day.

"Anyway, so now Paula and Kyle are an item and I'm single. After all that," Ash said. "Paula's such a jerk. I've always hated her."

Corpse felt the familiar sandpaper rub of Ash's remarks. I supposed Ash had texted us about breaking up with Kyle, but Corpse hadn't even turned on our phone since the dance. Ash obviously thought she was being ignored. I guess we were ignoring her, ignoring the world, by not even opening that beaded purse. How had we been so blind to how her every word ground us down?

Gabe and Corpse said at the same time, "It's your turn, Ash."

"Okay," she said, like *whatever*. She leaned forward, her

fuzzy, V-neck sweater flashing cleavage, and spun the plastic wheel in the board's center. It whirred like a gear. Ash counted out her spaces and moved her tiny orange car forward. They were all halfway across the board; had careers and starter homes, were just building their fortunes.

When had Ash started wearing low-cut shirts every single day?

"Payday and a raise. Goodie! Give me ninety-thousand dollars," she said.

Gabe counted out the money as Corpse spun the wheel.

"God, I don't want to go to school tomorrow. Mondays suck," Ash said.

Corpse couldn't even think about school. She still tired like she was a thousand years old, and her missing digits wailed. Faint purple crescents hung below her eyes, and though the bandages were off, her cheek resembled a tilled field. Mostly, though, we weren't ready to face the stares that had nothing to do with her appearance. We'd accumulated enough credits to graduate after first semester, so it didn't matter if she was there. Besides, it had dawned on us last spring, just before Gabe arrived in our life, that Yale would never deny us acceptance—Dad had established a monster scholarship fund for immigrant students there. All our hard-earned A's had been for nothing. Actually, that's not true; the A's had come easy.

"Olivia and Dylan broke up too, did I tell you?" Ash said. "I've always thought he's such a hottie."

Corpse moved her car along the spaces, feeling Ash's

gossip turn the world gooey. *You got the looks, but I got the cleavage,* Ash had said the night of the winter formal, when we'd given Ash's dress a double-take. She'd changed so much.

Or had she? Maybe we'd changed. Ash had been our best friend since kindergarten, after all. I reached back and found memory after memory of her bossing us around. Each time, we settled into a glazed place, a translucent barrier that numbed us.

Mom entered, carrying a silver tray with a pitcher of Sugeidi's *limonada*, three glasses, and a bowl of barbecue chips. Gabe moved the pistachios, and Mom negotiated the tray onto the coffee table.

"There. Enjoy," she said.

Gabe and Ash said, "Thanks."

Mom dropped her manicured hands to her sides, thumbs rubbing her fingers. A shaft of sun from the window veered off her face, making her seem miles away.

"That was nice, Mom. Thanks," Corpse said.

Mom recognized the game, the only one in our house. We didn't even have cards. "Didn't you get that for Christmas?" she said.

"Yes," Corpse said, real careful.

All of a sudden, Mom seemed to get it. Her eyes met Corpses's:

Mom: That game was for me.
Corpse: Yep.

"Well," Mom said, and she left, trailing a sense of longing.

57

"Since when does your mom do that?" Ash whispered. "She wasn't wearing makeup, either. Just mascara. Wow! You really got to her."

"Ash!" Gabe had been reclining back on one arm, and he lunged forward.

"Gabe, it's okay. Really," Corpse said. She noticed how Ash's face had taken on an oily sheen that she'd masked with powder. "Mom's trying. All right?"

"Where's my crown, anyway?"

"I'm sorry, Ash." Corpse paled as I pictured the doctors and nurses standing around her on the operating table, guffawing at that crown.

"Ash." Gabe's body looked like a weapon.

Ash studied him for a moment. She fluffed her hair. "My mom said your mom hasn't been to ski group or Foundation meetings or yoga since … you know. Hanging close, I guess. Where's your dad?" Ash said this last with a toss of her head. She knew just how to hurt us.

"Working. Downstairs," Corpse said.

"Well, at least one thing hasn't changed," she said. "Your turn, Gabe."

He glared at her, then spun the wheel, that sound spraying out between them. He didn't move his car, though. Instead he lurched up and stalked to the window, a view of our front yard, the wall, the mountainside where we'd tried to kill ourself.

Ash watched him with one eyebrow raised. "Touchy."

He turned on her. "It's nothing to joke about!"

"What are we going to do? Spend the rest of our life

tiptoeing around Oona's problems? Besides, we all know she just did it for attention."

Gabe was at Ash in three strides. He loomed over her, and she recoiled in the chair.

"She died, Ash! Do you get it? She was dead! See if that will stay in your empty head!"

We'd never seen him like this. He stepped back, chest rising and falling in that same light Mom had stood in, except Gabe looked velvet, illuminated motes dancing around him.

Was this the rumor Ash was spreading? From where I'd drifted, in the ceiling's farthest corner, it was obvious Ash viewed Corpse with a sense of entitlement. As if she were a low-cut sweater, or a car. Mom had been the same way. I remembered Mom standing there moments ago, looking so new, so unsure how to behave. Corpse felt herself settling into that glazed place. She sat up straight, forcing it back.

Ash rose. "Okay. I'm done." I had to admire her nonchalance. "I'll leave you two lovebirds alone. It's not like I was invited anyway." She strolled to the door, lifted her fitted pink parka from its hook on the wall. Pulled it on. Zipped it to her cleavage.

"Ash," Corpse said and limped to her. Ash gripped the knob.

"I'm sorry," Corpse said. "I can't explain anything right now. Not even to myself."

"Look," Ash said, "I know you think I'm an idiot."

"I don't think you're—"

"Admit it."

"Ash—"

"You're my best friend, Oona. You've always been my best friend. Couldn't you have even texted me?" Ash's eyes turned glassy.

"I just . . . I can't . . . something about the way life used to be made me do this. I'm afraid to go back. Does that make sense?"

"You think I—"

"No! Ash, I just . . . after something like this, who's dating whom . . . It just doesn't matter."

Ash looked down and wiped her nose. "*Whom*? Wouldn't Ms. Summers be proud. You always were a brainiac." She looked up, and her cheeks matched her coat. She shut the door. From the window beside it, Corpse watched her climb into her little Audi and zip away.

Corpse averted her eyes from the mountain where we'd frozen, but she felt the cold on her limbs, the hardness of that rock under her butt. She sensed me then, watching her.

"She doesn't get it," Gabe said from his window.

Corpse turned at the sound of him putting away the game. She knelt beside him and helped clean up, glancing over her shoulder. Toward me.

"I have that Physics test tomorrow. I really have to go. Are you okay?" He reached out, stroked Corpse's neck. That touch sent a jolt through her, a heat she'd never felt. In all the time we'd been dating, depression had blocked us from offering Gabe anything more than vacant kisses. She sensed me again—reasoning, doubting, judging. She rolled her shoulders.

"I'm fine. But Ash is right," Corpse said.

"About what?"

"About Dad."

"That he still works all the time?"

"That he keeps us miles away. Even now, when he's right here. In the hospital he was different. He said he was 'a new man,' that things would be different."

Gabe's face turned grim. "Oona, he ..."

"What?"

Gabe sighed and looked around the room, seeming to relive what had just happened with Ash. "Nothing."

---

Our backyard sloped down to Crystal Creek and the golf course fairway on its far bank. The basement opened through floor-to-ceiling glass doors that folded away onto stone patios with comfy furniture. In summer the whole area became indoor-outdoor. Flowers spilled from copper boxes and pots. Even when the river froze over, the snow drifted high, and people Nordic skied along the golf course on groomed tracks. We liked those glass walls. There were two rooms along that glass: the library and Dad's office.

Corpse didn't loiter in Dad's office doorway. Just limped straight in with LIFE under her arm, me trailing like a speech bubble in a comic strip. LIFE's pieces bounced inside, sounding like a tiny marching army.

"Hey, Dad."

He was typing something into a chart and looked up.

"Oona. What a surprise!" He said this like she'd travelled from New York instead of from upstairs. I wished we were up there, that she'd just leave things be.

Corpse settled into the tufted leather chair that faced his desk. She'd never sat in that comfortable-looking chair before, and its hardness surprised her. Dad sat very straight, watching. She watched him.

"What are you doing?" she said.

"Updating a client's portfolio." Boundaries surrounded his words.

Discomfort swelled the air. He clicked off the mur-muring TV with the remote.

"Do you like being a financial manager?" Corpse said. I retreated toward the window wall.

Dad looked as surprised as I was. His chair squeaked as he settled back and considered her question. "It's lucrative."

"What would you do if money didn't matter?" Corpse said.

Dad smiled slyly and his eyes glinted. "Money matters."

"Why?"

"It keeps us safe. Free."

"Safe? Free?"

"We have a roof over our heads, insurance, clothes, food."

Corpse studied the game's upside-down lid in her lap. Warning laced the air, and she tilted her head against it. Her left hand rested on the *I*, with the *E,* the *F,* the *L* surrounding it. "I was wondering"—she felt her nervous words hovering at the edges of themselves—"if you wanted to hang out, play LIFE or something."

Dad looked at the game, and she thought how to him it would appear right-side-up.

"Isn't Gabe here?"

"He left." In a green square on the box's bottom corner, Corpse read *Family, Ages 9+*.

Sweat beads rose on Dad's brow, and though the house was hot, I knew that wasn't why. "Oona, I—" Not a hint of those chocolate eyes.

"That's okay." She bolted up, moving toward the door, that little army marching under her arm. "No worries."

In the hall, Corpse leaned against the wall and shut her eyes. What was she afraid of? A memory rose up like connect the dots: us, a first grader, wanting to hold Mom's hand, but scared and looking up at her as she leaned against this very wall, eyes closed just like this.

# Eight

FROM OONA'S JOURNAL:

*In its liquid form, water's hydrogen bonds are fragile,
lasting only a few trillionths of a second before
bonding with a new partner. This constant, rapid
change creates a phenomenon called cohesion. It is
structure not found in most other liquids.*

—Biology: Life's Course

"So you'll call me if you want a ride home. Or if you need
to come home early." Mom drove her Range Rover slower
than the spitting snow warranted, and the wipers screeked
across the windshield.

"Gabe and I will walk."

"Okay, but if you're tired—"

"I won't be," Corpse said.

"You might get cold."

"I won't."

Mom's look said *Sure you won't*.

She turned into the Crystal High parking lot and

64

steered to the drop-off lane at the front entrance. Gabe waited there, his breaths warm puffs rising on the cold. Corpse watched several puffs disappear. I thought of *The Daily Crystal* article after our suicide, of the angry rumors Ash had probably spread in the month since the winter formal. Today's headline: *DEAD GIRL RETURNS.*

"Oona," Mom said. She reached over and grasped Corpse's hand, and they seemed to look inside one another. The words for something big hung on Mom's lips. Instead she said, "Good luck," and let go.

Corpse nodded and climbed out. Gabe took that hand. They walked up to the entrance. As we crossed through the first set of doors, Mom still watched, and Corpse waved back in the space between her and Gabe's heads. Through me.

My first touch. An electric shock brimming with confusion and longing.

I'd always hated being touched when I was in Corpse, but that was skin. This was way worse. Like touching a person's soul.

Corpse rubbed her two fingers and thumb together like they itched, then rubbed them against her jeans. We passed through the second set of doors and into the building.

We'd forgotten school's smell. The cafeteria's fake butter mixed with the janitor's barfy cleaner. Dr. Bell, the principal, stocky and shorter than half the guys in the school, stood outside his office speaking with two freshmen, but his face lit up when he saw Corpse.

At her shoulder, I reeled. All those years inside, I'd

never allowed her feelings to seep into me. I mean, I knew them intimately. Manipulated them daily. Felt them? Never.

In the school's entrance lobby, across from the main office, stretched a sitting area made of two knee-high carpeted steps. Here, the kids of workers from Mexico or South America hung out. Some mornings they'd all be bawling because a raid at work the day before had rounded up their parents and sent them back home.

"Serves them right," Ash would say, but we understood that sense of no family, of scrambling for footing in air. Even so, I hate to admit we'd felt superior to them. Now they saw Corpse walk in and swarmed together, whispering Spanish.

We climbed the stairs to the first hall of lockers, the slamming and buzz of voices yanking us back to just before we'd died. Corpse lifted her chin to hide that she was gulping air. Gabe squeezed her hand, but she didn't look at him, just squeezed it back.

We moved in a buffer of silence, and Corpse imagined smoke rising off her from the burning gazes. A couple people said, "Hey, Tunes," but everyone else was mute. Tanesha's friends, who ever since we'd started dating Gabe had sent *bitch* barking at our heels, studied Corpse with calculating eyes. As we turned the corner toward the Student Union, I understood that every look, no matter its skin's hue, held fear. This brand of fear could care less about prejudice.

We passed the Student Union's tables and chairs, where Mr. Handler stood, mug of coffee in hand.

"Oona," he announced. "Welcome back!" His kind face just about killed us. Eyes at tables looked up.

"Thanks," Corpse said, not like *thank you* but like *thanks a lot.*

He knew what he'd done, and he chuckled. Like I said, he was smart as a fox.

Ash had the locker beside ours, and she was there, banging books from her backpack into it.

"Hey, Ash," Corpse said and spun her lock's dial. I drifted to the breath-crowded ceiling. Risk getting touched again? No way.

Ash assessed Corpse. "Coming to the Student Union?"

"I'm sorry. I can't do that anymore," Corpse said.

Their eyes had a conversation:

Ash: "You're serious?"
Corpse: "I've always hated it. I just did it for you."
Ash: "Duh."
Corpse: "I'm not trying to be mean."
Ash: "Well, you are."
Corpse: "Still not going."
Ash: "Go to hell!"

Ash slammed her locker and stalked off. Gabe put his hand on Corpse's back.

Taped inside our locker door was our schedule and posters of two soccer players: Lionel Messi and Alex Morgan. Corpse studied them like she was seeing them for the first time. Everything seemed foreign.

"You okay?" Gabe said.

"*Chingado!*" Manny yelled from across the hall. Gabe waved to him.

"Come on," he said, "let's get you to Bio."

Tanesha shot us a vicious look from her locker down the hall. Her mouth resembled a wound as she spoke, and the girls around her turned and looked at Corpse and laughed.

Corpse pulled out her textbook and folder and she and Gabe started back toward AP Bio. Our English class with Ms. Summers was AP too. Last year, we'd taken AP Physics and AP History.

"Gabe." Corpse halted. "I can do this. Your class is right here."

"That's okay," he said.

Corpse didn't budge. "No. I need to do this alone."

His head tilted toward her and he almost smiled. "All right." He slid his hand behind her neck and kissed her forehead. "Be strong."

Everywhere: eyes. Judging Corpse's face, her missing fingers, her limp. As Corpse crossed the Student Union, Ash held court at her usual table near a bank of windows framing Crystal Creek. Two girls flanked her, and popular guys lounged around the rest of the table. One of them leaned on the table and flicked a little triangle of folded paper with his middle finger at a guy who held up his fingers in the shape of a goalpost.

We'd sat right there day after day, in that glazed place, as Ash flirted and schemed and ordered us around. Had we ever been like her? We searched for but could not find a memory of Ash that didn't look through that glaze, and it was weird, seeing her now with such clarity.

"Yes, I'm playing soccer," Ash said real loud, her glance a knife. We'd played soccer together since kindergarten, moving up through Club to high school, where we'd been a starter, left fullback, and Ash had warmed the bench.

Corpse entered the hall to AP Bio, our favorite class. But Ash was our lab partner, and as we approached the room, I dreaded how uncomfortable that was going to be. How Ash even got into the class was a mystery; she wasn't the greatest student. The bell rang as Corpse limped through the door.

Mr. Bonstuber stood at the lectern. He nodded to her and returned to scanning some papers, but everyone else watched Corpse limp to her seat, watched surprise register as she found Clark Millhouse on the stool next to hers. Corpse set her books on the cool black tabletop and slid onto her metal stool.

"Hey," Clark said.

"Hey," Corpse said.

Ash whisked in, giggling, but everyone watched Corpse as Ash rushed to her seat at the back with her new partner.

Clark glanced at Corpse's hand. Mr. Bonstuber started explaining Mendelian genetics in his German accent as he drew a diagram on the whiteboard. Corpse pulled out *Biology: Life's Course* and a blank sheet of paper, tuned out her screaming digits, and scrawled notes with her left hand.

Clark grimaced at her scribble. He leaned close and whispered, "You can borrow mine."

"Thanks," Corpse said.

Mr. Bonstuber might have been the one who switched our partner. Ash was a C student, while Clark was all A's. I wouldn't have put it past Mr. Bonstuber to notice Ash gossiping about us or saying something cruel, and moving her for that reason too. He was that way.

He wore a wrinkled dress shirt, slacks, and some sort of science tie every day, even though most of the faculty was in jeans. Corpse studied the way his shirt, though he was slim, puffed out the back like a water balloon. I noticed a thin gold wedding band on his left hand, couldn't believe I'd missed it before. What would his wife be like? Were they happy together? I had an image of him cradling a faceless woman in a sheer nightgown. Corpse shook her head to banish the thought. We owed Mr. Bonstuber a lot.

Last fall, before class had even started, he'd assigned the textbook's first chapter. About water. Maybe we were bored after a summer of brain atrophy, I'm not sure, but water's properties fascinated us. Its role in all life. When school started, Mr. Bonstuber showed us this YouTube video of a property called "coalescence cascade."

In the video, a drop of water was deposited gently onto the surface of a pool. The drop dipped below the surface, making a ring, and shot back out as two drops. One drop disappeared below the surface. But the smaller, second drop bounced twice and dipped below the surface. We couldn't see it divide this time, but again two smaller drops popped out, one disappearing below, the other bouncing twice and disappearing, shooting out even smaller.

It did this four times, until the tiniest drop disappeared and did not shoot back out, and the pool's surface was eerily still. Mr. Bonstuber explained that as the drop impacted the pool at low speed, a layer of air was trapped beneath it, preventing it from immediately coalescing into the pool. That air layer drained away, and surface tension pulled some of the drop's mass into the pool, but a smaller drop was spit back out. It bounced off the surface of the pool again, and the process was repeated until the viscous properties of the pool became too strong for the drop to withstand coalescing completely.

Later, in a lab on surface tension, we deposited water on a quarter with an eyedropper till there was a towering bulge. We couldn't pull ourself away from the microscope, from how that bulge trembled, and to the beat of Ash popping her gum, we kept seeing that video's drop being spit back out, bouncing on air, until that eerie stillness.

During our lab on capillary action, Ash had surreptitiously checked Facebook and whispered gossip, but we couldn't stop watching how water crawled up the glass tube till it was higher than the beaker's water it stood in. That afternoon we started seeing water migrating up every plant stem, up every tree trunk. We wondered where they stored water for the winter, imagined their long, cold thirst.

After we studied evaporation, we'd picture water rising off those plants and trees, off Crystal Creek and the pond behind Chateau Antunes, off the bodies in the golf carts. The clouds seemed comprised of swirling bits of all these things. When it rained, we'd stand in those cool drops and feel everything around us touch our skin. Then we realized that rain held parts of things from far away, maybe even lingering bits from other continents, and we felt touched by the world. We wondered if events were washed from the air, and even felt history's touch.

Water murmured an answer. An answer to why we were wheeling apart. Just softly enough that we couldn't make out its words. It sucked, that whispering. Once you start sensing water, really sensing it, you can't stop.

We'd been unable to pull away from our last water lab too, amoebas from Crystal Creek, gathered behind school, wriggling between slides. When the bell had rung, Ash had rolled her eyes, said "You're such a geek," and left.

"It's my planning period next," Mr. Bonstuber had said. "Take your time, Oona. I'll write you a pass to your next class. I hate to hinder a fascinated student."

"That's okay," we'd said. "I have the next period free."

"Then take all the time you like." He grinned. "You like biology?"

"I like water. It's so cool."

"Icy, tepid, steaming," he said, that grin twisting on his pun.

We talked about water. He seemed as fascinated with it as we were. We started thinking how he probably needed to get work done, so we started cleaning up. Mr. Bonstuber walked to his desk and, from a shelf behind it, pulled out a soft-cover book.

"You might enjoy this." He handed it to us. "This author explains the life and work of a scientist named Viktor Schauberger. He was born in the late 1800s, and he was unconventional. He believed that water was best studied outside a lab, in its natural environment. Personally, I think both modes are helpful. He's still considered unorthodox, yet his insights are brilliant, profound, and gaining more acceptance as they're being proven true over time. If you like this book, read it and tell me what you think."

That night, after we'd finished our homework, we opened the book and didn't close it till after midnight, copying Schauberger's ideas and words into our journal. *Water must be treated as something alive*, we read, and we leaned close to the page, could see the paper's pores as we said, "Yes." We traced the edges of Schauberger's words and ideas, sensing pieces of ourself defined there. All we knew for sure was we understood that bouncing drop's despair as it diminished, sucked down toward that motionless pool.

# Nine

FROM OONA'S JOURNAL:

*Where water and air meet, the hydrogen molecules*
*bond to one another. This makes the water seem to be*
*protected by an invisible film. This is surface tension.*
*It can be observed when water stands just above the*
*rim of an over-full drinking glass or when a raindrop*
*holds its shape.*

—Biology: Life's Course

Mom waited in the Range Rover, sparse snow whirling down, the clouds too cold to let loose. Corpse climbed in, settled back against the heated leather seat, closed her eyes, and sighed. Mom pulled out, not saying anything. Not even *Buckle your seat belt.*

When we turned off the short road that led to Crystal High, Corpse said, "You were right: I wasn't ready for a whole day. I'm wiped out." I hung near the Range Rover's rear window, wiped out too.

"How'd it go?"

Corpse shrugged. "As good as it could, I guess." She studied the effortless strides of a woman jogging along the plowed sidewalk as they approached her from behind. The woman's ponytail bounced out a hole in the back of her knit hat. She must have been running a while, because the back of her jacket was rimed white with frozen sweat. Corpse tried to imagine the sensation of that woman's strides in her own thighs, in the balls of her feet. "I think everyone's afraid of me," she said.

Mom snorted.

"Mom?"

"Yes?"

"How did Ash and I ever become friends?"

Mom ran her fingers through her hair, seeming to gather her words with the action. "Back then, Cheryl and I were best friends. We were both new in town. Enchanted with being moms in Crystal Village." She glanced at Corpse. "We've drifted apart over the years. People change. You know?"

Corpse nodded.

School had been so busy that I hadn't had a chance to recover from Corpse touching me as we'd walked in, and I tried to dispel that jolt of her pain by relaxing and letting it drift away. But no. It clung to me.

Mom followed the frontage road past the ski village. Cars zinged by on the interstate parallel to us. Corpse scanned Crystal Mountain, the colorful specks shushing down its wide white ribbons through the forest.

"I don't know if I'll be able to ski anymore," she said. "Or play soccer. Or hang with Ash."

Mom pressed her lips into a line. The same bus we'd taken from the dance pulled out of the Transportation Center, and Mom steered around it. At noon, in the lull between the rush to and from the slopes, it was nearly empty.

"No more family ski days." Corpse loosed a high-pitched laugh. Like our family had ever skied together in the first place. "I'm sorry," she said. "You're really trying. I can tell."

Mom sighed but didn't speak, just drove beyond town. The golf course's white expanse stretched out beside us. I could feel Mom's mind racing. She swerved into a pull-out and stopped where people parked to go climb a frozen waterfall that dove off the red cliffs on the golf course's far side. Corpse straightened.

For a minute Mom just looked ahead, but her right eye squinted almost imperceptibly. "Listen," she said. "I got off track. It started shortly after we moved here, and I could blame your father, but the truth is I have no one to blame but myself. Cheryl fed into it; she's been miserable in her marriage for years. We had this hateful pact of suffering that must have fed into you girls. I'm sorry, Oona. For everything. Especially that you felt desperate enough to try to kill yourself." She looked at Corpse with eyes bulging water. Surface tension.

Corpse willed that water on Mom's eyes not to give way. Didn't want to find out she, herself, had no more tears left. "It's not your fault."

The lie seared her tongue. It would burn for Dad too.

A clumsy skate skier glided past, and Mom watched him. Corpse studied the frozen waterfall, and I wondered why frozen water was sometimes white and sometimes translucent as glass, while water suspended in air was invisible.

"No." Mom said. "I'm sure I had a lot to do with it. I know this is hard to understand, but I was stuck for so long. My parents have always been miserable. It just seemed natural." She shook her head. "When I think that I pushed you to suicide—you can't have any idea how that feels. There's that saying about how awful it is when parents outlive their kids. But to outlive your kid because you pushed her to suicide? I'll never forgive myself."

"Mom—"

She held up her hand. "I've thought about this a lot. Any parent of a suicide will forever bear guilt. There's no way around it. It's my penance." She tightened her grip on the steering wheel and peered at the gray sky. "I'm going to be a better mother. I have to hope."

All those years, Dad had always been away in Chicago. When he'd come home, he'd secluded himself in his office or his observatory. Mom must have been so lonely. Maybe lonelier than us. Except instead of spinning apart, she'd spun inward, churning tighter, tighter, till she'd turned to stone. A wave passed through Corpse, like that buckling chill on the beach.

"Are you going to divorce Dad?" Corpse said. Little voice.

Mom shrugged. "Either way, I'll be a better mom."

Corpse remembered Sugeidi saying "Heal her," and one thing finally made sense. One thing was something. Something to hold onto. Mom's hand rested on her thigh. Corpse took it and squeezed.

"Good luck," Corpse said, just like Mom had said it to her that morning.

Mom barked a laugh and brought the backs of her other fingers to her mouth. Those tears still bulged on her eyes. I had to respect Mom: she didn't blink.

We pulled into the garage alongside Corpse's white Range Rover. Corpse wanted nothing to do with that vehicle, never wanted to drive again. Mom caught her staring at it, and their eyes had a conversation:

Mom: Your father wants you to have that.

Corpse: I know.

Mom's eyes traveled across the garage ceiling and walls as if she could see all of Chateau Antunes, and Corpse understood that this house was Dad's idea too. She thought how he'd been gone for so much of her life, and I saw ourself and Mom as women he'd kept locked away. Like possessions. Corpse blinked.

They trudged from the garage through the mudroom into the kitchen and surprised Dad.

"You're home early," he said. He looked between Mom's red-rimmed eyes and Corpse. Suspicion took over his face. "How'd it go?"

Sugeidi appeared in the archway from the hall to our room.

"I just got tired is all," Corpse said.

Dad nodded in that not-knowing way, and we all watched him.

"Sugeidi, will you make Mom and me smoothies for lunch?" Corpse said.

"*Sí.*" She trod toward the fridge.

"Care to join us, Dad?"

Dad backed toward the hall, nodding. He held up his coffee mug like a toast and left.

Mom and Corpse exchanged a glance.

"Give me your coat," Mom said. She took it and stepped into the mudroom.

"*Bueno*, Oona," Sugeidi whispered as she poured berries into the blender. "*Bueno.*"

Mom and Corpse sat at the counter, and Sugeidi served them the smoothies. It was awkward, but also just right.

"What else I make for you?" Sugeidi said.

"That's all I need," Corpse said. "Mom?"

"I'm fine."

Sugeidi took the blender to the sink, rinsed it, and set it in the drying rack on the counter. She dried her hands and started to walk away.

"Sugeidi," Corpse said.

"*Sí?*"

"Have you eaten? Would you like to join us?"

Mom stiffened but she said, "Yes. Join us, Sugeidi."

Sugeidi faltered, a thing I'd never seen, and she walked

to us. "I lunch already," she said, yet she lingered at the counter.

"How many of those dresses do you have?" Corpse said.

Sugeidi looked down at her maid dress. "Three."

"Don't you have to wash them a lot?"

"*Es* nothing."

"Mom, could Sugeidi wear regular clothes to work?"

Mom looked hard at Corpse. "You think I make her wear that dress?" Now she did cry.

Sugeidi studied her hands on the counter. Heat rushed through Corpse.

"Oona," Sugeidi said, "I like wear this. *En* Mexico, *es* uniform of the maid."

Corpse slumped back. After a minute she said, "I'm sorry."

"Was I that bad?" Mom studied Sugeidi's immaculately pressed dress and her lower lip trembled.

"Actually," Corpse said, "maybe I've been worse." I remembered how making Mom suffer had been one of our last freezing thoughts. The day weighed Corpse down, and she bent till her forehead rested against the counter.

Mom's hand came to Corpse's back and rubbed it in a tentative circle. Corpse heard Mom sigh and felt that circle grow firmer. Corpse watched for tears to rain onto her jeans, but felt only her eyes' dryness.

# Ten

FROM OONA'S JOURNAL:

*Compared to other liquids, water loses a large
quantity of heat for each degree of temperature
change, though water resists changing its temperature.
The measure of how a substance resists changing
temperature is called "specific heat."*

—Biology: Life's Course

Mr. Bonstuber had written *Genetics of Drosophila* across the white board. *Drosophila* meant fruit flies. Beneath that, he'd written each step of the lab. Corpse finger-combed her hair into a ponytail and maneuvered it awkwardly through a tie she'd pulled from her jeans pocket. When we used to do this before labs, Ash would roll her eyes and say "Dork." Corpse imagined Ash rolling her eyes at the back of the room.

Clark returned to his seat with the foot-long wooden mount holding four tubes of flies that he'd prepared the week before, while Corpse was still at Chateau Antunes waiting for her face to become socially acceptable. Special blue food filled the bottom of each tube. "Mating pools," Mr. Bonstuber called them. Over the last two weeks, those pools had laid eggs, hatched larvae, pupated, and were now flies, ready for study to determine how certain genetic traits were passed down. Corpse's left hand rested on a sheet of paper with the heading *Female Wild, Male Vestigial*, brilliantly white against the black lab table. On it were six columns, titled *Eyes—Ee, EE, ee,* and *Wings—Ww, WW, ww*. Below the sheet on top were three other sheets differing only in their headings: *Female Vestigial, Male Wild; Female Wild, Male Wild; Female Vestigial, Male Vestigial.*

Clark read step two on the board. "You want to do this?" he said.

Corpse held out her right hand, just a couple Band-Aids masking the healing gaps now.

"So what?" he said. "It's not rocket science. You just slide this brush with the FlyNap inside the rubber stopper."

Ash's giggle drifted to them, and then her voice saying "Ew!" Corpse glanced her direction, and their eyes glued. For a second, Ash's expression matched the one when she was six and had fallen from an aspen tree in Chateau Antunes's front yard. Corpse wanted to rush to her, but Ash straightened and turned away.

"How about I do the first one?" Clark said.

"Okay."

He lifted out a tube and read its label: "Female Wild, Male Vestigial."

Corpse checked the heading at the top of the paper to make sure it matched. Clark took the Q-tip-like brush and pinched back the stopper at the top of the tube as he slid it in. They leaned close to watch the flies conk out; they were supposed to pull out the brush when 90 percent were asleep.

"Clark," Corpse whispered, "how did you become my partner?" She could feel him concentrate on the flies to keep from looking at her.

"Bonstuber stopped me after class. Asked if I wanted to switch."

"You're not afraid of me?"

Clark grinned. "I've never been afraid of you, Oona." He turned quiet, and she could hear him worrying that he'd insulted her by referring to when she was gorgeous. "I'd have been a fool not to switch. Come May, you're undoubtedly valedictorian."

Corpse snorted. "*Was* valedictorian. *Was* everything."

*Was*. Our life had become past tense. I hovered just above everyone, had learned where to linger so I'd be nowhere near a touch. It was trippy looking down at all those black tables from above. The tops of all those heads we'd known most of our life but never seen.

Clark shrugged. "Fact is, you're super smart and a whiz at science."

Corpse grimaced. "I'm not a whiz at anything. Not anymore. Anyway, thanks for doing this."

"They're ready." Clark read step three on the board. He pulled out the stopper and inverted the tube onto a petri dish. "Tap that, will you?" He reached for the dissection microscope and a tool like a fine paintbrush.

Corpse tapped the tube with her two fingers.

"Besides," Clark said, "missing fingers are sexy."

Corpse laughed.

"Don't tell Gabe I said that. He'd kick my ass, and considering his kicking abilities, well…" Clark looked into the microscope, craning his neck and tilting his head the funny way people do when they peer into that invisible world. "Wow!"

Corpse noticed Mr. Bonstuber watching them and understood exactly why he'd made Clark her partner. She smiled at Mr. Bonstuber and scooted her stool closer to Clark.

I thought about the smallness of things making them invisible, and I wondered if the bigness of a thing could make it invisible too.

"Okay, ready?" Clark said.

She picked up her pencil, poised over the paper.

"The red eyes are wild, remember?" he said.

"You just said I was smart."

"Okay, okay. Female wild, female wild, male wild, female wild…"

Corpse made a hash for each type of eye color and then for each type of wing.

They repeated the process for the second tube. When she faltered before sliding the brush inside the stopper, Clark said, "They're fruit flies," and her hand steadied.

She looked into the microscope to count, and was stunned. Fruit flies equal annoying black specs, right? Wrong. Their bodies were almost translucent. The males had darker abdomens, the females striped, yet they were still far lighter than she'd expected. Their thoraxes and heads were orange. Most of their eyes were brick red. Their wings were what transfixed her, though. Gossamer, with four curved veins, they reflected rainbows. Fairy or angel wings.

"Oona?" Clark said.

"Sorry. Male wild, male wild, male vestigial, female wild . . . "

They compiled their data, determining what was dominant, recessive, sex-linked. Later, Corpse would make two graphs from their data and Clark would make two—graphs that would "predict the passing of traits to future generations," according to number eight, the last step on the board.

Finished, Corpse opened the "morgue," a bottle of alcohol clogged with flies. She couldn't move her eyes off all those dead bodies with rainbow wings. Her hands started to shake.

"Can you do this part, Clark?" she said.

When the bell rang, Clark and Corpse gathered their textbooks and folders.

"Yep, missing fingers. Sexy," he said. "That was good for me. How about you?"

A laugh burst from Corpse, and Ash glared at them from the door as she was leaving. That glare felt good, yet Corpse remembered Ash's injured expression.

Gabe was waiting in the Student Union. "Hey," he said.

"Hey, Gabe." Clark mugged a guilty face as he kept walking.

Gabe chuckled. "How was the lab?"

"Really cool. Clark's a great partner."

"He's a lot brainier than your last one," Gabe said.

"That's for sure." Corpse thought how Ash's grade would probably drop now that they weren't paired, thought of how mean she'd been when playing LIFE. That glare as Ash left class started feeling even better.

Gabe assessed Corpse's lingering grin and put his arm around her. She leaned her head against his shoulder. "Should I be jealous?" he said.

"Don't be silly. I'm not dating you for your brains."

"Oh really?" Gabe grinned.

I noticed Tanesha scowling from across the room, and Corpse straightened. "You know," she said, "I have to make graphs of the lab data, so I'm just going to get it done now. In here."

"Okay. See you," he said.

She looked at Gabe's relaxed face and realized how tense it usually was with worry. She touched his dimple.

"Did you get this from your mom or your dad?" she said.

"Neither."

"Recessive." She kissed it. "See you."

The passing bell rang seconds after he left, but all his teachers were being lenient with him in these first days that Corpse was back.

She retrieved her laptop from her locker and settled at a table in the Student Union. The graph was fascinating, and I hovered at her shoulder, watching it take shape.

"Good morning."

I shot to the ceiling, which was littered with gum

wads and pencils from guys having contests to embed them in the Styrofoam tiles. Beside me stretched a brown spray, probably from a can of soda.

Mr. Handler stood at Corpse's elbow. He sipped from his coffee mug. "What are you working on that has you so engrossed?"

"A genetics graph for Bio."

"You do love science." He patted Corpse's shoulder. "Have a minute?"

"I need to finish this."

"It will only take a minute."

"Okay," she said. "I'll be there in a second."

He strolled to the Counseling Center and disappeared through the door.

The Counseling Center had a wall made completely of one-way glass that looked out on the Student Union. It made the office feel open, but everyone knew the glass was really for policing activity. I wondered if he'd been watching her.

She finished the graph and closed her laptop. Now that she wasn't focused on the drosophila, she felt eyes assessing her every move and wished she could shrink into that invisible world. She gathered her papers and tried not to limp as she walked.

The reception area in the Counseling Center was hung with posters—some for colleges, most just cheesy inspirational sayings with solitary people strolling down forested paths or on beaches with seagulls winging against sky. One, of a kitten hanging from a tree branch, proclaimed *Hang in there!* Mrs. Peña, the secretary, smiled at Corpse as she passed through.

"Good," Mr. Handler said as Corpse entered his office. He closed the door but for a crack, and I retreated to a corner near a window. He sat at his desk and crossed his hands. "How are you faring?"

"I'm okay."

"And your parents? How are they?"

Corpse shrugged. "Mom's okay. Dad?" She looked out the window at bare aspens in a courtyard that nobody ever used because there were no doors to it. *Dad's eerie*, she thought, and pushed it away.

"Are you seeing the prescribed therapist?"

"Therapist?"

"I take that as a no." Mr. Handler looked at his hands, pressed them flat against his desk, then recrossed them. Corpse saw that he'd already known this. He was building toward something. "You're eighteen, so you can make your own choices, but if you or your family need counseling, let me know."

Corpse snorted.

Mr. Handler was still for a minute.

"Listen, I know college is probably the farthest thing from your mind right now," he said, "but have you checked your email lately?"

He was right. College?

Miles from our mind. Corpse turned shivery. She concentrated on Mr. Handler's green golf shirt, couldn't quite read the little logo on its breast. Did he get all those shirts from tournaments? Did he buy them from courses he liked? How many golf shirts did he own?

On his hand was a wedding band, and she heard herself ask Mom, "Are you going to divorce Dad?" I wondered if Mr. Handler was a good husband. What made a good husband anyway?

Corpse noticed a desktop photo of him with his two sons when they were both in high school, each holding a golf club and standing in front of a black-and-white checkered flag on a putting green. Blinding smiles on all three as the younger son, who graduated last year, held up a golf ball. Where had that son gone to college? Where had his older brother gone? I couldn't remember.

"I haven't checked my email," Corpse said, sensing Mr. Handler was about to rock her world.

He took a deep breath. "I was copied on an email they sent to you. You're accepted to Yale. Hearing from them this soon without requesting Early Action is unusual. Congratulations."

"Yale," Corpse said.

"Yes, an accomplishment," he said.

She laughed, this weird sound, like stumbling over rocks. "Not for me."

Mr. Handler's brows rose.

"My dad got me in."

"I see," he said. "You shouldn't have a decision from Princeton and Cornell for a month or two."

No decision. More like our life right now.

"I hope this isn't overwhelming, but I thought it might help. Knowing."

"I'm not sure if I want to go to college anymore," Corpse said. "I don't know what I want."

"If you do go, decide what's important to you. Not to anyone else, just to you. You're strong and you're smart, Oona."

Her eyes shot to him, and I heard Sugeidi telling her a similar thing. What did these two see that I didn't?

Mr. Handler nodded. "I leave in two weeks to be a guest counselor at that Native American school. Remember? The one from the convention last fall?"

Corpse straightened, sensed something like a train chugging toward her. Her heart seemed far away, and she strained to hear its thread of beat.

"I wonder if you'd like to come along." It sounded like he was speaking underwater.

"Pardon?" she said.

"I've inquired, and you're welcome there. I've also checked with Dr. Bell, and he's granted permission for you to be gone. Your parents would just need to sign a release. I think it could be beneficial for you. You could help the juniors research colleges, attend a few classes if you feel up to it, or just hang out in a different environment."

"No!" Corpse shot up from her seat. "No way!" She lunged to the door, her head shaking nonstop. "No!" She flung open the door and it banged against the wall. That flute seeped up, making the carpeted floor waver. She felt us imploding in that bathroom stall and swayed. Mr. Handler steadied her by the arm but she yanked it away.

"Just consider it." His words followed her down the hall.

# Eleven

FROM OONA'S JOURNAL:

*As the water in the cylindrical measuring jar is stirred with a rod, the ping-pong ball just wobbles at the bottom. It exhibits no quick tendency to rise, but will eventually do so if the stirring is vigorous enough. However, when an egg, which has a natural tendency to spin on its longitudinal axis, is used instead, it rises very quickly and will stay at the top of the jar for as long as the stirring action is maintained.*

—Coats, Living Energies

Once Corpse had started back to school, the Antunes family began eating dinner together at the long glossy table beneath the dining room's beamed ceiling. Sugeidi would set three cozy seats at one end, light a candle between them, and flick the switch for the gas fireplace that filled the wall behind Mom and passed through to the kitchen. Yep, Chateau Antunes had three fireplaces. At the table's other end, a wall of windows displayed the storybook view of the valley's jagged peaks. This is how we'd eaten for thirteen years' worth of Saturday nights, the one night Dad had been home. Otherwise we'd eaten at the bar in the kitchen, just Sugeidi and us mostly.

Now, Dad strolled in late every night. Mom and Corpse would sit at the table to wait as the sun breathed a golden sigh on those peaks, setting the golf course, the pond, anything white aglow. Corpse would study the fire, how those peaks echoed the flame, until Dad arrived. Mr. Suave, smiling and joking. But his body would be rigid, as if two different people lived in him. It gave Corpse the shivers. Mom seemed to ignore it. Each night went something like this:

Mom: How was your day, Tony?
Dad: Good.
Mom: Good?

Her eyes would study him like a Calculus problem.

Dad: Good.
Mom: Can you elaborate?
Dad, in a technical voice as though humoring a child:
    I increased a client's portfolio by 1.2 million dollars.

Each night, what he'd done would change, but it was always to do with money. Loads of money.

Mom: That's great. Your client must be happy.
Dad: I hope so.
Mom: Didn't he thank you or anything?
Dad: Yes. He thanked me profusely.

Mom: So he was happy?

Dad, with an edge of impatience: Yes, he was happy.

Mom would look at her plate, fingers working the napkin in her lap.

Dad, like he was thrusting back in a sword fight:

How was your day, Muriel?

Mom would study him again and tell us about her day. This would take a while, because she'd be careful to describe it fully.

Dad: Good.

His face and tone: Are we done with this?

Mom would stare at her plate and eat.

I had to admire her perseverance.

The first week, Corpse was so stunned by her new view of Dad that she didn't speak, just kept her head down at a weird angle. As far back as I could remember, dinners had been like this, but now it was like she saw our world through a microscope and our parents' sickness was in sharp focus. She could feel how these exchanges had entered her body over long years and settled like accumulating bacteria. The weight of it numbed her. She'd gaze up at the beams and imagine each night's words gathering there, trapped in a vaporous battle, till they took over the room.

Now, on the third night of the second week, Corpse felt she might suffocate. She blurted, "I heard back from Yale." Her first words at the dinner table.

Mom and Dad stopped chewing and looked at her. Mom set down her fork.

"And?" Dad said.

"I'm accepted."

Dad returned to slicing his steak. "I don't know why you're bothering with the others. Yale was a sure bet."

"I might want to attend those others," Corpse said.

"The others are good schools," Mom said.

"Nonsense," Dad said. "Yale is the best school in America."

"I don't even know if I want to go to college."

Dad sighed. "Oona—"

"Tony!"

"Muriel, can't I express my values to my daughter?"

"Of course you can." Mom spoke in tiptoeing steps. "But she's still healing. Just trying to figure things out."

Dad nodded. Not like "yes," but in that not-knowing way. He ate for a minute, but then a battle waged in his face. He set his fork on his plate, his napkin beside it. He stared at his half-eaten baked potato and medium-rare steak like they were something else. It was creepy, yet I remembered that Dad from the hospital, and I felt sorry for him.

"I'm done." The sound of his retreating steps lingered in the room.

Mom and Corpse looked at each other. Mom's eyes mounded with surface tension again, and Corpse saw reflected there why she, herself, had grown so despondent. Saw Mom had been safer, so targeted with our frustration. Corpse's shoulders sagged.

"Don't divorce him, Mom." That little-kid voice.

Mom tilted up her chin, and the arrow of her jawbones was lit by the table's candle. "We moved here to change things. So he could relax." She slumped back in her chair. "*Relax?*" Her voice grew quiet, like she was speaking to herself. "He'll never relax. Never let me in. I'm afraid I'll go my whole life without ever knowing love."

Corpse felt how her body fit against Gabe's, and I searched for but could not find a memory of our parents in an embrace.

"He's working at home now," Corpse said. "That's a start. Give him some time."

"How much time, Oona? How long do I keep waiting?" Mom's skin was so fair, so different from Dad's and Corpse's. Against her temple zigzagged a purple vein.

"Just a while longer. Please?"

Mom smiled weakly. "Is this a sign you're planning to live?"

"I guess so."

Mom sighed. "Graduation, Oona. I'll give things till then."

*Three months.*

They were quiet for a while, their minds zooming around.

"Mr. Handler invited me to go visit a Native American school with him."

Corpse had planned keep mum about this, had held it inside for days. I considered Corpse and trust, and felt acutely her awareness of the hollow space I'd left.

"A what?" Mom said.

"He's going as a guest counselor to a school for Native American kids. I saw them speak at that leadership conference I went to in the fall."

"I thought all you did there was shop."

"Yep. Sorry. But I did go to this session, and the students from there, well ... " Corpse searched for words to express the profound thing that had happened. "They were cool."

"For how long?"

"A week."

"When?"

"Next week."

"I love Native Americans," she said.

"You think I should go?" Corpse worried about what might happen between our parents without her there; hated to give up a minute, with only three months to set things right.

"There's a saying, something about not regretting the things you've done, rather the things you haven't done. I'd have liked to be an anthropologist."

"You never told me that."

"Never allowed myself to fully realize it until this past month."

"So that's why there's all this Native American stuff around the house?"

"Yes, I suppose."

Mom looked so solitary, so beaten down. Corpse rose,

limped behind her chair, and wrapped arms around her. I drifted closer, lingered at the fireplace.

"Oh, you're cold," Mom said, and she covered Corpse's hands with her own.

"Don't worry. It's just the new me. Things are going to get better, Mom. I promise."

I remembered being in that bathroom stall at the leadership conference, wishing Mom would comfort us, just like Corpse was doing now. Corpse closed her eyes and hugged Mom tighter.

———————

Later, Corpse couldn't sleep. She took our journal from our nightstand and once again read through its pages. Every day leading up to the winter formal had an entry about water, yet now she hardly wrote in it. Why?

She read page after page and saw we'd been flailing for a key to unlock our spiral. It came to me that I'd been the one recording these things. She sat straight and sensed me sensing her. She came to the last written page: *orbits, breathe,* and *home*. Words she'd written. Without me. She stared at that page a long time.

Before I knew it, she'd tugged on her robe and limped to the mudroom. She slid on her boots, their sheepskin soft against her bare feet. She tugged on her coat, went through the garage door, and walked to the driveway's end. Ten steps down the street, she stood at the spot where Gabe's father had repaired the wall.

She traced the rocks with her eyes and thought how instinct had led her, that day last May. She cursed how *I love you* would not pass through her lips. I thought how last May she'd caught me off guard, how I was what had blocked those three words. She took a gulp of icy air and regarded the stars.

A car approached. An Audi. It slowed and stopped.

"Ash?" Corpse said.

Ash rolled down her window. "My parents are having another knock-down-drag-out. I couldn't sleep." She shrugged. "I was thinking about you."

Corpse reached in and rested her palm on Ash's flannel shoulder. She wore a robe too.

Ash trained her eyes down the road. "It's almost over, you know."

"What?"

"Living at home."

"I guess so."

"Our parents suck, Oona. They always have."

Corpse sighed. "Mine are getting better. I think. At least Mom is. Dad's going to take some figuring out."

A tear trickled over Ash's cheekbone, rushed down her cheek. "Every college I applied to will probably turn me down. Guess I should have tried harder in school. Like you." She pressed her lips. "I *need* to go away. Far away." She glanced at the stars. "Maybe the moon isn't far enough." A laugh-sob rushed out of her.

Corpse squeezed Ash's shoulder gently. "If there's one

thing I've learned, it's things change. What seems awful now might not be so bad a few months down the road."

"Right."

"No. Really."

They were silent but for Ash's sniffle. She wiped her nose with the back of her hand.

"Ash, I'm sorry. I'm not trying to hurt you. I just can't go back to how things were."

"Honestly, Oona."

Their eyes had a conversation:

Ash: Isn't that a bit dramatic?

Corpse: I'm not like you.

Ash: Whatever.

"You act like I'm the devil or something." Ash rolled up her window and drove away. Corpse watched her taillights till they disappeared on the road's curve.

Inside, she toed off her boots and hung up her coat. She started toward her room but stopped. She crossed the kitchen and limped down the long hall to the observatory. Dad lounged in his recliner, staring at the sky with that depressing woman singing.

What did he see up there? Maybe it wasn't those points of light that captivated him, but the void between. Corpse tried to construct a world through Dad's eyes but she couldn't, and she felt fully how little she knew him. She tried to make herself enter, speak a word, but her heart sped and that day in his office with LIFE was a wall. Instead her feet turned and limped to the living room.

She settled on the couch in the dark, gathering her cold legs beneath her robe. She studied the murky outlines of the peace pipe over the fireplace, the moccasins hanging on the wall above the bookshelf, the kachinas below. They still whispered *bullshit, bullshit, bullshit*, but she realized the bullshit had been her own assumptions about Mom.

She scanned the peace pipe's long shank, the rawhide strips dangling those feathers. I thought how smoke rising from its bowl would not look so different from the steam rising from the creek each morning as Mom drove us to school. Or from Gabe's breaths as he waited for us to arrive.

She thought about college. A dorm? A roommate? Studying hard for classes? No way. She pushed college from her mind, and there was Mr. Handler's offer. It kept whirling around in her head. She liked him, but going alone with him into a foreign world? She heard Mom's voice with that little catch. It triggered that flute music, and its notes swelled around her. She shivered as it summoned the three promises she'd made. The one to Dad, to stay alive? Not excruciating anymore. The promises to Sugeidi and Mom? Those were a challenge. Heal people? Make life better? Three months.

She studied the pipe again, thought of the inhalations rushing through that carved eagle-head bowl and along that shank. It occurred to me that the flute's music was nothing more than the master's exhalations released as notes. She wondered at the notes of ordinary breaths. Was there some creature that heard breath's music? Maybe the stars listened. Or maybe that inky space between them.

Corpse bolted up, listening to her breaths, and moved

to the fireplace. She lunged up onto the hearth, gripped the carved mantle, and reached high with her right hand. Her two fingers grazed the pipe's bowl. She hopped and hit it with her fingertips. The bowl bounced off its nail and struck the crown of her head. She caught the trailing rawhide with her clumsy two fingers and thumb, and it raced through them till her grip closed on the feathers. She lifted those feathers to her face, rubbing her head, and grinned.

# Part Two

*To Die Of Thirst*

# Twelve

FROM OONA'S JOURNAL:

*Water must change and transition and renew itself.*

—Viktor Schauberger

Mr. Handler exited the highway and barreled down a ramp that led to nothing. Literally. Corpse couldn't even see a road. Just endless Utah desert. Panic crept down her neck. She swallowed against how people at school would gossip about her leaving with Mr. Handler. *DEAD GIRL SUCKS UP.*

The ramp's asphalt ended, and Mr. Handler's Prius bounced onto dirt that hooked left, under the highway in a one-lane concrete tunnel. They burst into light at its far end, and still there was nothing but junipers, piñon pines, and sagebrush. Here and there a skiff of snow yawned in a tree's shadow. On a sign faded from blue to mostly white, Corpse read through bullet holes the name *Sego*

*Ridge*, and, beneath it, *Pop.* Sego Ridge's population was just a shot-out hole.

Mr. Handler glanced at Corpse as he gripped the steering wheel with both hands and navigated the washboard road, veering around rocks like land mines. An open bag of pretzels skittered off the console and hit Corpse's feet. She retrieved it and set it in her lap.

The road started climbing, growing steeper, steeper, till it seemed they drove into the sky, the dash inches from Corpse's chin. She listened to the blood rushing in her ears, the tires' thump over washboard. A steeple appeared, and as the road flattened, it became a tiny church sagging toward the dirt, faded beyond any hint of color. A pink house-trailer stood two hundred yards to the right. A rusty tin shed was tacked to its side. A beat-up orange truck, one rear panel primer gray and its back bumper wired on at an angle, was parked out front. A mammoth cottonwood stretched its winter limbs over the trailer and the truck.

As the Prius climbed again, Corpse leaned forward for balance till the dash neared her chin again, and then the road leveled off. Here perched two more house-trailers, one faded yellow, one faded green, worn tires scattered over the roofs. The rusted-out bodies of old cars surrounded both.

At the yellow trailer, a sheet of plywood covered a big window, probably the living room, and the front door was open. Two kids stood outside, one in just a diaper. A skinny black dog sprinted to the Prius and chased it with vicious barks. The dog gave up and Corpse twisted round, looking through me, to watch it out the rear window. It barked and bared its teeth.

I thought of the trailer park down the valley, where Sugeidi's kids lived. Where she spent her days off. Though we'd never visited Sugeidi's family, we'd studied that park as we'd driven by it. Those trailers were painted cheery colors and had little patches of lawn. The only time we'd seen poverty like this was on vacations, when we'd ridden with Mom and Dad in limos from foreign airports to five-star hotels. We'd never considered that people lived this way in America.

Just before the road curved left, a crisp black-and-tan sign announced *Sego Ridge School*. A paved road branched right, and Mr. Handler turned onto it. The Prius bucked, tires ringing, over a cattle guard. Sudden loud silence filled the car. The asphalt's smoothness was unsettling.

Corpse closed her eyes and tried to slow the rushing in her ears. She rubbed her eyelids, and the ache of her fingers and toes returned.

The Prius tilted down.

Corpse opened her eyes to a panorama of successive pine ridges, each a shade lighter till they merged with the horizon. A valley lined with reaching bare branches rose around them. On the right, nestled against the earth, an adobe building materialized. It matched the dirt's red color so closely she might have missed it if she wasn't watching. Another low building appeared on the right. Another. A common area, the lawn dormant, with a dry swimming pool and tennis courts bordering it.

"This looks like one of Mom's spas," Corpse said.

Mr. Handler nodded. "It's a corporate retreat. They've leased it to the school as a tax write-off." He steered the Prius left into a five-space parking lot in front of a building crowded against the hillside. A white sign above its door read *Office*.

"Okay," he said and unbuckled his seat belt. "Home sweet home." He climbed from the car and stretched the six-hour drive out of his limbs. Leaning down into his open car door, he said, "Come on."

Corpse scanned around for students. Staying right there in Mr. Handler's Prius might be just the plan for the whole week.

"That dog back there might bite you, but nobody here is going to," Mr. Handler said.

He knocked on the screen door of the office. Corpse set the pretzels back on the console and climbed out. She squinted up and saw wings circling, blocked the sun with her palm. I tried to make out what type of bird it was but could discern only its silhouette.

"Well hello, Perry!" a woman said. "Welcome back! You don't have to knock."

"Oona?" Mr. Handler held open the screen door. Corpse eyed his black golf shirt. She closed the car door and walked toward him.

The office had a reception counter across the back like a hotel. Perpendicular to it was a desk with a computer on one side, piles of papers and college brochures balanced on the other. Two upholstered chairs occupied the lobby's other side. A copy machine and printer were stuffed behind the counter.

A stout woman in a purple broom skirt and a white blouse said, "You must be Oona. We sure can use the help."

Corpse glanced at Mr. Handler. How was she supposed to help anybody, wreck that she was? She hadn't agreed to anything.

"I'm Louise," the woman said. "Just Louise. No Mr. or Ms. in here. Right, Perry?"

Mr. Handler nodded.

"Not much has changed since you were here last. You'll be in this back room again."

I hovered just above the beaded barrette that clasped Louise's ebony hair in a bun as they followed her into a small office with an empty desk. Shelves brimming with college brochures lined one wall. Corpse tried to place Louise's familiar, clean smell: Ivory soap.

"You were such a help, such a great mentor last year. I'm really looking forward to this," Louise said. "Do you need to put anything in here now? Otherwise I'll show you to your rooms."

"Show us our rooms," Mr. Handler said, glancing at Corpse, who looked like she might run for the hills. "I'm sure Oona could use a rest."

"Do you remember where the dorms are?"

"I do," he said.

"Drive on over. I'll get the keys and meet you there in a minute."

When we were in the Prius, inching past the common

area, I slunk to the back seat. This was going to be a long week.

A woman in a blouse and jeans and a man with a dark braid bisecting his gold T-shirt strolled along a sidewalk that bordered the common area, deep in conversation.

"Isn't it late to be applying to college?" Corpse said.

"They're just doing research now. It would be great to come in the fall and help out, but it's a madhouse during that time back home."

The road forked as the valley fanned out, and Mr. Handler followed the left side that hugged the mountain and climbed gradually to two single-story adobe buildings. They faced southwest and looked like hotels, with tall, south-facing windows and sliding doors to patios that were bordered by waist-high adobe walls.

"Where is everybody?" Corpse said.

"In class. They should be out soon."

"How many students go here?"

"Around forty. Just juniors and seniors."

"Why?"

"They apply from schools across the country. Most are from reservations; most want to go on to college." He pulled into a parking space against the mountain, sighed, and looked at his lap. "They're just kids. Trying to figure things out. Like you."

"Like me?" Corpse said.

He nodded. "Like you." He climbed out of the car. "It's gorgeous here, isn't it?"

She got out. The sun was warm but the air had a cold bite.

Mr. Handler took a deep breath. "Smell that juniper? There's nothing like it."

Corpse heard voices and looked up. Louise and a group of Indian students were walking along the road toward us. Shoes scuffed. Laughter rose. A swan-like girl slapped a boy's shoulder, more of a caress, reminding me of Ash. Maybe half the school was there. They wore jeans, cords, T-shirts, jackets, sneakers; could have been kids from anywhere in America. Corpse kept the Prius between her and them. I sunk behind her.

"Perry!" one girl said.

"Hey, Perry," another one said.

"Lone Ranger," a boy said.

"He *no sabe*," said another, and they all laughed. A joke I had no clue about.

The girl from the reading, the one who'd held the feathers, stepped out, and Mr. Handler put his arm around her in a half-hug. "Angel," he said.

The girl who'd slapped the boy stepped forward, and he hugged her too.

"You're gonna be mad at me," she said.

"Uh-oh, Roberta," Mr. Handler said.

"*Uh-oh* is right," said the boy she'd slapped, and she slapped him again. There was muffled laughter.

"It's good to see you all," Mr. Handler said. "I can't wait to hear how things have been. And I look forward to meeting you juniors."

A few glances skidded across the Prius's maroon roof to Corpse.

"This is Oona," Louise said. "She goes to Perry's school back home. She'll be helping out in the office."

Things got quiet, and it took every bit of strength Corpse had to stand in their scrutiny. Recognition sparked in Angel's gaze. In the gazes of a few others.

Louise jangled the keys. "Your rooms are next door to each other."

The students took this as their cue. "See you," and "Bye," they said and moved on. Angel glanced over her shoulder at Corpse.

Mr. Handler opened the trunk and pulled out our suitcases, his computer bag.

"The rooms have Internet, but remember there's no cell phone coverage down in this hollow. If you want to make a call, you have to hike up there." Louise pointed to the top of the mountain behind us. A double-track road ran straight up it. Corpse sighed. We'd promised Gabe we'd call.

Mr. Handler laughed. "I remember well."

Our rooms were on the near end of the closest building. Louise opened the first door and we followed her in. "This will be your room, Oona," she said.

Two single beds, a kiva fireplace, a pine dresser, a bathroom sink with a mirror; the toilet and shower were in a room beyond. The wall of windows displayed that panorama of ridges. The afternoon sun splashed in. We stepped onto the patio.

Mr. Handler took another deep breath and savored the smell. "It's so good to be here."

We headed back in, and Louise showed Corpse how to control the heat in the room.

"Dinner is at six. Breakfast at eight. Lunch, noon," she said.

"I remember," Mr. Handler said. "Great food."

Corpse thought how she'd miss Sugeidi's cooking.

"Okay," Louise said. "See you at dinner then."

She left and Mr. Handler said, "Need anything?"

Corpse trailed behind him, running her fingers along the dresser. "No."

He turned and caught her looking around the room, saw her doubt. "It's good you're here, Oona." He closed the door.

Corpse ambled to one of the beds, plopped down on its edge, and buried her face in her hands. Pathetic. After a while, she peeked through her fingers, ran her pinkie down her new nose. She walked to the mirror over the sink. She'd been avoiding mirrors since that first day Gabe came by the house. Now Corpse stared at a stranger—still strikingly pretty, yet her nose seemed all wrong. Her gaze trembled. Traces of scar laced one cheek. The other cheek, her chin, her forehead were still faintly mottled. I'd noticed that people's eyes bounced around her face, unable to take in the whole, as if searching for one trustworthy place to land.

She listened for the screeching that had accompanied mirrors for so long. Heard only silence. She pressed her two-fingered hand against her cheek, moved it until her chin rested in the gap where her ring finger and pinkie had been. That made her smile.

She recognized herself then. The Oona from way back, troubled, but able to laugh and crave soccer and have a purpose. She reached out, traced her mirrored nose on the cool glass. She peered into those eyes till it seemed she'd crossed a boundary.

# Thirteen

Corpse served herself tamales, beans, salad from the buffet and settled beside Mr. Handler at a round table in the school's dining hall. It had obviously once been a restaurant. Eight tables were spread across the half-moon-shaped room, and a bank of windows looked out on the panoramic southern view. A swinging kitchen door was on the back wall. On one side stretched a buffet table. On the other, a table with bins for dirty dishes and silverware.

"Oona," Louise said, "this is Dr. Yazzie, our headmaster." Dr. Yazzie was the guy in the gold T-shirt with the long braid we'd seen earlier. Now Corpse saw the symmetry of his forehead, cheeks, and chin; a movie-star face, smooth but for creases at his eyes.

"Dr. Benson, our flute master," Louise continued. "Ms. Cole, who teaches history, and Mr. Gonzalez, who teaches science."

"Hello," Corpse said. First names applied only for the counseling office, it seemed. The flute master's face surprised her. It was light-skinned, and angled enough to cast shadows on itself, even in the dining hall's low light.

"Oona is here with Perry to help me out," Louise said.

Corpse took a bite and paused. Mr. Handler wasn't joking about the food being good. While she ate, Mr. Handler asked about students he'd counseled last year. Corpse inventoried the room.

About forty students were sprinkled across the eight tables in groups of four or five. Several students were lighter-skinned than Corpse. At one table, a girl she'd have guessed was white talked fast, her face a storm, while the girl sitting with her nodded. At another, guys threw something small and silver, and the girls around them giggled and squealed. But for the shape of the tables and the quality of the food, it could have been Crystal High's cafeteria. I drifted toward the beamed ceiling, took stock of all those dark heads.

"You know the statistics, Perry. These kids are smart, but most need to feel they have a place within the school." Dr. Yazzie's words drew Corpse back. She studied him but thought of Gabe, whose friends picked on him ceaselessly for being a good student. *Chingado* they'd call him: "Fucked." It was good natured, sort of proud really, yet Gabe endured a constant current of banter. She thought of the Chicano students she knew who cared about grades and wondered why Gabe didn't hang with them instead. We'd avoided talking about it with him. Our being together was a similar thing. Except he'd been the farthest thing from *chingado*. Corpse snorted, and eyes around the table zinged to her.

Mr. Handler cleared his throat. "What about Susan?"

"She's doing great," Louise said.

"She's a survivor, that one," Mr. Gonzalez said. He resembled a young Albert Einstein: broom moustache, frizzy hair.

"You know her aunt is on the Navajo police force? That aunt's been a good role model," Louise said.

"Cindy made it, didn't she?" Mr. Handler said.

Dr. Yazzie and Louise glanced at each other, then at Corpse, in the way adults do when they're trying to decide whether to divulge a thing in front of you.

"Her father died." Louise's mouth, which arced down naturally, stretched down in a real frown. "Her mother had to get a job, so Cindy went home to help out with the kids."

"She's so smart," Mr. Handler said.

Louise nodded. "But her family needed her. Her father drove his truck in the ditch. Drunk. Tried to walk home on a frigid night. They found him sitting, frozen, at the entrance to their driveway. Apparently neighbors were driving past, waving."

Ms. Cole shook her head. "I hadn't heard that last part."

Mr. Handler cleared his throat.

Corpse focused on her tamales' texture, hoping to hide

her flush. Did the teachers know she'd frozen to death? From the corners of her eyes, she could see students glancing at her and talking to each other. She imagined them saying *Why is she here? Have you seen how she walks? Look at her hand!*

"What's Roberta done that she thinks I'll be disappointed in?" Mr. Handler said.

Louise laughed. "She skipped that summer internship you arranged at the hospital. Didn't even call to let them know."

"Damn," Mr. Handler said.

Louise looked at Corpse frankly. To Mr. Handler, she said, "You know, she's older than the rest. Turned eighteen last May."

"Yes," he said.

"She took a job as a stripper instead. Still goes back and works weekends. Calls herself 'Destiny.'"

Corpse realized her tamale-laden fork was suspended in air. She moved it to her mouth.

Mr. Handler set down his fork and slumped back in his chair. He scanned the students in the room. Some of them had finished eating and were bussing their trays. Corpse followed his eyes to Roberta, who sat with her shapely back to us. I had an image of Roberta in a string bikini, slithering along a pole over an audience of salivating men, some hungrily waving dollar bills.

"Doesn't she have to be twenty-one?" Mr. Handler said.

Louise gave him a look.

We were eighteen too.

Angel sat across the table from Roberta, and I noticed how she watched Corpse. Corpse's eyes met hers. Angel's mouth turned down, but like Louise's, it was natural. Her eyebrows arched on the same path, a silky brow above. Then Angel pushed her tray forward, leaned on her elbows, and focused her attention on the guy next to her, the one who'd read about his grandmother at the conference.

Corpse forced herself to look out the windows at the stretch of dormant grass and sidewalk illuminated by foot-lights. It was trippy, being in a room with these people who'd settled in our mind as an ideal. Like peering through a dream. A dream you couldn't wake from. These weren't the people we'd imagined inhabiting that flute music. The ones who'd made us feel poor. Maybe the bullshit had been those conference readings. And then she thought, *Or maybe it was us.*

"You know," Mr. Handler said, "I read the statistics. You even told them to me, but the reality is a lot harder to swallow."

"Yes, it is," Dr. Yazzie said. He studied Corpse's two fingers holding her fork, and his hand slipped into the pocket of his chinos.

———

After dinner, Corpse and Mr. Handler strolled along the road back to their rooms. The moon was new, and stars commanded the sky. Each step along the asphalt was like walking blind. Mr. Handler was quiet. I imagined I could see the students he'd discussed at dinner hovering in his thoughts as Corpse studied the inky gaps between the stars. We neared the dorm, which cast a frail light. A girl's playful shriek and then muffled voices reached into the night.

At Corpse's door, Mr. Handler said, "Why don't you take your time tomorrow morning. Get homework done, relax, whatever. Come by the office in the afternoon. We should have some work for you by then."

"Okay," Corpse said.

"I'm going to get an early start. They serve breakfast till nine. See you at lunch?"

"Okay."

He pursed his lips and nodded. He swallowed, and his Adam's apple went up, down.

Corpse wanted to say *I'm sorry* about those kids, but I got in the way. She unlocked her door with the key. "Good night," she said.

"Sleep well, Oona," Mr. Handler said.

Before she closed the door, I saw Mr. Handler take three steps toward the mountain, cross his arms, rock back on his heels, and peer up. I supposed it couldn't have hurt, that kindness.

# Fourteen

FROM OONA'S JOURNAL:

*Right in the middle of this rushing cold
water... Schauberger pointed to the motionless stance
of a so-called "stationary trout"... holding a stick
over it, or even the shadow of the stick, was enough to
make the trout dart upstream. The direction of escape
was never downstream, but it always accelerated
upstream. Very odd, because one would normally
consider movement downstream to be the fastest
avenue of escape...*

—Coats, Living Energies

Corpse's noisy breaths rose white before her. She continued her long strides up the steep double-track, hoping to get warm. The valley, shaded from the morning sun by the mountain, trapped the cold. She pictured Gabe's breath clouds, hoped to reach them before he walked from his five-room, well-tended house along Crystal Creek, the one his family had owned since before the ski area arrived fifty years ago, to Manny's bass-thudding Blazer for his ride to school.

She worked to lessen the bob in her gait, willed her phantom pinkie toes to disappear. Halfway up she pulled her phone out of her fleece jacket pocket and found she had coverage. Five minutes till Manny arrived. She speed-dialed Gabe and, as his phone rang, scanned the landscape. She unzipped her fleece and fingered her heart necklace. I perched in the branches of a juniper.

She'd emailed with Gabe last night. Emailed with Mom too, and learned Dad had fled to Chicago for the week. Corpse had lain staring at the ceiling, unsettled by his leaving, then wrapped herself in a blanket, ambled onto the patio, settled into a plastic chair, and gazed at the night sky like she was reading Braille. She'd woken hours later, stiff and craving Gabe.

"Hey," he said, surprised.

"Hey," Corpse said. I imagined her sliding along that strip-club pole. She rubbed her forehead. "I needed to hear your voice."

Gabe chuckled. "So you hiked up that mountain?"

"Partway."

"I must rate."

"You rate," Corpse said.

In their silence, she sensed me sensing her. She glanced around at the arid forest and listened to Gabe's breaths, imagined inhaling his presence through the phone. Was his breath still breath when it reached her ear? She wanted to tell him that Dad had fled to Chicago. Yell it across the expanse. But she couldn't even whisper it.

Gabe said, "I heard back from Harvard yesterday."

"And?" She pictured him standing in his entryway, wearing his letter jacket with the big *C*.

"I'm in!"

After visiting Yale last summer, Dad striding around like he owned the place, we'd ridden the two-hour train to Boston, near Harvard. We'd told Gabe about that train connecting the two schools, thinking he'd never get accepted.

"Wow, Gabe! That's amazing! Congratulations!"

"Yeah, thanks. I know soccer helped because they said I wasn't really supposed to hear yet, but they wanted to confirm I'd play. Offered a monster scholarship. Dad's flipped out. Even with the scholarship it costs a fortune. Well, a fortune to us. Anything's a fortune to us. But I tell you one thing—I'm not sticking around here to be a stone mason the rest of my life."

Corpse traced her nose. She wondered how to be a new self. She hunched over, felt like she crumpled on the hollow space I'd left.

A hawk lit from the tree beside mine. I darted to Corpse as she flinched to the side.

"You okay?" Gabe said.

"Yes." Her hand came to her heart. "Gabe, I got into Yale."

Her keeping it from him stretched between them as silence.

"How long have you known?"

"A week."

Silence again. The hawk soared out over the flat area at the mountain's base and began a giant spiral.

"I just..."

"It's all right, Oona." She could hear his hurt.

"You must be so excited. I mean, Harvard. Nobody gets into Harvard."

"Nobody gets into Yale."

"My dad made that happen."

"Yes, well, being Chicano didn't hurt me either. You've got to take a break when it's there. Life is hard enough."

The hawk hovered at eye-level a half-mile out, adjusting its wings in small movements to stay in place. Corpse imagined riding its back, felt herself right there in its feathers, the wind whipping her hair. It dove, so suddenly she felt suspended and stepped back. It disappeared into the sagebrush, only the tips of its stretched wings visible.

"You wouldn't chose your college just to be close to me, would you?" she said, and heard Manny's car honk.

"Look, I was never interested in anyone till you, Oona. I've never told you, but my dad has a saying: *No macho here. Hernandez men love big, and they love once.*"

A plane spewed a contrail across the sky. Corpse noticed contrails written by gone planes, fuzzy as they dispersed. She listened to Gabe's front door close and the bass of Manny's Blazer grow louder. The hawk's wings disappeared into the sage. I wondered at the evaporation rising off the desert panorama before us: Water, a ghost here.

"Will you call tomorrow?" Gabe said.

"*Chingado*," Manny said. "Hang up, married."

I pictured Gabe flipping Manny the bird.

"I'll let you go," Corpse said. She slid her phone into her coat pocket. "I'm such bullshit," she said to the air. After a minute, "*Rest of my life.*"

Graduating from high school was the end of being not-adult. Gabe, eighteen and hardly kissed. I pictured him beneath Roberta's stripper pole, looking up at Corpse. Corpse barked a laugh. Felt it tumble down the hollow space inside her as the hawk burst from the sage with something dangling from its beak. It climbed, crossing one contrail. Two. Three.

She turned away from the landscape, toward the school's valley, and pulled out her phone. She took a deep breath and pulled up her texts. Forty-two. Mostly from Ash. Corpse opened the most recent one. Two weeks ago, our first day back at school: U r a user!!! She opened the next, two weeks before that: Where's my crown???!!! The day we returned to Chateau Antunes: Wat hav I dun? The day we woke in the hospital: Text me!!!!! Pleez!!!!!!

Corpse's hands fell to her sides. That tear trickling over Ash's cheekbone rose in her memory: Ash's pain laid bare by the moonlight. I pictured Ash on the stage at the winter formal, balancing that crown in front of her up-do. Saw that crown bobbing on Corpse's head as the paramedics hustled our stretcher along that suicide trail, their moonglow shadows cast long. That crown growing looser, looser, till it bounced off, the paramedic in back stepping on it. Mashing it into the soft snow without noticing.

Corpse blew out her breath and erased all the texts. No way could she go back to being best friends with Ash, but she could at least show some compassion and smooth things over when she got home.

The sun lit her shoulders, making them tingle. She thought how Gabe's handsome father had never remarried. Didn't even date.

She heard steps. Angel, wearing navy blue sweatpants and a gray sweatshirt, jogged down the double-track.

"Hey," Corpse said.

"Hey," Angel said.

They stared at each other.

Corpse held up her phone. "Making a call. You?"

"I was greeting the sun." Angel's voice was just as we remembered it: slow yet soft, lilting.

"Oh," slipped out of Corpse.

"I have to get going." Angel grimaced and resumed descending, then paused. She looked at the ground. Kicked a rock. It sailed before gravity grabbed it. She didn't turn around, just said, "I dreamed of you three nights ago."

"Me?" Corpse said, but there's no way Angel heard. She was hopping over rocks and rough spots, her braid swinging like a pendulum.

———————

In the dining hall, two white women—one with a ponytail and one with gray hair like a scrub brush—sat talking, their trays pushed to the middle of their table. From the buffet

Corpse noticed Angel, in jeans and an orange T-shirt now, sitting alone with a full plate. Angel saw Corpse, and her eyebrows pressed close.

Corpse spooned scrambled eggs and refried beans onto a plate, ladled chunky salsa down the side, and started toward a table near the windows. She stopped. Turned.

"May I join you?" Corpse said.

Angel nodded once.

Corpse sat two chairs away. "Why aren't you in class?" she said.

"I don't have first period. I have enough credits to graduate already."

"Me too," Corpse said. I wondered why she'd spend the morning ahead doing homework but knew she wouldn't be able to stop herself.

"Are you an urban Indian?" Angel said.

"A what?"

"An Indian from the city. One who maybe doesn't know traditions, Indian ways."

"No. How could *I* be Indian?"

Angel shrugged. "There's a lot of mixed-blood or northern Indians here that don't look Indian."

"My dad's Portuguese. I inherited this olive skin from him."

Angel examined her. "When the newspapers or television or magazines come to report on the school, they always take photos of the kids who look Indian. They never take photos of the kids who don't. We get pretty sick of it."

Corpse felt dumb again. "I just needed a change of scenery."

Angel took in the red scars on Corpse's hand holding her fork.

"People visit here all the time," she said. "Journalists, educational researchers, other teachers. Almost every week we have a visitor." Angel pulled a face. "People like to visit Indians. It makes them feel like they've done a good deed or something."

"Then why does everyone keep staring at me?"

"You're a legend: the girl who ran out during our presentation."

Corpse set down her fork and put her hands in her lap.

"We tease William."

"William?"

"The guy who'd just read when you left the room. 'Beauty Repellent' is his nickname now."

"It wasn't his fault."

They analyzed one another. Angel's high, silky forehead and the forward tilt of her face made her seem honest. A pale line of scar meandered from her cheekbone to her chin. Corpse wondered at its history.

"You must be a senior then?" Angel said.

"Yes."

"Going to college?"

"Not sure."

Angel shot Corpse a questioning look.

Corpse shrugged. "I'm not sure if I want to go." I

heard her words' hollow ring. Away from home they'd lost their potency and sounded, well, spoiled.

"Where'd you get accepted?" Angel said.

Corpse told her.

Angel looked out the bank of windows. "I got accepted to Yale. It's a long way, Yale."

"Yale's nice. Have you been there?"

"I've been to Harvard," she said, seeming to watch something out the windows. Corpse couldn't see anything but the view.

Angel's eyes darted back to Corpse and then traveled directly to her shoulder. To me. I forced myself still.

"I need to get to class. See you around," she said.

"See you."

Angel walked to the table by the kitchen door and bussed her tray. Once in the common area, Angel didn't follow the sidewalk toward the dorms but a sidewalk leading right, past the empty swimming pool toward a big building. Probably meeting rooms converted to classrooms.

Corpse sliced me with a glance. "Bullshit," she said, like *I thought so.*

That glance shoved me to the ceiling. I remembered Angel looking at me, and I dreaded her dream.

———

After lunch, Mr. Handler and Corpse strolled toward the office. The valley bottom was warmer now, so Corpse carried her fleece instead of wearing it. Mr. Handler's face was still drawn, but his shoulders sagged less beneath his white golf shirt. I wondered what he'd encountered that morning. Corpse tried to make out the logo on his shirt, but couldn't. She searched for something to say that might lift his spirits. I let her. She remembered the photo on his desk in his office back home.

"Your sons," she said, "where did they go to college?"

Mr. Handler's shoulders straightened. "They're both at CU. Doing well. It's a good school."

"What are their majors?"

"Phillip is a business major. Paul is a freshman, so he has no idea, but I suspect he'll go into teaching."

"A teacher?" Corpse remembered Paul in the halls at Crystal High, could see him sucker-punching his buddies. How weird to consider him the opposite of student. Adulthood pressed close. I tried to shove it away, but Corpse drew it close and pictured herself in a white scientist's coat, hair drawn back.

Roberta sauntered toward them, and they turned to her.

"Okay, Lone Ranger," she said. "Save me."

Mr. Handler chuckled and we entered the office, the screen door clapping behind us. Louise was working at her desk and glanced up as Roberta sauntered to the back room.

"Louise has a project for you, Oona," Mr. Handler said. He followed Roberta, leaving the door open a crack like he did when we were in his office back home. I felt sorry for Mr. Handler and Roberta. I pictured them sitting across from each other like opponents: Mr. Handler offering Roberta opportunities and her repelling them. I had an image of Roberta's swan body slithering along that pole with an angry glare. Blaming everything in life but herself.

"Oona," Louise said.

Corpse blinked and turned to her.

"You all right?"

She nodded.

"Okay," Louise said. "I have a project for you. Since you've just done this, and must have done it well because I heard you got into Yale, I'd like you to review the online application pages and procedures for the schools on this list."

Louise handed Corpse a piece of lined paper with names as headings, short lists of colleges under each. "We'd like you to coach our juniors on filling out the Common Application and in looking at the requirements for the schools they're interested in. We'll save what we can and refer to it again in the fall. They may change their minds about schools, and that's okay. These applications can be daunting. Can you do that?"

"Sure." Corpse simmered with apprehension; she'd had a hard time with her *own* applications. These kids were plenty smart; she'd seem like a fool.

"Good. We have twelve juniors applying next year." Louise shook her head. "I wish we could get all twenty-one to apply. Let's plan for you to meet with three students each afternoon. Tomorrow you'll meet with ... " She walked to an appointment calendar on her desk and ran her finger to tomorrow's box. "Pauline, John, and William. See how I've listed the schools under their names?"

Corpse scanned the paper and nodded. *William. Beauty Repellent.*

"Excellent. Here's the computer you'll be using." Louise walked to where the two upholstered chairs had been pushed apart, a short wooden table squeezed between. "When they're finished, please print off their applications and store them in here." She pointed to a folder. "Save them on this flash drive too."

"Are you sure they need my help?"

"Can't hurt," Louise said without looking at her.

Corpse flushed. Louise and Mr. Handler were just creating something for her to do. She wondered what the staff was telling the students about why they'd have to endure this with her. I pictured them sitting there, bored, humoring her, thinking the whole time how screwed up she was. She wished she'd never come.

"Okay," Corpse said. She took a pencil from a tin can next to the computer and marked hashes next to *Pauline, John,* and *William.* She drew back the folding chair at the computer and sat down.

Louise returned to her desk.

Corpse pulled up the first school under the first name and began to navigate the site. The upholstered chairs on either side of the desk seemed like pudgy guards. From the inch-wide opening to Mr. Handler's office, voices trickled out. If Corpse strained, she could make out words, but she concentrated on not listening. I loitered around, nervous about Corpse's comment at breakfast.

She was well into the second college site, Gustavus

Adolphus, when Roberta swooped out, wiping her cheeks. Right through me.

She missed a step and froze.

I shot to the ceiling, jolted by her fury and confusion. Her touch mirrored Corpse's, yet emitted such sexuality.

Mr. Handler leaned against his office door frame. Roberta scowled over her shoulder like Corpse was a disease, then bolted. The screen door clapped behind her. Mr. Handler looked a hundred years old. He smiled sadly at Corpse and Louise.

Louise shook her head. "You're a god, Perry."

He patted Corpse's shoulder and disappeared back into his office. The chair's creak as he settled into it seemed part of his sigh.

# Fifteen

FROM OONA'S JOURNAL:

*In the moonlight falling directly onto the crystal clear water... the large trout disappeared in the jet of the waterfall, which glistened like falling metal. I saw it... dancing in a wild spinning movement... It then came out of this spinning movement and floated motionlessly upwards. On reaching the lower curve of the waterfall, it tumbled over and with a strong push reached behind the upper curve of the waterfall. There, in the fast flowing water, with a vigorous tail movement, it disappeared.*

—Viktor Schauberger

Though I'd willed Corpse to stay in that warm bed, she strode up the double-track through murky early light, partly to get warm, and partly because she didn't want Angel to see her. She was huffing when she reached the halfway point where she'd called Gabe the day before. It seemed a week ago that she'd made that call rather than yesterday.

She kept going. All this walking was great practice. Her missing toes still shouted, but her stride was definitely smoothing. What we'd thought was the top was actually a swale where the mountain flattened before continuing up. Angel kneeled in a clearing, facing east with her head bowed, silhouetted by a rising sliver of sun that ignited the horizon and the mountain's ascending edge. Corpse prowled behind a juniper and peered through its scented branches.

Angel began chanting in a language we didn't understand, and Corpse suddenly felt like a peeping Tom. She turned the other direction and picked a blue-gray berry. Sliced it with her thumbnail. Held its sharp, clean smell to her nose. It reminded her of the cleaner Sugeidi used on the woodwork of Chateau Antunes. Across Corpse's chest, a stick of longing seemed to connect her shoulders and tug toward the maid she wasn't supposed to call.

Angel grew quiet, and Corpse turned as Angel rose, brushing off her knees. She spotted Corpse and Corpse froze, looking like an idiot.

"Are you spying on me?" Angel said.

Corpse stepped out, but I stayed in the tree. Twenty yards stretched between them, and Corpse held up her palm to shield the sun. "When you tell a person you dreamed about her, it gets her attention. But I didn't spy; I turned my back."

Angel wore the same gray sweatshirt and navy sweatpants. She blew out her breath and started toward the road.

"Why do you do it?"

"I'm showing him I'm ready for the day. And worthy."

I wondered what the sun saw when it looked at Corpse.

"Do you do it every morning?" she asked.

"Most mornings. Sometimes I'm lazy."

"Do they greet the sun back home?"

"Yes," Angel said.

"Do you miss it? Home?"

"A little."

"Where's home?"

"Fort Defiance, Arizona."

"What do you miss?"

"What is this? Twenty questions?"

"Sorry."

Angel shrugged, but it seemed more like something inside her giving up. "I miss my family. Especially my grandfather."

"I used to hate my mom."

"You don't anymore?" Angel looked interested for the first time.

A breeze rose from the valley, draping Corpse's hair across her face. She hooked it back with a finger and returned that hand to blocking the sun. "I understand her now."

"What changed?" Angel said, really looking at her.

"I tried to kill myself."

Angel nodded. Her eyes swerved to me in my tree.

Corpse's hand dropped, and she went limp all over.

Angel glanced at the sun. "I've got to get going." She took two steps. "Want to come?"

*No!* I said. Enough was enough.

Corpse couldn't move. Her mouth barely worked. "I need ... to make a call."

Angel traced Corpse's sagging outline with her eyes. "See you at breakfast?"

"Breakfast."

Corpse listened to Angel's footsteps descend the double-track till they disappeared. I hung back, nervous. After a long time, Corpse turned to the sun. "What do you see? A dead girl? Bullshit?" She shut her eyes, and red ignited their lids. Her thoughts turned to flame, her hands made fists, and she rocked back and forth. "What's wrong with me?"

She willed the sun's energy to scour her like a laser beam. She imagined that searing beam inching from her toes to the top of her head, smoke rising off her.

Two magpies landed in a nearby tree and started a racket. She stumbled back like a drunk and opened her eyes. She reached her hands up and yelled, like sending a long ray back at the sun, and the magpies took to squawking flight. For a long time she stood, arms outstretched, her eight digits reaching like twigs. It was freaky, and I hoped nobody could see her from below.

She pulled out her phone. On the third ring, Sugeidi said "Hello," the word like a box in her mouth.

"*Hola, Sugeidi. Es Oona,*" Corpse said.

"*Sí, Oona. Cómo estás?* You are no hurt?"

"No, I'm fine." Corpse's voice rose to that kid voice. "I just missed you. That's all."

Before the muffled sound of fingers over the mouthpiece, she heard Sugeidi's breath catch in her throat.

————

At breakfast Corpse didn't talk much. She felt limp, exhausted, like she'd trudged a thousand miles. She wondered if it was from getting up so early and hiking up the mountain these last two days, but she knew better. This fatigue was from what had happened up there. Angel eyeing me in that juniper kept playing in her head like a song. Corpse sensed me sensing her and poked at her eggs with her fork. She felt Angel's eyes on her now. At a table behind them, those same two white women, the ponytail one and the scrub-brush-haired one, murmured, the only other people in the room.

"Did you already know I'd been dead?" Corpse said.

Angel shrugged and glanced my way.

"Try me," Corpse said. "If I'd said I was an urban Indian, would you tell me?"

Angel's face hardened. She rose and gathered her tray.

"Can I join you tomorrow? To greet the sun?"

Angel closed her eyes and sighed. "It's private."

Corpse set her hand on the table and studied her missing fingers.

Angel watched her, seeming to weigh things.

Corpse longed to ask about the dream.

"See you," Angel said.

Corpse watched Angel walk across the common area toward the big building. The women still murmured behind Corpse, and she peeked over her shoulder at them. They leaned close. Their hushed voices lured her attention.

"I'm just not sure what I'll do next year," the ponytail woman said. "This has been a great experience, don't get me wrong. But it's been a wild ride, and I've never been able to forget, even for a minute, that I'm an outsider."

"Don't you think you're overreacting?" the scrub-brush-haired woman said.

"Did I ever tell you about my first week here?"

No response. Corpse imagined Scrub Brush shaking her head.

"I think it was the second night. And one of the girls came banging on my door, whimpering about witches and *something* in her room."

"What? Like a ghost?"

"I don't know. It was the middle of the night, for God's sake, and I tried to calm her. I mean, a witch? I eventually got her to sleep—she spent the night in my room—and in the morning she seemed fine. At lunch Yazzie took me aside. Apparently I'd handled it all wrong. When something like this happens, you inform him immediately, and they call a medicine man."

No response again.

"I read the faculty handbook. It doesn't say anything about this kind of thing."

"But now you know. I'll take this place any day. I taught

at this boarding school for at-risk teens outside Chicago. Talk about challenges. Every school—"

"And then," Ponytail continued, "there was the time I was directing *A Midsummer Night's Dream.* I had all these kids that were sprites, and I was trying to get them to *sprite* across the stage. They were having a hard time with it, so I said, 'How about if I play some drum music?' Well, they all rolled their eyes and got pissed off, saying, 'Just let us be teenagers!'"

"Exactly. They're just teenagers," Scrub Brush said.

"No. Every day it's something. I won't ever get things right. I need to make up my mind. Oops, it's 9:10. See you at lunch," Ponytail said.

Students and adults entered the common area, most headed somewhere. Five students loitered together on the yellow grass. William was one of them, and he laughed, his whole big body shaking. The bright sun pushed sharp shadows from their feet.

I thought about being part of that joke on him. How you could hurt someone and never know. How hard it would to be to face him this afternoon. Corpse thought about living in Angel's dreams. She wondered how many selves she had out there in the world. She again felt caught in some weird dream. I hadn't known she was capable of thoughts like that.

————

"Lone Ranger." William nodded to Handler and then eyed Corpse like he was a fish that might dart away. She felt the same. William became more like a whale, though, as he settled into the chair at the computer, making it seem like a kindergartner's.

She looked at the two colleges Louise had listed below William's name: University of Colorado and Western State College, also in Colorado. I hovered in the ceiling's corner. Still in shock from Angel's glance and the talk of witches.

"I'm from Colorado," Corpse said.

How stupid—she'd come here with Mr. Handler. And hadn't William been with that first group of students we'd met, when Louise introduced her?

Corpse sighed at me.

William nodded.

She remembered his soft, high voice and thought of his grandmother. "Do you like Colorado?"

Could he hear how her words quavered?

Corpse glanced at me. *Go away!* she thought.

I turned silent.

"My dad lives there."

"Really? Where?"

William typed in "CU Boulder" and clicked on the site. "Leadville," he said. "He works at the Climax Mine."

Corpse had no clue where the Climax Mine was. Hated to sound dumb again, so she just said, "I'm from Crystal Village. That's about an hour from Leadville."

"I know," William said. "Mansions. Fur coats. Good ice cream."

"Do you ski?" she said.

"Me? Ski? Nah. You?"

She started to say yes, but stopped. "I'm not sure any-more."

William looked at her funny. Louise milled about behind them, and Mr. Handler shuffled papers in his office.

"My uncle drives a snowcat at Taos. He took me out once." William shook his head. "I was like an elephant on roller skates."

"Oh," Corpse said.

Laughter rolled out Mr. Handler's office.

"Okay, here's the site," she said. "Now, see this tab for Freshman Students? Click on it."

William took the mouse and clicked the tab as she tried to imagine him in glitzy Crystal Village, then in Lead-ville's thin 10,000-foot air. A hundred and fifty years ago, Leadville had been a booming mining city. Today it was a shell of its glory days. It had a neat main street, but most of the rest of town was run down, and all of it was cast in the odd slant of that high-altitude light. So different from here.

"Okay," she said. "Now open Forms and Downloads." She pointed at the button on the screen, then dropped her hand into her lap. William's eyes followed it. She held it up. "A dumb mistake."

His eyebrows rose and he studied her hand. Then he looked at the screen. "Application Packet?"

"Yes," she said.

A photo of CU's red-brick campus in summer appeared, the Flatirons, giant fins of red rock, jutting up against the mountainous background. Across the screen's top it said, *Find Your Place . . .*

Those words froze Corpse. She felt William watching.

"I'd like to fill out the CU application instead of the Common one," he said.

Corpse nodded. "You don't need my help."

William scrolled down and said, "My dad's missing a pinkie. He lost it in the mill at the mine."

"Oh," Corpse said.

He typed his personal information on the application. When she'd worked with the two students before him, their personal histories had already made her say "oh" a lot. One had both parents; the other was raised by her aunt. Each had filled out an Application Fee Waiver Request Form because they couldn't afford the application fee. To qualify, a student's family had to earn less than $27,000 a year with two dependents. That's kids. Mom probably spent that much in one year at spas.

Corpse remembered Gabe's white sock peeking through the hole in his sneaker that first time he'd walked us home. What was his dad's income? How poor were those immigrant girls who sat on the steps of school each morning? How much did Mom pay Sugeidi? Sure, we'd studied the rest of the world in school, but we'd never considered the poverty around us.

"What's a Major Code?" William said.

"It's what you want to study."

"I want to be a doctor."

"Okay, then pre-med. I'll look it up." Louise had tons of brochures, and she'd set the ones for CU and Western State on the table. Corpse opened the index and searched for Major Code. After a minute she read him the number. She sat back and pictured William in a doctor's coat.

When he got to the household income boxes, he clicked one in the middle: *$35,000-59,999*. Under *Next of Kin* he typed "Gina Cheveyo," and for relationship he checked *Other*, then typed "Grandmother" in the space provided. When the application said *Indicate the highest level of formal education attained by your parents or guardians*, he checked *High school graduate*. At *Academic Honors*, he paused.

"Lone Ranger?" he called out.

Mr. Handler appeared in his doorway.

"What do I put for that thing at Harvard?"

"Oh," Corpse said.

Mr. Handler told him, and he typed it in for last summer and the one ahead.

Corpse slouched back in her chair and studied the shaggy line of hair along William's neck, the thick strip of skin above his red T-shirt.

She noticed Mr. Handler watching. He smiled and disappeared into his office.

William finished the application. They saved it and put it on a flash drive. While they waited for it to print off, Corpse stood and propped her knee on her chair, resting her forearms on the back and leaning on them.

"William," she said, careful to keep looking at the beeping printer. "Sorry about running out after your reading at that conference."

Louise concentrated on the paper before her.

William shrugged, which moved the whole top half of his body. "It's been a good joke."

"It wasn't your fault. I was screwed up." She held up her hand again. "Dumb."

"You're not dumb anymore?"

Laughter rolled out Mr. Handler's office.

"Careful there, Lone Ranger, you'll fall off your horse," William said.

Mr. Handler laughed harder. William's eyes met Corpse's, and they grinned.

I envied that grin. Envied her petting Sugeidi's head. Envied her hugging Mom. Envied Gabe.

The printer finished, and she handed him the application for his file.

"About your essay," she said. "If I were you, I'd use what you read at the conference."

"Then I better hope someone ugly reads my application." When William laughed, even his ears lifted. She noticed that they stuck out and were tiny compared to his body, and she laughed despite herself. Corpse could tell that the teasing he'd gotten about her would have been like this. A liking kind of teasing. He'd be an excellent doctor. She slapped his shaking shoulder, more of a two-fingered caress. I envied that too.

Later, Corpse wrote in our journal:

*Find Your Place ...*

*—CU Undergraduate Application*

# Sixteen

FROM OONA'S JOURNAL:

*The process by which the trout stays motionless in
flowing water is as follows: The trout always seeks out
the part of the water-body, that part of the current
flow where the water is densest and coldest... Because
of its bodily form, as each filament of water passes
around the trout it accelerates and in doing so
exceeds the above critical velocity relative to
specific temperature.*

—Viktor Schauberger

In darkness, Corpse paused before the mountaintop. Some-thing scurried away from her. She hoped this wasn't one of the mornings when Angel felt lazy and didn't get out of bed. Her body started to cool, but nerves kept her warm.

Yesterday at breakfast, when she'd asked Angel if she could come to greet the sun, Angel had said it was pri-vate. But she didn't say she couldn't meet her on the way down. Corpse was figuring out that people here didn't look straight at each other very often. And they didn't just get to the point. They seemed to talk or wait their way around things. Corpse decided to be patient about the dream.

She heard approaching footsteps. The sky was lightening. When Angel saw Corpse, she rolled her eyes.

"I'm not spying. I promise. I'll just wait here."

Angel breathed in like Corpse required all her patience. She disappeared over the crest.

Corpse decided to greet the sun in her own way, found a flat spot beneath a tree, and kicked away the small rocks. She kneeled just as the sun breached the horizon and the mountain's edge, casting rays like a kid's drawing.

"Good morning." She held out open palms. "Am I worthy?"

She listened so hard her ears rang. She started sensing me again. This time like on steroids. I slunk into the high branches of a piñon pine.

Her thoughts zoomed around. Ricocheted between relief at this escape from the hate between Mom and Dad and how angry she was at Dad for fleeing to Chicago. She remembered him in the hospital, perched on the side of her bed, saying *Things are going to be different.*

Now Dad was at home when she was, avoiding them full-time instead of one day a week. She considered his not-knowing nod. The way his eyes travelled somewhere else as he nodded. What did he see? It was unsettling, like Dad had two selves. Or existed in two places at once.

She swallowed the crisp air, felt it inhabit lungs that not long ago had stopped. The despair that had led her up that snowy path after the winter formal arrived like an image on Chateau Antunes's theater screen. She saw Dad watching her pretend to sleep those first mornings after the hospital, saw the evenings when she was awake and how he'd fidgeted and left so quickly. She saw herself unable to stay in Dad's office and talk to him.

"Dad," Corpse whispered.

She strained to hear her heart's nervous beat. Even thinking of Dad this way felt dangerous somehow. Like a betrayal. She ran her thumb over her finger nubs.

"But he's the key," she whispered. To me. "The key, the key, the key," she repeated, willing the sun's rays to inject resolve into her.

At the sound of footsteps, she rose. "How come nobody else greets the sun?"

Angel shrugged. "Some do. In their rooms. Most don't want to get up this early."

"Why do you come up here?"

"I can't see him in the valley."

"Oh." I hated how "oh" kept slipping out of her. She rose and looked around, noticed a strip of pink surveyor ribbon fluttering from a juniper branch on the double-track's edge. Another fluttered in the distance.

Angel followed Corpse's gaze. "There's a cross country race up here in the fall. Dr. Yazzie coaches our team. He's a good runner. Does those ultra-marathons."

Corpse pictured school busses lugging past Sego Ridge, up the steep roads to get here, that dog snapping at their giant tires, their tangy yellow river parked along the valley floor. She saw kids wearing numbers safety-pinned to jerseys, suffering up this mountain. She rubbed her eyes. What was it with stupid assumptions in this place?

"Do you want to jog down?" Angel said.

"I can't. I lost my pinkie toes. When I died."

"So?" Angel said. "You made it up here in the dark, didn't you?"

Corpse shook her head. "I can't."

"What could happen? You fall down? Bleed a little?"

Corpse rolled her lip with her teeth. I slunk to her shoulder, willing her away from this.

"It's fun," Angel said.

"I'm going to call my boyfriend."

Angel shrugged and started down.

Corpse felt like a cheat, using Gabe as a crutch, an excuse. *It's fun.* Would she avoid things all her life? No. Not *things.* Happiness. She was avoiding *happiness.* Dad, Mom, they all were. Bullshit! How would she ever face Dad if she didn't have courage for this?

*No!* I said. She crinkled her nose. "Ugh!" She looked down at Angel. "Wait!"

Angel turned as Corpse took a jog-ish step. After three, she lengthened her strides. Running down employed her heels more, so she kept her upper body gathered, and the balance wasn't too bad. She took a reaching stride over a rock and grinned at the sense of soaring. Her toe caught and she really did soar, hands out like in a dive. She landed and skidded down the road on her chest. When she stopped, she didn't move.

*See?* I said.

"Are you all right?" Angel knelt beside her.

Corpse groaned but levered herself up to her knees. To her feet. One knee of her jeans was torn, and her skin inside bled. Her palms were raw. She wiped them on her thighs, leaving streaks. Wiped her cheeks and nose with the back of her hand and nodded to Angel. She took a shuddering breath and started down again.

After ten steps she laughed like she was insane. Angel caught up to her. Their steps were loud. Corpse grinned at the air's velocity against her skin and vowed to greet the sun for the rest of her life.

———

After breakfast Angel left for class, but Corpse stayed at the table in the dining hall and ran her sore hand over the oak branches carved into our journal's leather cover. She'd finished all her homework for the week, had emailed the assignments where they needed to go. Dr. Yazzie and the ponytail teacher, the one who'd calmed the girl scared by witches or ghosts, sat at a table across the room, speaking low. Dr. Yazzie's face was serene. Ponytail's was not. I could relate. I guessed the woman was giving her notice.

Corpse opened our journal to its first page. She read our name, address, phone number, written with all the fingers of our right hand. The blue ink, our writing's deep slant and close letters, seemed to shout confusion. She turned the pages, studied how notes or passages about water filled them. Like we'd been studying for a test. It had been driving us nuts, consuming us. She studied the margins between where she'd transcribed Dickinson's socially acceptable poems and the originals.

She reached the page with *orbits*, *breathe*, and *home*. At the bottom of that page, she now scrawled *promises*, then *Dad*, then *bullshit*, then *the key*, then *courage*. She was staring at the bumps in her pencil lines when Dr. Yazzie said, "Hello, Oona."

"Oh," Corpse said. "Hi."

"Are you doing all right?"

"I'm fine."

"May I join you?"

"Sure."

He wore khaki chinos and a yellow T-shirt that said, *Western States 100*. Muscle traced his forearms. A tiny, puckered scar marked his temple, and Corpse wondered what had created it.

"Are you enjoying your visit?"

"Yes."

"I hear you're doing a nice job coaching students in the counseling office. The kids say you're okay, which is as close as we Indians come to a compliment.

"Thanks." Corpse smiled a little. "But they don't need me," she said, like *I feel like an idiot*.

He reclined back in his chair.

Corpse heard Gabe: *You've got to take a break when it's there.*

"Looks like it's been hard for you," Dr. Yazzie said.

Corpse dropped her hand into her lap. "Don't tell me you can see I've died."

He smiled. "I can see you're struggling."

Corpse glanced my way. I didn't budge.

"Mr. Handler told me your story before you arrived."

"Oh." Corpse looked at her lap. "I suppose he had to."

It was quiet but for the muffled sound of running water, pans clanking in the kitchen, and the beat of her stumbling heart. Its rhythm was a lifeline I clung to.

After a while Dr. Yazzie said, "I have a rock in my pocket. It speaks to me."

Corpse looked at his hand, concealed in his pocket.

"It tells me you're a good person. That you're going to be okay."

Corpse tilted her head. Their eyes had a conversation:

Corpse: Really?

Dr. Yazzie: Yes.

Corpse: I'm asking about me, not the rock.

Dr. Yazzie: I know.

"Thanks," she said.

"Will you come to Circle today?" he said.

"Circle?"

"You didn't know?"

She shook her head.

"We hold Circle each Wednesday at ten. In the gymnasium. Over there." Dr. Yazzie pointed toward the side-walk leading to the big building. "It's like a town meeting. Join us." He rose.

Alone, Corpse opened her journal to the next blank page. She wrote:

*You're a good person. You're going to be okay.*
—*Dr. Yazzie's rock*

———————

Corpse entered the double doors to the big building. She walked past a room containing two long tables that housed three computers each. A room on her left, then one on her right, held about fifteen desks facing a white board. In one, students were stuffing their books in backpacks.

Ahead was a door with people milling around it. Corpse stepped through them, feeling her unIndianness like a neon sign, and entered a small gymnasium with a circle of thirty chairs. A few people were already seated. Angel was there. She nodded toward Corpse. Corpse walked to the chair beside her and sat down. Mr. Handler entered the room, saw Corpse, and came to sit beside her. I rose to the high ceiling, trying to put distance between us.

"My favorite part of the week," he said. "Be warned, this first bit will be like the conference."

Their eyes met. That moment after we'd come out of that conference hall bathroom, a total wreck spiraling down, was suspended in their gaze.

"Don't worry," Corpse said. "I'm past that now."

"Really," he said, like *I don't believe you.*

"Really," she said.

"What happened to your hands?" he said.

"I fell. Running down the mountain."

"Really?" he said.

"Really," Corpse said.

"Running." He said it like it was something good to eat.

Dr. Yazzie strode across the room and sat on the floor. An inner circle was forming since the chairs were full.

"Dr. Yazzie is quite a runner," Mr. Handler said.

"I heard," she said. "He has a rock in his pocket that speaks to him."

"Yes," Mr. Handler said.

Their eyes met again. They smiled in a way that showed they both believed in that crazy rock.

William lumbered in and sat on the floor beside Dr. Yazzie. Corpse studied him as the lights dimmed. I drifted to the ceiling's farthest corner.

No introduction this time. Dr. Benson rose from his chair. His hair was loose, and I worked to get used to the profile of a man with silky, flowing hair as he put his wooden flute to his lips in that clarinet way.

A reedy note seeped out. Goose bumps rose on Corpse's flesh. The flute dove to lower notes, then arced high. So graceful. So simple. Just like I'd dreaded. Though seated in a chair, Corpse felt herself kneeling against the mountain, the sun's warmth radiating through her. The flute was sound-wave honesty again, yet this time it seemed to embody the sunrise. She considered Yale and how hollow her words about not going to college had sounded. Her mind darted to Mom, how they'd grown to understand each other. To Sugeidi in her maid dress. To her promises. To the self she'd recognized in the mirror. To how her view of life was changing.

She sensed all my warnings and fears, and she pictured Dr. Yazzie and Angel as they'd looked at me. Corpse saw herself from *my* perspective. She felt how I constantly reasoned, doubted, judged. She whispered, "You have to stop."

She heard Sugeidi say *You are wise and strong.* She heard Dr. Yazzie say *It tells me you're a good person. That you'll be okay.* She thought of Gabe, and felt, for the first time, worthy of his love.

The flute swelled, making her hunch forward, and she discovered that knife-of-honesty slice in her chest, the one I'd escaped through at the winter formal. She traced it, fury at me simmering. She whispered, "I am who I am." She started from its bottom edge, sealing it together with her thumb and two fingers.

I rushed down before her. She glared at me, hand inching up. Would I become a ghost? I shot through the bit left of that slice. Corpse sucked in air and bolted straight.

My world turned murky. I ricocheted in her boundaries. So dark. So confining. This was my future? I shot back out, careening against the ceiling, just as Corpse closed the slice. She hunched over again. Our link diminished to threads and a hollowness consumed me. A tear leaked across her cheek and down her nose, then splashed onto her leg in the emptiness next to her right hand's middle finger.

The flute music ended. She looked up from her feet as the room's lights brightened. Dr. Yazzie was watching her. One side of Angel's mouth turned up as she watched too. Roberta gaped. Around the circle, many eyes watched. I huddled in the corner.

"I need some air." She lunged toward the door, glancing at Dr. Yazzie. He nodded once, like she'd won a race. I followed her, a balloon dragged by a string, and not a shiny new one. A deflating one, like from a dance long over.

# Seventeen

FROM OONA'S JOURNAL:

*Water vapor in the form of clouds covers half the
Earth's surface. Clouds form when microscopic
droplets or ice particles suspended on the air
condense and gather.*

—Mr. Bonstuber

Corpse skipped lunch. As she approached the office, Mr. Handler was waiting for her out front. "You okay?" he said.

She shrugged and pushed back her hair.

"That flute music always gets me," Mr. Handler said. "I asked Dr. Benson to play today."

Corpse glanced at him and snorted.

They listened to some jays and the clack of bare branches in the breeze.

"So you fell running?" he said.

Corpse held out her palms. "With Angel."

Mr. Handler grinned.

Before I knew it, Corpse said, "I heard some teachers talking about a student scared by witches, maybe a ghost in somebody's room here. Do you believe it could be true?"

Mr. Handler regarded the sky. "I hoped this place would help you see things in a different light. I hadn't counted on it happening so fast."

Corpse kicked a pebble. "I died once already. Remember? So maybe I'm part ghost."

"It's not a thing I'll forget."

"Well, do you? Believe? In witches? Ghosts?"

He sighed. "Here, I do. In our world, it's not so easy."

"Why do you think that is?"

He scanned the common area. The panorama out the valley's funnel. "A quick, glib answer comes to mind, but I'd rather think on it and let you know."

"Okay," Corpse said.

"What do you believe?" Mr. Handler said.

She had my full attention. She shrugged. "I'm not sure. I'm realizing I was wondering about things like this before I got here. I just didn't understand I was wondering. You know? Like, I think water is alive somehow. Sort of the key to..." Footsteps approached.

Mr. Handler winked at her. "Hello, Tina," he said. Tina was another other girl who'd been at the conference. The one we'd never heard read. Corpse pressed her palms together like prayer and then followed them into the office.

―――――――

Corpse scooped mashed potatoes next to the baked chicken on her plate. She spooned out green beans and put those in her plate's remaining third. She filled a glass with water, grabbed silverware and a napkin, and looked around for Mr. Handler and his faculty table. Instead, she saw Angel and William. Angel patted the space between them.

As Corpse passed Mr. Handler's table, she felt Louise and Dr. Yazzie watching too, all of them like proud parents.

Angel and William were in a conversation. They kept talking as she sat down. Next to Angel sat Pauline, who Corpse had helped with her applications the day before. Pauline came from Oklahoma, but she'd applied to Arizona State University and University of Arizona. She wanted to be an engineer.

Corpse dug into the mashed potatoes, self-conscious about her wobblier-than-usual fork. After one bite she switched to her left hand and wondered if she'd ever be normal.

"Harvard this summer again, huh, William?" Pauline said. "I thought you hated it."

"The program was really good. There were just some lugheads there." He shrugged. "Good chance they won't be back."

"Brave." Angel snorted.

William let out a war-whoop.

They all laughed.

"What are you doing this summer?" Angel said to Corpse.

She shrugged. I hadn't even considered summer. Would

it be the usual shopping spree in New York followed by a month on a yacht? We actually liked that camp, the way they lived on and in that turquoise sea, ate mostly fish. She especially liked the dolphins that would dive with almost no splash around the boat. "Not sure," she said. "I usually I go to New York and then to a camp."

"Camp? Like with counselors? Where?" William said.

Corpse couldn't make herself say St. Lucia. She shrugged. "What happened at Harvard?"

William watched her for a minute, but went along with her change of subject. "Just some students who'd say things like 'I didn't know Indians wore normal clothes,' or 'I didn't know Indians cut their hair.'" He took a thoughtful bite of potatoes. "I don't think they were trying to be mean. I think they were just that dumb."

"Right," Angel said.

"Seriously?" Corpse said. "You believe they knew that little about Indians? That's impossible." She remembered how many times she'd said "Oh" and bit her lip.

"Honestly?" William said. "We're the last ethnicity where it's still okay to be racist."

Angel blew out her breath and let her hand drop. "Here we go."

"What do you mean?" Corpse said.

"Well, for starters, our nation's capital has a football team called the Redskins," William said.

"How about the Cleveland Indians logo?" Pauline said.

"Or Kansas City?" William said.

"Chiefs?" Corpse tried to remember if that was football or baseball.

"Can you imagine the riots if a team was named the Washington Negros?" William said. "The Cleveland Asians? Maybe the Kansas City Rabbis?"

Corpse laughed with everyone else. But it wasn't actually funny at all. How had she not noticed this before?

"That doesn't bother me," Angel said, dismissing it with a wave. "The comments bothered me."

"You were there too?" Corpse said.

"Well, they should," William said.

"For a writing program."

Corpse slouched back. "I've just been going to camp in summers."

To Pauline, Angel said, "What did you decide to do?"

Pauline opened her mouth to speak, but Roberta arrived, thumping down her tray and slouching into her seat. She picked up her fork, rocked it in her fingers. The anger and confusion from when she'd stormed through me came right back.

"Louise just offered me five hundred bucks not to dance anymore." Roberta poked her potatoes twice, pushed her tray forward, crossed her arms on the table, and rested her forehead on them.

Money, Corpse thought, created a lot of problems. As I studied how Roberta's hair fanned out on the table, Corpse felt her butt against that hard leather chair in Dad's office.

# Eighteen

*Water covers most of the planet, and its high specific heat holds the Earth's temperature within a range that allows life. Organisms, made mostly of water, also benefit in the same way.*

—Biology: Life's Course

"It's already Thursday," Corpse said.

"All day," Angel said.

"Time is different here," Corpse said.

"Uh-huh."

They strolled toward the dorms through moonless black. After living next to two rivers, one of water and one of cars, Corpse couldn't get used to the quiet, and she realized her ears had been straining to hear rushing since she'd arrived. Such darkness, no water. Her mouth felt dry, and she tried to count the number of times in her life she'd been in a place this still.

One. Now.

A coyote darted across the road. Another flashed after it. Moments later, eerie howling rose from the mountainside. Angel looked toward the howling, then ahead, seeming to think hard. I was thinking hard too. About Roberta. About money. About my future. They arrived at our door, and Corpse dug out her key.

"Well, good night," she said.

"Want to come to my room?" Angel said.

"Sure."

Corpse followed her to the building's far end. The coyotes sounded again, each yip and howl so unique, so mournful, it churned her guts. Angel unlocked the door of the room on the building's other end.

Inside, it was like our room, except crowded and lived-in. One bed had a bedspread with big poppy blooms. The other, a bedspread with zebra stripes. There were two desks squeezed along the wall with the dresser, one on each side, and on them were framed photos and books. Another dresser stood against the wall before the bathroom. Covering the walls were posters of movies and bands. Angel walked to an iPod in an alarm clock on her nightstand and turned it on. Hip hop music pulsed out. Above the nightstand, her feathers hung from a rawhide cord tied to a nail.

"My roommate's gone this week," she said. "That's her bed." She pointed to the one with the zebra spread. "She went home."

"Is everything okay?" Corpse said.

"Yes," Angel said. "Sometimes we just need to get back home. You know?"

Corpse sat on the zebra bed and flopped onto her back, felt a little out of control. "No, actually, I don't." She could feel Angel studying her. She looked at the photos on Angel's roommate's desk. One showed six people in formal attire, corsages pinned to the girls' dresses, boutonnières to the guys' lapels. They stood in a line, arms around one another, obviously having a great time.

"Do you have prom here?" Corpse said.

"Sure." Angel followed her eyes to the photo. "They hold it at the Oasis House. It's really fun."

"Where's the Oasis House?"

"Farther down the road along the valley's other side. It's lush there. Pretty."

In the photo, Angel's head rested against William's shoulder. "Was William your date?"

"Yes," she said. "But we're just friends."

"I like your dress," Corpse said. "Blue is my favorite color. My prom dress was blue." My mind travelled to last April. To prom and Richie Leevers, our date. We'd hated Richie Leevers. Ash had insisted we go with him because he was best friends with Paul Thomas, who she was dating at the time. We'd met Gabe in the hall the week afterward, and it was strange to think of a time before him. I remembered our last dance with Gabe. How Corpse had kissed him for real because I'd left her. She moaned and sat up.

"We had a winter formal back in January," she said to Angel's puzzled look. "I left it, took the bus to a trail by my house, hiked out, and let myself freeze to death in a pink satin dress and strappy heels dyed to match. I was wearing a freaking crown. My heart stopped. The doctors said I was dead for twenty minutes. Twenty minutes."

Angel didn't say anything.

"I hate pink. My Mom made me get that dress. They must have sliced it open because they had to cut holes in my groin and pump warm fluid into me before my heart would start again." Her fingers went to the tiny, precise scars. She'd forgotten those incisions. Funny, she thought, how these saved her body, while that slice in her chest saved her soul.

I had to think about that. Did she mean my leaving was good?

"I keep picturing the paramedics, the doctors, working to revive me and me wearing that crown." She snorted. "Dad always called me princess. I made him stop."

"So you're on your second life."

Corpse cocked her head. "Yes, I guess I am." *Second life.* She liked the sound of that.

Would her second life include me?

"When do you go home?" Angel said.

"Saturday morning."

"So you just have tomorrow left," Angel said.

"I guess so." She considered asking Angel about her dream but decided not to. "I never heard what you're going to do this summer."

"I'm going to work in the movie theater at home. I need money for college."

"Have you decided where you want to go next year?"

Angel looked at Corpse with a funny expression. "I think so."

A knock at the door made them both jump. When Angel answered it, Dr. Yazzie stood there, hand in his pocket.

"There's a wildfire down across the highway." He gestured with his chin, as if they could see through the building across the miles out there in the dark. "This one's spreading. We may have to evacuate. Pack a bag just in case. Stay in your rooms, so we know where to find you. It's a ways off, and it would have to jump the highway, but the wind's blowing this way."

Angel closed the door, grinning.

"This is good?" Corpse said, but Angel didn't answer.

Into a backpack, Angel stuffed a pair of jeans, two shirts, two pairs of underwear and socks, and two framed photos from her desk. She grabbed her toothbrush and a hairbrush. She took the prom photo from her roommate's desk. She lifted the feathers reverently from their nail, slid them into a gauzy bag she pulled from her drawer, and zipped them into the front pocket. They went to Corpse's room. Corpse packed the few things she'd taken out of her suitcase while Angel paced on the patio. Corpse joined her.

"I can see the flames." Angel pointed ahead and left. Sure enough, there were flickers of orangish-yellow.

"I've never seen a forest fire," Corpse said. "Let's watch it." She pulled the bedspreads off the beds and handed one to Angel. Smoke clogged the air.

Corpse wrapped herself like a burrito and settled into a

plastic chair. Angel set her bedspread in the other chair and walked to the low wall bordering the patio, staring at the fire. The flames, an arm's-length wide and tall as Corpse's thumbnail, were hard to imagine as dangerous, yet it was mesmerizing, watching them waver in that space halfway to the invisible horizon.

"I wonder how it started," Corpse said.

"A smoker, probably. Flicking his butt out the window. Butthead," Angel said. "This happens a few times a year."

A set of red and blue flashing lights appeared for a second and disappeared. Corpse imagined all the firefighters and emergency workers. How loud and chaotic it must be, while for her and Angel it was so still.

I thought how there must have been a circus of pulsing lights parked at the trailhead back home as rescue workers hauled us out. I imagined the pajama-and-bathrobe-clad occupants of the houses nearby, gawking out their windows. A scrap of our history we'd never see. Corpse rubbed her forehead, sighed, and surveyed a sky muted by the moon's light. She thought of Dad, imprisoned in his recliner.

Angel blew out her breath. "I'm going down there."

"To the fire?"

"My cousins are firefighters. They might be down there."

"Oh."

Angel strode into the room.

Corpse shot to her feet. "You won't get caught?"

She shrugged. "I miss them."

Corpse eyed the line of flame. "I'm going with you."

"You didn't even want to run down the mountain."

I forced myself quiet.

"There's a bunch of people who have a memory of the dead me," Corpse said. "Of the flashing lights and the rescue workers. I don't have that memory, and I need to know what it was like. That fire there. Maybe it's as close as I'll ever come."

Angel shrugged again. "It's a long hike. You won't get much sleep tonight."

Corpse flexed her fingers, feeling all ten. "I'm starting to see things more clearly, the things that made me do what I did. But there's so much about my life I don't understand. I guess that's why I was following you up that mountain. I have to start figuring out some answers. Does that make sense?" She didn't mention that she also craved seeing Angel's people.

"I'll be right back." Angel left Corpse's room and returned with a flashlight and two down coats.

This time I hung close. I needed to see that fire and Angel's people just as much as Corpse did.

————

Angel kept the flashlight off till we were away from the campus. Even then, it cast a wan light the size and shape of a soccer ball. The trail descended steadily, sometimes dropping into a draw and climbing steeply out. It was hard to gauge when the rocks or sticks or whatever Corpse saw in the flashlight's beam would arrive underfoot, so she tripped about every twentieth step.

After an hour the air turned strangely warm, conjuring Chateau Antunes's warm air as she'd wobbled, in that mask of bandages, down the hall toward Gabe. The night sky glowed, and a roaring sound filled it. Ahead of them reached a wall of white smoke. Shouts sounded, faint against the roar. The smoke made Corpse blink and take shallow breaths.

The highway appeared a hundred yards down a graded hill. On its far side, weirdly enticing flames took over the night. Sheriff cars, state patrol cars, fire trucks, and trucks with Forest Service and Bureau of Land Management emblems filled the inside lane, their strobe lights slicing the dark. The roaring came from the fire, but it reminded Corpse of a river's sound. And something else she couldn't place.

Angel and Corpse settled behind a clump of sagebrush. A thwapping consumed the air, and their hair swirled. A helicopter, its light a knife of daylight, dropped water from a huge, dangling sack onto the fire's length. It turned and passed again. In its path, Corpse saw firefighter after firefighter step back and look up.

The breeze toward us stiffened. A tall pine exploded, sending a spray of orange branches and bark. The tree swayed and fell, an arc of yellow against the night, and a scream pierced the fire's roar. Corpse scanned the scene frantically: one firefighter lay trapped beneath the trunk, another beneath its branches.

Firefighters rushed forward, hurling dirt onto the tree

with their shovels, able to safely reach only the branches. They pried out that firefighter from a web of flame. Angel glanced at Corpse, but Corpse was fixated on the body trapped beneath the trunk.

In Bio, during our cellular respiration lab, Mr. Bonstuber had told us that when organic things combusted, they rose as carbon dioxide and steam, invisible but for suspended soot and ash. Before her eyes, that firefighter was evaporating.

Within minutes the fire was gnawing the highway's edge. Two paramedics and two firefighters shot onto the pavement through a gap in the flames, carrying a yellow stretcher. The injured firefighter was jostled along, but his eyes stayed closed. Angel rushed toward the stretcher, but Corpse froze and touched the top of her head, where Ash's crown had been.

I was right there with her, and in our mind's eye, that guy's brown jacket and pants transformed to a pink dress, his bearded face to ours. Something about how he lay wasn't right; we peered at death.

The back of an ambulance opened, a bright geometry, and Angel returned to Corpse's side as the stretcher slid into it. The doors slammed. The paramedics raced to the cab's doors, and the firefighters milled in the red glow from the ambulance's taillights as it pulled into a paved connecter between the east-bound and west-bound lanes. Its siren sounded, and Corpse covered her ears. At the road's edge, the vehicle's headlights swept across them.

"Hey!" one of the firefighters shouted.

"Sherman!" Angel called.

"You can't be here! It's not safe!" he shouted.

Corpse and Angel were in two headlamp beams that started toward them.

"It's me, Angel!" She walked toward the lights. Corpse followed.

One of the lights said, "Angel! You shouldn't have come. It's dangerous!" and then it became a tall guy hugging her.

"You stink!" Angel said.

Sherman chuckled. Corpse could make out a long, serious face below the beam.

"Where's Kenny?"

"I'll get him. But then you have to go. Promise?"

Angel nodded, and Sherman took off in a tired boot-jog. The other firefighter followed him, but walking. Angel wiped her cheek with the back of her hand. Corpse stepped beside her. A minute later, two headlamps bounced toward them again—one shorter, resembling an off-kilter car on a bumpy road.

"Straight A!" called the shorter beam. It picked Angel up and spun her. She squealed. Sherman watched them, grinning, and then his eyes landed on Corpse.

Kenny set Angel down, and Angel held up her hand against the light. Kenny turned off his headlamp. He was round-faced and jolly with eyebrows that matched Angel's, and their eyes had a conversation. Corpse felt she should look away, but she gobbled up the bond in their gaze.

Then Kenny saw Corpse, squinting in Sherman's headlamp.

"This is Oona," Angel said as Sherman extinguished his

light. The fire's incendiary glow cast their faces in ghoulish shadows. I thought how all light, even the sun, was released energy. Corpse attempted a smile, but the burning guy pressed around her. The guy on the stretcher seared her gaze, and the bond connecting Angel and her cousins was a thousand pounds on her chest. Angel's people. Corpse swayed and gulped the smoke-clogged air. Everything started to churn. A hacking cough bent her.

"You shouldn't have come," Kenny said.

Angel shrugged.

A shout made the cousins look back, toward the combusting man. Their faces turned grim.

"Things good?" Kenny said.

"They're okay. I miss home."

They fell silent against the fire's roar.

"You know that guy?" Angel said.

Kenny shook his head, but his eyes held pain. He reached out a filthy hand and petted Angel's cheek. "We've got to go."

Angel nodded. "Be careful," she said to their backs.

"Always," Sherman called over his shoulder.

A smudge from Kenny's touch marked Angel's cheek, but she wore a serene expression. She walked to where we'd emerged on the highway, scaled the hill halfway, and sat down. Corpse stood for a minute, then settled beside her.

Angel stared into the flames. "Just being close helps."

———

We hiked back in silence. Corpse felt the burning guy under the tree press around them, and the guy on the stretcher scorched her vision. Had Gabe and Dad run ahead of or behind our stretcher as it moved along the trail? When the ambulance slammed closed its rectangle of light, did they stand grieving in the dark? Knowing we were dead?

Guilt and smoke churned so hard in Corpse that she stopped and puked. I hovered near her, wishing I could puke too. When she turned, Angel stood a few feet away, still gazing at the fire like it was a lifeline.

She seemed to sense when Corpse was ready, and they moved on. Corpse cleaned her mouth on the back of her sleeve, realizing too late the coat wasn't hers. We seemed to trudge out of a nightmare.

Corpse pictured the water falling from the helicopter, the burning body returning to the clouds. "There's no water here. I keep listening for it, but there's no water. It makes me thirsty. For months I've been fascinated with water." She spoke loudly so her words would reach Angel. "I don't know why. It just seems to be whispering an answer. I can't figure it out. It's driving me crazy."

"There's water," Angel said over her shoulder. "Beneath our feet." She scanned the sky. "In Navajo tradition, there's a water god. He's responsible for rain, sleet, snow. Thunder and lightning. Maybe he's been speaking to you, trying to heal you."

Corpse thought of Circle, and I squirmed. "Maybe," she said. "Sherman and Kenny. Are they brothers?"

"Nah," Angel said. "They're the sons of my mom's

sisters. They live together in Albuquerque, but they're fighting another fire near here."

"How many cousins do you have?"

Angel seemed to count. "Seventeen."

"I can't imagine it. That sense of family."

They walked in silence again.

"Those guys were dead." Corpse said. "It'll kill their families." She took a shuddering breath, coughed, and surveyed the stars. "Things are so wrong at home. My family is dying. I think my Dad's the key. When he was ten, his family died. I don't know how. He won't talk about it. That was in Portugal. He was sent to live in America. I think it screwed him up. And money."

"Money?" Angel said.

"Yes. Money's like a drug for him. He's addicted. God, it's such bullshit. You wouldn't believe how rich we are. We live in a freaking castle. I have my own car. A Range Rover, and not a used one. No, one right off the lot. I figured out that Mom spends the annual income of most of the families here just going to spas. We have a maid. Yet in every other way, in the important ways, we're so poor. That's what I figured out at the conference during William's reading. That's why I bolted. Does that sound crazy?"

"A little."

"Your cousins are great. You're so lucky."

"Lucky." Angel seemed to weigh the word. "Maybe your dad just needs to go back to his people."

"Huh?" Corpse said.

"Like my roommate. Maybe your dad just needs to visit home. Remember who he is."

"Oh." Corpse started to dismiss her words, but then remembered Dad in that recliner searching the stars, or on the beach when we were nine as he peered across the sea. She considered that new nodding, how he seemed two places at once. "His people," she said. She stopped and gazed at the flames, again the height of her thumb. "That's it, Angel! You're brilliant!"

"It's just common sense."

One flame flared high as Corpse thought about spring break. She ticked through ideas, and each shadowy rise of the moonlit hills before her evolved to steely gray waves that merged with the horizon. Beyond that horizon lay another continent. I kept silent, nervous as hell about what she was considering. Yet maybe I didn't know so much after all.

They returned to their journey back. A few points of light from the school appeared through the trees.

"I hope the fire doesn't reach up here. I like this place," Corpse said.

"Me too."

They came to the dorms. They went into Corpse's room and back out to the patio. Wrapping themselves in the bed-spreads, they settled into the chairs. Corpse's legs ached. Her lungs burned. Her scabbed palms pulsed. So did her head.

"Thanks for taking me down there," she said.

Angel was asleep.

As Corpse gazed at that smudge on Angel's cheek, I couldn't get rid of the terrible image of Gabe and Dad staring after that ambulance. Corpse clicked through how she'd make spring break happen. Pictured Portugal and Dad and healing. After a long time her mind turned gooey, and she yawned. In the distance, the coyotes howled, a thread on the air that raised goose bumps on her skin.

She saw again the bond in Angel's and Kenny's gaze. I thought about the years our family had spent avoiding each others' eyes. Thought of our nocturnal prowling in Chateau Antunes. How the scariest dangers stemmed from love.

Corpse woke to sprinkles against her face. Her head was cocked over the chair's back and drops tickled her throat like intimacy. When she finally moved, her neck was rebellious and sore. Angel was gone. Corpse massaged her neck. The fire's width had shrunk to the length of her finger.

"Good job," she whispered to the firefighters and police. "Good job," she whispered to the clouds. She willed her words to travel to the paramedics and the doctors who'd saved her. Wished for the guts to tell them in person.

She shuffled inside and closed the sliding glass door. Angel slept on one bed. Corpse settled on the other and drifted off to the rhythm of Angel's breathing.

# Nineteen

FROM OONA'S JOURNAL:

*Schauberger's view of the world contradicted the accepted rules of science.*

—Oona

Angel returned from bussing her breakfast dishes. Her eyes were puffy like Corpse's, and she rubbed them. Otherwise she seemed refreshed. At peace. I envied her.

"Do you want to see the Oasis House?" she said.

"Don't you have class?" Corpse rolled her head, try-ing work out her neck's soreness.

"I'm taking the morning off. Dr. Yazzie gave me per-mission."

Dr. Yazzie and Mr. Handler were deep in conversation at a table across the room. Corpse could see Dr. Yazzie's hand in his pocket. He wore a faint smile as he watched her, and she wondered if that rock had tattled about last night. How had he ended up with that rock anyway? Did he pick it out?

Was it a gift? And how could a person know if a rock was wise? Maybe he was just pulling her leg. She hoped not; she liked what that rock had said.

They strolled across the common area and onto the road. Corpse wore her fleece against the chill. Angel wore a jean jacket, and her hair riffled on the breeze. Corpse looked around and thought how this place reversed ordinary things.

"Angel," she said, "who was scared by witches, maybe had a ghost in her room at the beginning of the year?"

"How do you know about that?"

Smoke hung in the air. That morning, when Corpse had looked out her room's sliding doors, the fire had become just rising gray scarves.

"I heard two teachers talking. White ones." Corpse slid her hands into her fleece's pockets, pressed her fingers together to blot the missing ones' wails.

"The girl's not here anymore. Her father died. She had to go home."

"He froze to death?"

Angel looked at her funny. "Yes."

"What room was it?"

"Yours."

Corpse stumbled, and Angel caught her arm.

At the road's fork they followed its right side. It descended more than the road to the dorms, and they walked in long strides. With each step Corpse tried to push forward off the balls of her feet to eliminate that bob. Over her shoulder, the climb back up taunted. Her sore legs were already arguing with the downhill. Since she and Angel had slept in, they hadn't greeted the sun.

"A medicine man cleansed my room?"

Angel didn't respond.

"Does that stuff linger? Like, could his power cleanse me?"

Corpse had my attention.

Angel seemed to sort out her thoughts on the road ahead of them. "When you first came here, you scared me."

"What exactly is a ghost in your culture?"

Angel shook her head. "It's not good to talk about these things."

"What do you mean?"

Angel just shook her head.

"Could a medicine man cure me? My hands and feet have been tingling since Circle."

Angel gave her a serious once-over and then broke into a sly smile. "Seems like you're healing yourself."

"Really?" Corpse smiled, but I swore myself to silence. At least for a while.

The road descended a half mile, till a hillside curved before them and the Oasis House appeared, a sprawling porched building nestled in the valley floor. Leafless trees towered overhead, but lush vegetation quilted the ground.

Corpse followed Angel up three front steps onto the porch and around the building's side to the back, where a huge deck reached out to the green shore of a pond. She descended steps to the pond's bank, and her reflection stared back at us from the water.

Pretty was coming back to her. Something in her eyes

had changed. I looked closer. Recognized courage. She reached out to trace that reflected nose, sending waves across that girl.

"How can this be here?" she said.

"There's a spring," Angel said.

Corpse returned to the deck and peered through glass doors into an open room with a wood floor, leather couches and chairs. A regal painting of a Native American chief in a headdress, whose name she couldn't remember, hung on the wall opposite her. She recognized a corner of the gilt frame from the background of the photo on Angel's roommate's desk, and she imagined the people in that photo posing in there, laughing.

She turned to the pond, lined on the far side with cat-tails and bud-laden bushes. "This is like a different world."

"I like that about the desert," Angel said. "How it holds hidden worlds. Sometimes I hike that way along the valley floor." She pointed beyond the pond. "Hawks live in a tree down there. Sometimes they leave these on the ground." Angel held out a feather. "This is for all the things you've survived. And for our friendship."

The feather's reddish-brown tip was followed by a thick dark-brown stripe, then thirteen stripes below that, reminding Corpse of a tiger. At its end, a fluffy white tuft abruptly became the shaft held by Angel. Corpse's hand covered her mouth.

"You have to treat it with respect," Angel said.

"No problem." Corpse took the feather, ran her two

fingers up one side and down the other. "Thank you."
She leaned her elbows on the deck railing and admired it.

Angel joined her at the rail.

One stripe had a break in the middle. Corpse decided
that was ours. She traced its break and mentally thanked
the emergency room doctor.

"William wants to be a doctor," she said.

"Yes," Angel said. "He always has."

"You've known him a long time?"

She shrugged. "My grandfather and his grandmother
are old friends. We've been hanging out at powwows since
we were in diapers."

"Oh," Corpse said. "What do you want to be?"

Angel shrugged. "A writer maybe. Someone who helps
my people somehow."

*My people.* I pictured Sherman and Kenny. All we had
was our screwed-up family. I pictured Ash glaring at us.
Tanesha scowling at us. Manny shouting, "*Chingado!*" All
those eyes in the halls.

"How about you?" Angel said. "What do you want to
be?"

Corpse twirled her feather, head tilted, and thought,
Happy, loved, a scientist. "No clue."

On the pond were lily pads. The breeze gently tex-
tured its surface, rocking the pads.

"I wonder how charred it is down there by the highway," Corpse said. "I keep thinking about those guys' families." Her voice broke, and before I knew it, I hovered over
her shoulders.

Angel pressed her lips and leaned on the rail.

"That was lucky. The rain. To lose all this would be a shame," Corpse said.

"I didn't want to know you." Angel smiled in the way that transformed her face. "I didn't like that dream I had, and I only remembered you from the conference. When you got here, I tried to keep my distance, but I kept running into you. I finally decided to stop fighting it. I'm glad I did."

"Me too," Corpse said.

"My dream," Angel said, "was that you were my room-mate at Yale."

Corpse stiffened.

"I think I'll listen to that dream. I've decided to go to Yale."

"Even knowing how screwed-up I am?"

"You seem okay. And my dreams are never wrong."

Corpse looked at her sneakers. Gabe at Harvard, Angel, probably, at Yale. I didn't know what to think. Maybe after spring break we could consider college. Maybe then we'd feel worthy of these people who risked themselves on us.

"I can't commit to anything until my family is better."

"And if they heal apart?" Angel said.

"Then they heal apart," Corpse said. "Right now things are not okay. It would be like abandoning that guy under the fire last night."

Their eyes met.

Angel: He was already dead.

Corpse looked down.

Angel shrugged.

They leaned on the rail, taking in the scenery. Down the valley, a hawk appeared above the cottonwoods. It rose in a sleek, soaring curve.

"Maybe your feather came from that one," Angel said.

Its wings adjusted in slight movements against the currents.

––––––––––

William, Angel, and a few other students stood at the back of Mr. Handler's Prius. Louise came out of the counseling office, the screen door clapping behind her.

"Well," she said, "go if you must. Thanks for everything." She hugged Mr. Handler.

"No, thank you. I gain far more than you do when I come here." He turned to the rest of the kids. "From all of you." He looked worn-out but content.

Roberta marched up. She and Mr. Handler regarded each other.

Angel stepped from Corpse's side and hugged Mr. Handler. A couple other kids did the same. William shook his hand, and Corpse noticed his grip was light, like he was giving Mr. Handler something delicate.

"Good luck this summer," Mr. Handler said to him. "Good luck to you all."

Roberta hung at the back of the group, studying the asphalt. Corpse had an urge to slap her. To shout, *Hey! These people care about you!* But I remembered Roberta's scowl in the counseling office after she'd passed through me, her astonished face at Circle.

Mr. Handler and Corpse walked to their sides of the Prius. They opened its doors.

William, with Angel at his elbow, followed Corpse. "Angel has my number," Corpse said to him. "If you're in Leadville, come for some ice cream."

"I might be on a diet. Slimming down for college." He grinned.

"Bye," Angel said, and she and Corpse hugged. "Let me know how it goes with your dad."

Mr. Handler seemed to absorb her words as he watched them across the Prius's shining roof.

"I will," Corpse said. She started to get in the car but felt as if she was leaving something important. Too important. She turned to Angel. "Maybe you can come visit me this summer?"

Angel's eyebrows rose. "I have to work."

"A few days?"

"Maybe."

Corpse got in and closed the door. She rolled down the window. Mr. Handler started the car, and Angel said, "You had a sky blue bedspread. With clouds. Okay. I'll come see how rich white folks live."

Mr. Handler pulled from the lot and waved his arm out the window. The Prius ascended the road, and Corpse craned around and looked through me out the back window.

The kids were talking in a group, but Louise and Angel watched the Prius.

"Amazing place, isn't it?" Mr. Handler said.

"Yes."

Angel grew smaller. Corpse held up her thumb, and Angel was the size of its nail. Her eyes rose to where the fire had been, across the ridges' waves to the horizon. The Prius crested the rise, zinged over the cattle guard, and started bouncing along the washboard dirt road.

"In the middle of nowhere," Mr. Handler said, shaking his head.

The dog sprinted out to them.

"Crazy animal," Mr. Handler said. "I wish they'd tie it up. I'm afraid I'm going to hit it."

Corpse pictured the dog chained up, yanking and choking itself as it snapped and barked, frantic to get to Mr. Handler's car. This dog would break its neck trying to chase them.

The dog's fierce barking trailed off, and she watched it in the side mirror, braced in the road, fangs bared. Did that dog ever curl by the fire and let itself be petted? She craned around, looking through me again at the space where she imagined the school to be, curled in its valley. *Middle of nowhere. DEAD GIRL GOES NOWHERE.* In nowhere, we finally started to puzzle ourself out.

# Twenty

FROM OONA'S JOURNAL:

*Ice floats because it expands as it solidifies. If ice sank,*
*all ponds, lakes, and oceans would freeze, and life on*
*Earth, as we know it, could not survive.*

—Biology: Life's Course

Chateau Antunes smelled of Corpse's favorite enchiladas. Sugeidi stood at the kitchen sink, water rushing from the tap into a sudsy bowl, and her hands disappeared into white bubbles. Her skin was the same hue as Angel's skin, and this made Corpse smile. She tried to picture the distance between Fort Defiance, Arizona, and Monterrey, Mexico.

"Smells good," she said.

Sugeidi's hand flew to her heart.

"Oona! No sneak!" Then she grinned. Across the chest of her maid dress was a handprint outlined in bubbles, and Corpse laughed. Sugeidi dried her hands in her apron, and Corpse saw that dress in the way Sugeidi did, so she didn't hug her like she'd planned. Instead she walked to her, put one hand on her shoulder, and kissed her cheek. In the corner of her eye, Mom appeared in the doorway but stepped back.

"I missed you, Sugeidi. It's good to be home," Corpse said.

Sugeidi assessed her, and Corpse straightened under her scrutiny. "You mend," she said.

"I'm getting there."

"*Bueno*, Oona. *Bueno*."

"*Bueno*," Corpse said.

Mom came in. "You're back." Her words sounded rehearsed. She stopped at the breakfast bar.

"I'm back."

I noticed Mom had caverns in her cheeks and around her eyes, even rivulets between the bones of her wrists. Though taller than Corpse by three inches, she seemed breakable. Corpse walked to her and hugged her. Cautiously, I blanketed them. It felt okay. Nice.

Mom sighed and her arms circled the low part of Corpse's back. She laid her hollow cheek against Corpse's hair.

"You can stop worrying now," Corpse said.

Mom pulled back. Her right eye quivered, and she wiped her cheek. "I see that." She looked over Corpse's shoulder at Sugeidi. "Tell us about your trip."

"Where's Dad?"

"He'll be back from Chicago late tonight," Mom said.

Corpse touched Mom's arm, and Mom looked down.

Part of Corpse wanted to flee back to Angel, to anywhere. This seriousness, this much suffering, was a disease. She climbed onto a stool and Mom took the one next to her.

"I'm starving," Corpse said. "Are those enchiladas ready?"

"*Sí*," Sugeidi said. She pulled the pan from the oven and turned the knob from *warm* to *off*. With a spatula she dug out the red-sauced enchiladas and filled two plates that she carried to them. She drew two glasses of water, set a bowl of corn salad between their plates, and stood at the counter.

"None for you?" Mom said.

Their eyes had a conversation Corpse couldn't decipher. I realized it was Saturday, a day Sugeidi was usually with her family in the trailer park. What had gone on with just them here?

"I eat already," Sugeidi said. "Tell, Oona."

Corpse told them about greeting the sun, and the rock in Dr. Yazzie's pocket, and the dead guys in the fire, and the feather Angel gave her. Neither of them spoke or even blinked with doubt. Instead they leaned close, hanging on her every word.

"Thing is, I'd held them on some sort of pedestal. An ideal," Corpse said. "But William and Roberta and Dr. Yazzie and Angel, they're just people. Regular people. Like us." Her eyes met Mom's and Sugeidi's, all their struggles suspended there, and they burst into laughter.

Day faded to night, and in the dimming kitchen, the triangle of their heads seemed lit.

Gabe's arms felt so good. They were made to fit together, I decided.

"You look better," he said. "I'm not sure what it is."

"I am better."

He kissed her and she kissed him back, like on the dance floor. She weaved her fingers into his hair.

"Wow!" he said. "Much better."

"I thought a lot about you. About us," she said.

"It must have been good."

They kissed again. Corpse pressed closer, and he pulled her tighter. Her kisses moved along his cheek to the stubble at his jaw. Seemed to crackle across his dimple. She kissed his ear, and they looked at each other in a way that had never existed before. One of his hands ran up her back into her hair. He peered over her shoulder through the living room and into the kitchen.

"Where is everybody?"

"Sugeidi just left to visit her son. Mom's watching a movie downstairs. Dad's flying back from Chicago."

"That sucks. That he left. Your mom's great."

"Really?"

"Yes. She's really trying."

"I've never said thank you, Gabe. For loving me through it all."

"If this is how you're going to express it, thank me all you want."

They kissed again, whole bodies kissing. I drew back,

kept seeing Roberta. Gabe's hardness shouted beneath his jeans, and Corpse molded herself against it. How did she know to do this?

"What happened at that school?" He fingered the heart on her necklace.

"I figured some things out." She snuggled closer.

"I don't have anything with me. Like rubbers," he whispered.

"Why would you? I've been like a corpse." She stumbled on "corpse" and her eyes darted around, then over her shoulder.

"What is it?" Gabe said.

She shoved my judging aside. "I'm going to go on the pill. I'll see the doctor next week."

"Wow!" he said. "Things are really looking up."

"I'll say."

They laughed like they'd robbed a bank, and he hugged her closer.

"Are you really a virgin?" she whispered.

"Yes. I told you, Hernandez men love once. You're the one that's hard to believe is a virgin."

"Believe it."

She ran her thumb across his dimple. She thought how Gabe had his people, too, how they anchored him. She took his hand and led him to the velvety couch.

"Oona—"

"It's okay. I promise."

I squirmed as she lay on the couch and pulled Gabe to her. He settled carefully between her and the couch's back. His hardness pressed her hip and she turned toward it, wanted it in a way that had nothing to do with reasoning or doubting or judging.

He traced the plane of her cheek. Moved down her sweater and slid his hand underneath it. She arched her back as he tried to unclasp her bra, but he couldn't figure it out.

"Gabe Hernandez not good at something?" she whispered, unclasping it for him.

His fingers trembled against the flat of her belly and stayed there, memorizing it. He reached up, noting each of her ribs, till he found her breast. Breathing hard, his finger haloed her nipple and everything disappeared but Gabe and her and their pulse. She lifted her sweater and he looked at her, leaned down. She felt his warm mouth. He moved to her other breast, and she thought she'd explode. She pulled Gabe on top of her.

*Humping*, I thought, and the word drifted to the back of her skull. *DEAD GIRL HUMPS.*

She paused. Gabe's mouth hovered over hers. They exchanged breaths, and she reached down to his pants. "Just our jeans," she said. She unbuttoned and unzipped both their pants.

Gabe took on an intensity we'd seen only on the soccer field. This, along with underwear on underwear, put Corpse over the top, and her breathing rose an octave. Gabe's too. Their humping grew furious, and it became her favorite word. Her head bloomed, and she gasped and dropped back on the couch. Gabe lay limp on top of her, and wet spread into her pubic hair.

"Wow!" he said against her ear.

"And we're still virgins."

He laughed gently.

I sighed on their intimacy.

The door between the kitchen and the garage opened and something heavy clunked against the stone floor. They bolted up. Gabe zipped and buttoned his jeans. Corpse zipped and buttoned hers. Their eyes met, realizing how this would look, and they lay back down.

Dad closed the door, walked through the kitchen, paused at the doorway to the dark living room, and continued down the bedroom hall, suitcase rolling behind him.

Gabe and Corpse burst into muffled laughter.

# Twenty-One

FROM OONA'S JOURNAL:

*Most living cells have an internal pH of 7.*
*A change in pH, even minor, can be damaging.*

—Biology: Life's Course

Corpse walked to the bank of dining room windows, knelt before the peaks, and held out her open palms just as the sun shot rays over the mountains' jagged line. "Good morning," she said.

I dropped back to study how the sun's rays traced her body. She closed her eyes and considered how Sugeidi had stayed on her day off to welcome her home with her favorite meal. How Mom, Sugeidi, and she had been a trio. She thought of Gabe and flushed.

Today: Dad.

She tried to plan how she'd start their conversation, but her mind ricocheted to Ash. Tomorrow she'd work things out with her. Corpse crinkled her nose, knew they'd never be friends like they were, but she could at least make things, well, nicer.

She took a deep breath and cleared her mind. "Courage," she whispered.

Though it was Sunday, Dad was already in his office, she was sure. She'd carry in the LIFE game as an excuse. Keep her butt in that chair and chitchat about Chicago and her trip. She'd gently lead their talk toward Portugal.

Nervous as hell, I clung to silence.

In the living room, she took LIFE from the cupboard. She passed through the kitchen on the way to Dad's office. Mom ambled in, still in her fleecy robe and rubbing her eyes.

"You're up early," she said. "I just woke up. My head hit the pillow and I was out. I didn't even hear your father come in. Did Gabe stay long?"

"An hour." Corpse turned away to hide the heat rising up her neck, hoped Mom wouldn't notice the LIFE game, but Mom just moved to the coffee machine and poured herself a cup. She opened the fridge, poured half-and-half into her coffee, and stirred it. Corpse tried to imagine what it felt like, sleeping with someone who wouldn't talk to you. She pictured Mom and Dad hugging their bed's edges, their backs like armor. Last night Corpse had slept face-down so the wet of her underwear pressed into her. She wore them still. Maybe she'd wear them for a week.

Mom leaned her hip into the counter and sipped her steaming coffee. Her eyes glittered and she looked so pretty. "I haven't slept like that in years."

Corpse moved down the hall toward Dad's office on watery legs. Each bobbing step rocked the game under her arm. Return of the little marching army. She bent her hips, her knees, her ankles and stayed lower with each stride, trying to eliminate that sound. It didn't help. She straightened. Maybe this was just her new walk.

She came to Dad's office door and paused. She filled her lungs and reeled herself back to that mountaintop with Angel, the sun bursting over that horizon below. She conjured the warm splash of its rays and wondered why it was harder to confront the people you loved than it was to confront strangers.

Dad's phone rang, that annoying regular-phone ringtone, and he answered. He talked more on that phone than he talked to us and Mom put together. She understood a little of the finance jargon.

Dad laughed. A rare thing. "Thursday?" he said. "Thursday would be good."

Dad never said "good" that way. Who listened on the phone's other end? Why was he, or she, lucky enough to hear him talk this way? Corpse turned furious that Dad refused to laugh with Mom or her. She strode into his office, to that chair, and sat down, erect as a soldier, LIFE across her lap. I hung in the doorway.

Dad studied her as he talked into the phone. He really was handsome, especially with the gray peppering his temples, but his eyes had taken on a slinking look. He was so successful. People trusted him with their money. To them he must be smooth, polished, charming. Who was he to that person on the phone's other end? Did anybody really know him?

"Okay," Dad said into the phone. "Talk to you Thursday then. Goodbye." He set his phone near the top of his desk. "Oona. How was your trip?"

"Who was that?"

"A business associate."

"You laughed. You *laughed* with him. Or her."

Dad just stared.

"You promised things would be different."

He didn't flinch. I admired his composure. "That good," he said.

"That good. What are you doing?"

"Working. I—"

"Where's the 'new man' who sat on the edge of my bed in the hospital?"

So much for gentleness.

He examined two papers, bright against the dark wood of his desk and framed by his hands.

"How have you tried, Dad? Have we gone to a show? Out to dinner? If anything you've gotten worse. You don't even come into my room to say good night anymore."

"I stopped working in Chicago." He stared at those papers. I envied that Angel-Kenny bond. "I'm here. For dinner each night."

Corpse snorted. "That's going well. Dodging conversation with Mom. Retreating down here. What are you hiding from?"

"Hiding?"

"Why won't you laugh with us?"

"Laugh?"

"What are you afraid of?" Corpse realized the question was actually more to herself, and she lifted her chin to hide it.

"I'm not afraid, Oona. I—"

"Bullshit."

Dad raised his eyebrows, but his eyes had turned razor black. He nodded in that unknowing way, stopped and scratched the back of his head. "Thanks for that assessment." Would he lunge at her, slap her?

"Coward."

"I'm doing the best I can."

"Coward."

Dad's phone rang and he reached for it, but Corpse got there first, LIFE hitting the floor with a jingle-bang.

"Hello," she said.

A voice like Ms. Authority said, "I'm looking for Tony Antunes."

"He's busy." Corpse hung up. I wondered if Dad had been faithful to Mom.

"Oona!"

"Dad?" She'd never said anything more bitter. She didn't care how sharp he seemed. She picked up the LIFE box, opened it, dropped his phone in, and forced down the groaning lid. Dad settled back in his chair, his mouth slightly open and cocked left.

"Would it kill you to play this game with me?"

Last night with Gabe. Now this. She was out of control.

"Oona!" His face was pale.

That flute music seemed to swell beneath her feet. She closed her eyes and pictured Angel handing her that feather. Sugeidi sitting on her bed, washing her blistered feet. Mom so pretty this morning.

"I may have been the one to kill myself," she said, "but you, me, Mom—we've all been dying for a long time. I'm trying to *live*, Dad." She watched those words ride the edge of her voice and register in his face.

He looked at her like she'd stabbed him. He leaned forward, clunked his elbows on the desk, and rested his head in one hand. He ran his fingertips across his forehead. I slunk to him and hovered near his shoulders, fascinated. From here Corpse looked older, completely in control. Not like the girl I understood.

"Must have been some school." His words fell to his desk.

She didn't say anything, just kept that truth-stare boring into him. I squirmed.

Dad's hands landed on his desk with a thump, and he shot up. Through me. His eyes lost their focus as a yawning inkiness surged into me. I stifled a scream.

He strode to the window wall, opened a glass door, and left.

Corpse blew out her breath. She turned back around

in her chair. With sheer will, I forced back that darkness, yet it hovered at my edges.

Dad's phone rang inside the game, weird, muffled, like from far away. On his shiny desk were those papers. His computer whirred. She stared at those papers and listened to that whir. Numb.

The carved wooden clock on the credenza behind Dad's desk said 7:37. Corpse stared at nothing. She looked at the clock again: 7:57. If she listened carefully, that flute played on. She rose, walked to the middle of room, and set out the LIFE game on the Berber carpet.

She selected a blue car and a red car. She put a little blue man in the blue car and a little pink woman in the red car. I urged her to flee, tried to make her understand, but she tuned me out. She set the cars on the start space. She sorted the money, the cards, and spun the dial, its whir taking over the room, slowing to that *tick, tick, tick* till it stopped.

Icy air from the open door flowed across her, but she wasn't cold. She chose the *Start Career* route over the *Start College* one, realized she needed to select a career, and chose *Mechanic $30,000*. She moved the red car eight spaces and landed on *Snowboarding Accident, Pay $5,000*. She paid the bank.

Dad appeared, and she watched him amble along the windows. His hands were deep in his pockets and he watched his feet, which were hidden behind the window frames. When he stepped through the door, she saw he wore slippers. He closed the door, walked to her, and looked down at everything. He sat at the board's opposite side.

"You're the blue car." I trembled, but her courage rippled like that pond behind the Oasis House.

He nodded.

"It's your turn," she said. "You start by spinning the dial."

# Twenty-Two

FROM OONA'S JOURNAL:

*The total amount of water in a human of average weight is approximately 60 percent, but this amount progressively decreases from birth to old age. During the first ten years of life, the greatest decrease occurs.*

—Mr. Bonstuber

Mom pulled away from the curb in front of Crystal High, and Gabe and Corpse waved. Corpse could drive herself to school now, but she loathed driving, and besides, Mom liked this new ritual.

Though snow was piled high around them, the morning held spring's warm promise. As they strolled up to the entrance, Corpse leaned to Gabe and whispered, "I'm still wearing that underwear. From Saturday night."

He raised his eyebrows and smirked at her. After two more steps, he looked at the clear sky and laughed out loud. They entered the double doors, grinning.

On the big, carpeted stairs, the immigrant girls were huddled. Two bawled. Corpse stopped. She started toward them. They looked at her with surprise. Their faces closed. Gabe took Corpse's hand and led her to the stairs. As she and Gabe ascended, she tried not to look at those girls, but her neck betrayed her. She watched them, and they watched her.

That first long hall was loud with talk and shouts and laughter and lockers banging, yet a bubble of hush followed them like on her first day back. I trailed along, out of reach. All those heads seen from above made Crystal High seem like a documentary, and I marveled at how different this was from the Indian school. Was this always what happened when bodies were squashed in one building with bells and classes and cafeteria food? What rumors had spread in our absence? Gabe squeezed Corpse's hand and kept walking.

"Hey, Oona," Clark said. "See you in Bio."

Her thankful hand touched his arm.

They crossed the Student Union and Corpse searched for Ash, ready to make things better with her. But Ash wasn't at the table by the windows where she usually held court. She wasn't at her locker either. Corpse stowed her books, stored her backpack, and pulled out her AP Bio textbook and folder.

Gabe set down his backpack, pulled her close, and kissed her. He looked down, beyond her books pressed between them, toward her underwear. She did too. They laughed.

"Bye," he said.

"*Chingado!*" Manny called. "Get a room!"

Corpse rolled her bottom lip with her teeth. "Bye." She banged shut her locker and took one last glimpse of Gabe. He was locked in a glare with Tanesha and Brandy. She couldn't see his face, but his shoulders were braced and the girls sneered at him. Tanesha seethed a word Corpse couldn't hear, and Gabe shook his head. Everything around her turned to echo and slow motion, yet Gabe could take care of himself.

She started toward Bio. In the Student Union, "Why don't you play with your own kind?" stopped her. Tanesha.

Corpse kept moving on the same watery legs from yesterday's walk to Dad's office. The clack of Tanesha's heels stayed close behind her. A few of the immigrant girls stood on the Student Union's far side, hugging one another goodbye. They stopped and watched with tear-striped faces. Corpse glanced around for Ash, who would love this, but she wasn't there.

"Hey, rich white princess. Like the taste of our skin?" Tanesha said, almost yelling, and Brandy laughed. I shot to the ceiling.

Corpse stopped. She closed her eyes. She heard those coyotes on the hill at the Indian school. She saw those nighttime flames across the highway. That dead guy on the stretcher.

"User bitch," Tanesha said.

Before I knew it, Corpse had dropped her books. She spun and rushed at Tanesha with her hands out. Tanesha recoiled, but Corpse's arms wrapped around her. Tanesha smelled like shampoo.

"Get off me!" she said, but Corpse held her tight.

Corpse said into her ear, "I love him. He loves me. Can't it be that simple?" She stepped back.

"You're crazy!" Tanesha said.

Corpse nodded. "*Loco*."

Mr. Handler arrived, in a lavender golf shirt. "What's going on, ladies?"

Corpse looked from Tanesha to Brandy. "Why can't we just get along? It's only skin."

Tanesha's eyes narrowed. "It's more than skin."

"Is it?" Corpse said. "We use the same shampoo."

"Ladies—" Mr. Handler said.

"You're not Chicano," Tanesha said. "You're not one of us."

Corpse's spine lost its resolve. She stepped back and looked down.

"Stay with your rich white boys," Tanesha said.

"Tanesha—" Mr. Handler said.

"What's *white*, exactly?" Corpse said. "And you're way richer, Tanesha. You have family. People."

Corpse gathered up her book and folder. Eyes everywhere. Tanesha and Brandy stood with their mouths cocked open. Mr. Handler looked about a thousand years old. Ignoring the watchers at tables, the gapers lining her path, Corpse headed to Bio.

At the classroom door, she leaned against the wall and pressed her forehead to the hall's cool cinderblocks. Might Tanesha be right? I thought of that hole in Gabe's sneaker the first day he walked us home. How we hadn't told him about Yale. Were we using him? She opened her eyes.

Mr. Handler stood in front of her. "You all right?"

She nodded.

"You sure?"

"I've been dead. Nothing's worse than that."

The bell rang, and Mr. Bonstuber nodded to them as he shut the door.

Mr. Handler took a breath that filled his chest, and he pressed his lips. "I thought you were going to slug Tanesha. But that hug might have been even better. Brilliant!"

Their eyes met.

"I had an email from Louise this morning. Roberta's giving up dancing."

They both knew what he was doing: bringing Corpse back to that Indian school. But she was glad for the news. She straightened. "That's great."

"She said seeing a white girl as screwed up as you helped somehow."

Corpse bit her lip. I'd never considered that he'd invited her to that school for anyone but us.

"Also …" His face turned serious. "Witches. Ghosts." He smiled and frowned all at once. "Let's keep believing."

───────

Across the white board in AP Bio, Mr. Bonstuber had written *Genetic Engineering* and underneath that *Bacterial Transformation*. Mr. Bonstuber walked down the row of lab tables, setting a chart for recording data on each. Lab day. One predictable thing, at least.

Mr. Bonstuber set the chart at Ash's vacant seat, and her lab partner slid it in front of him. Everyone else watched Corpse and whispered to each other like a beach-ball-sized tumor had sprouted on her forehead. She hunkered down, prepared to ride out the storm of gossip after that scene with Tanesha.

Mr. Bonstuber returned to the lectern. "At each of your tables are five petri dishes. One has the starter colony of E. coli. The other four have Luria broth agar in them. That's food for E. coli bacteria. As I said before, E. coli is the most common bacteria found in the human gut. This E. coli is naturally sensitive to ampicillin. Two of these dishes will be controls. The other two, the experimental ones. For those we are going to try to get these bacteria to take on ampicillin resistance through a humanly engineered plasmid. Remember, plasmids are circular pieces of DNA that carry their own genes for specific functions. To get the E. coli to take on the plasmid, we must make them *competent*. What does that mean? We must make the cell walls susceptible or ready to take on plasmids. We'll do this via calcium chloride and heat shock. What I'm saying is review, people, right? The steps are here on the board."

Corpse had missed class discussion last week, but Mr. Bonstuber had assigned her the reading about the experiment. He didn't usually recap like this, so she was sure he'd done it for her benefit. She eased a hair tie from her jeans pocket and finger-combed her locks into a ponytail.

She and Clark spread out the four petri dishes for the starter colonies and labeled them *Control 1, Control 2, Experimental 1, Experimental 2.* All the while, Corpse felt eyes boring into her. The usual hum of discussion on lab days was laced with whispers.

Clark leaned over. "Don't worry; it's not you they're interested in, really. It's Ashley."

"Ash?"

"Well, I wasn't there. I'm not her favorite person anymore. Actually, I never have been. But lately she's taken to calling me 'dork.'" Corpse gaped at him and he shrugged. "Fine with me."

"I'm sorry, Clark. You're not a dork."

"We all can't be brilliant *and* beautiful, Oona." He grinned at her slyly. "Ashley's always had a ... an edge that made me ... nervous. Anyway, Saturday night her parents were out of town, and she had a party. A rager. Apparently she got drunk. Drunk drunk. The cops came. Most of the baseball team was there, and they're going to end up suspended."

Corpse looked at him.

He raised his eyebrows. "Some of the soccer girls too."

"Oh, Ash." Corpse inventoried which girls Ash would have corralled. She missed soccer, felt awful for abandoning the team.

Clark fixed his attention on the petri dish and test tubes in their wooden rack as he poured calcium chloride from a beaker into each tube. "But what everyone's really talking about..."

"Clark? What?"

"You know I say this as a friend, right?"

Cold breathed up Corpse's spine. "Yes."

He opened the petri dish with the starter colony of E. coli. He lifted the straw-like inoculating loop and scraped some of the bacteria into each tube.

Corpse sensed he was working up to something, so she took the calcium chloride beaker, rinsed it out in one sink, walked to another sink Mr. Bonstuber had filled with snow, and scooped the beaker into it. She set the beaker on the lab table, and Clark pushed all four test tubes into the snow.

"Apparently Ashley shouted something like, 'Oona Antunes sucks! She does everything for attention! A user! That's all she is!'"

Corpse froze.

"She was really drunk." Clark added the plasmid to test tubes three and four. He cleared his throat. "Word is, she yelled this as she was dancing on her dining room table." His voice cracked as he said, "Topless."

Corpse imagined cops pulling Ash down, her boobs jutting around. She'd had countless dinners with Ash and her parents at that polished oval table.

"She slugged a cop. No clue how she wasn't arrested. My bet is she's being suspended today."

Corpse pushed a second beaker forward, crossed her arms on the chilly black tabletop, and let her head drop into them. Eyes everywhere. She didn't care. She pictured Ash's moonlit tear. She felt Mr. Bonstuber standing before her on the lab table's other side.

"Everything okay?" he said.

Corpse saw the puff of his dress shirt, the triangle end of his purple tie. She sat up and pressed her wrist against her jeans, her underwear into her skin.

"Not feeling well?" he said.

"I'll be okay."

"Mr. Handler told me you had a good trip to the Indian school." His German accent bouncing over "Indian school" sounded exotic. Their eyes had a conversation:

Mr. Bonstuber: Be strong.

Corpse: Thanks.

Did the entire school know about Ash's party? She heard Tanesha spit "user bitch." How about the rest of Crystal Village? Maybe some tourists too? Maybe she was ridiculed in Spanish, French, Japanese. *DEAD GIRL DECLARED USER.*

Mr. Bonstuber tapped the table twice before he moved on.

Mechanically, silently, they transferred the test tubes into the shock bath at 42 degrees Celsius. After sixty seconds, they transferred the bacteria to their respective dishes.

Clark gathered the dishes. "I'll put these in the incubator."

"I wonder how many plasmids got through," Corpse said.

"We'll see tomorrow," he said.

Corpse dumped the starter colony and the inoculating loop into a biohazard trash can. She gathered the beakers and test tubes, washed them out in the sink, and set them in the drying rack. No one came near her.

Clark watched her return. "You all right?"

"I'm not sure. I'm glad you told me, though. You're a good friend."

Clark shrugged. "It's easy to be friends with nice people." He leaned forward so Corpse would look at him. "Oona, Ashley has been headed toward this for a while. In my opinion, she's been dragging you down."

Corpse slouched back. "Clark, it wasn't her. I know why I tried to kill myself now, and it wasn't Ash."

"Well, simple observation would indicate she was hindering your development."

———

Gabe waited for Corpse in the Student Union.

"You didn't tell me," she said.

"I just found out myself. Ash and I don't exactly hang out anymore." Behind his eyes was tightness, caused, Corpse was sure, by Ash's poisonous words.

Corpse touched his dimple. "This is my favorite part of you."

His face relaxed. "Really? I was under the impression there was another."

Their eyes had a conversation:

Gabe: Say you love me.
Corpse: —

"I need to speak with you right away." Mr. Handler's face was ashen, and he started toward his office without waiting for a reply.

"See you later," Corpse said to Gabe. She followed Mr. Handler.

Mrs. Pena, swollen-eyed, watched them pass through the reception area, and Corpse turned shivery. Mr. Handler closed his door but for a sliver. He sat down and stared at his hands. Corpse wanted to tell him he could relax, that she already knew.

"I didn't want you to hear this through gossip," he said. "Ash had a party Saturday night. Her parents were out of town, and apparently things got out of control."

"I heard."

"They were supposed to arrive home very late that night. Around two a.m., I believe."

Corpse relaxed. Mr. Handler would tell her about Ash's suspension next. His upper lip clung to the lower, and he seemed to force his mouth open.

"Ashley took an overdose of her mother's sleeping pills. Seems, from her note, that she'd planned for her parents to find her when they got home. But their flight was delayed, then cancelled. They arrived home Sunday, mid-morning. Ashley was dead."

Corpse's hands flew to her mouth. She doubled over, and her screams squashed me against the ceiling.

# Twenty-Three

Corpse lunged into Mom's Range Rover. "Mom—" That little girl voice.

"I know," Mom said, her eyes red pillows. "Mr. Handler called, right after you did."

Corpse made a noise like a gear shearing off its bolt. Mom reached across the console and hugged her.

Corpse bawled. "How could I ever have tried to do this to you?"

Mom pulled a mini-box of tissues out of the console and offered one to her. Mom took one too. They blew their noses. She put the idling Rover into gear and pulled away. Corpse watched the school. Gabe would be pissed at her for not telling him she was leaving, but this way he could have a few more hours without knowing. Corpse turned on her phone and typed Feeling sick, couldn't lie to him and deleted it. She wrote Went home and pressed *Send*. Her first text since we'd died.

She'd gotten out of the habit of using our phone, had turned it off when we got home from the Indian school on Saturday. Now it sounded, *ding-dong*, as a text arrived. From Ash. Saturday night, 1:10 a.m.

Corpse set our phone on her leg like it was a grenade. I moved to the back of the vehicle, wanted nothing to do with that text. Out the window passed the parking structure, the busses. We passed the golf course. When we came to the street where we turned toward Chateau Antunes, Corpse peered right for the first time since we'd died and tried to make out our trailhead. Mom pulled into the garage and the door clanked closed. She climbed out.

"You coming?"

"In a minute," Corpse said.

Mom eyed the phone on Corpse's leg. "Okay." She started away, and I longed to follow. She paused. "I'm back here in five minutes if you're not in by then."

Corpse listened to Mom enter the mudroom. She eyed her own white Range Rover parked next to Mom's, and a slide-show of Ash in its passenger seat played across her vision. The vehicle's interior light blinked off above her and she lifted our phone: Here's to attention, user!!!

Eight hundred people stuffed the Interfaith Chapel, its balcony, and its reception area, where a big-screen TV would broadcast. We'd had to park in an outlying area and ride there in a shuttle that felt like a hearse. Dad knew the driver from all his time at the airport, so he sat up front and they chatted about how the shuttle company had volunteered their services, how most of the things had been donated for this memorial service.

"Damn shame," the driver said, then caught himself and glanced at Corpse in the rearview mirror.

She sat beside Gabe and his dad. In front of her sat Mr. Dressler, our PE teacher and soccer coach. We hadn't said boo to him about not going out for the team this year. Corpse's stomach writhed. I hovered just in front of that writhing, narrowly avoiding being touched in the crowded vehicle.

Out the window the Hawk River flowed past beneath ice. Every spring someone drowned in that river. Corpse glanced at Dad, and I remembered his touch. Lethal currents flowed in people too.

Gabe took Corpse's hand and kissed it. Their eyes had a conversation:

Gabe: I'm psyched we didn't have to do this for you.
Corpse: Ugh.

A constant urge to barf up guilt blocked Corpse from any speech.

Mom and Sugeidi were already at the church, comforting Ash's mom and setting things up. Mom had spent a lot of time with Ash's mom, and Corpse had worried she'd get even thinner. Instead Mom grew sturdy and her skin took on a peachy glow.

When we arrived, she was waiting at the entrance in black pants and a black blouse. Corpse remembered how she'd pictured Mom at our memorial, but Mom didn't need a clingy designer dress to show she was gorgeous. Her hair was pulled into a barrette. She and Dad exchanged an unfriendly glance, and she held out her arm to Corpse.

Corpse slid into it and inhaled Mom's soft, tropical-flower scent. I hovered just above Mom's arm and felt calmer too.

"Mrs. Antunes," Gabe said. "This is my father."

Gabe's father looked just like him but older. No dimple. He held out his hand. "Frank."

"Muriel," Mom said, and their hands clasped. "I'm ashamed that we haven't met before today. We'll have to remedy that." She let go his hand.

"That would be great," he said.

"And this," Mom said, gently guiding Sugeidi forward, "is Sugeidi, our ... friend."

We'd never seen Sugeidi wear anything but that maid dress. Today she wore an elegant black dress that accentuated the gray conquering her dark hair. I wondered if it was the dress she'd worn to her husband's funeral.

"*Con gusto*," Sugeidi said as he took her big-knuckled hand.

"The pleasure is mine," he said.

"Sugeidi rocks," Gabe said, and she looked down but smiled.

As they started to move inside, Mom and Mr. Hernandez's eyes lingered on each other. Gabe noticed too, because his dimple flashed and he looked at Dad, who was taking inventory of the people in the reception area.

School was bad, but this audience numbed Corpse's legs. Her gait bobbed as she turned cold and stiff. Gabe was walking beside his father, so Mom moved to Corpse's side like a shield and took her right hand. *DEAD GIRL KILLS BEST FRIEND.* Corpse glimpsed Mr. Handler across the room, speaking to some parents from school and looking like he'd stared at sleep all night. Everyone else was a blur.

Mom had saved seats in the chapel's second row. At the altar, two life-size photos of Ash were propped on easels. One her senior portrait. One from first grade. We'd listened to Mom on the phone, ordering and paying for the vibrant flowers filling the space between.

Ash's kindergarten soccer jersey, number seven, hung before them on a hanger from a wooden rack. Her skis were propped beside it. When we'd waited in line for that school photo, Ash had poked her tongue through the space where her two front teeth had been, and we'd been jealous because we hadn't lost any teeth yet. After school, donned in crowns, we'd sung to the aspens in Chateau Antunes's front yard, willing the birds to flock down to us.

"Why won't the birds come?" Ash had said to Sugeidi.

"Sing *mas* beautiful," Sugeidi said, so we had. Long

216

after Ash had turned quiet and collapsed on her back in the grass, we'd kept singing.

"They're never coming," Ash had said sourly as she'd watched branches yield and clouds writhe.

I imagined our senior photo, with our hair carefully curled by Sugeidi. Our first grade photo with our ringlets sculpted by Sugeidi. In the years between, the Oona Antunes that everyone knew had evaporated till we were like a photo. Just an image. Yet inside, we'd divided. Me growing stronger, stronger, till that knife swooped down at the dance and our own photos, jerseys, and skis had been heartbeats away from filling that altar.

If they'd been there, would Ash be here now? Ash must have been sliced open too. *Maybe the moon's not far enough.* Corpse longed to hunch over and wail, but she forced herself frozen. We were practiced at this, had been doing it for years. I scanned the room's sad faces. Was the world filled with people pretending they were whole? I didn't see or feel any other selves hovering nearby.

Ash's dad stood near our seats at the front, and Corpse cringed at how much he looked like Ash, even down to the pouty set of his mouth. We'd been avoiding her parents, but now his eyes dissected Corpse.

Ash's dad: This is your fault.

Corpse's head grew too heavy for her neck.

They filed into the row in careful order—Mr. Hernandez leading Gabe, Sugeidi, Mom, Corpse, and then Dad, who nodded to Ash's dad and sat down. A balding man with a ring of gray hair stepped to a podium between the photos. He tapped the microphone. Everyone sat down. Ash's mom rushed up in a clingy designer dress, and her parents moved to the seats in front of Dad and Corpse.

Ash's mom noticed Corpse and leaned over her chair's back. Before I knew it, Corpse had leaned toward her. Ash's mom cupped Corpse's face in her chill hands, sending a shiver through her. She kissed Corpse's cheek, and then her lips quaked while her eyes were whorls of pain. Corpse turned dizzy. Ash's mom sat down, but Corpse was stuck, reeling. Mom helped her sit back.

"Greetings," said the man at the podium. "I'm Pastor Michael Wallford. We gather here on this glorious March day to celebrate a life." Corpse braced against his cheesy amplified voice. Who was this guy? Ash's family never went to church. Had she ever even met him? In the air above him, I pictured Ash rolling her eyes.

Mom glanced at Corpse and took her hand. She took Sugeidi's too. Ash's mom's fingers were ghosts against Corpse's cheeks.

She looked up at Dad, who sat as rigid as one of those British palace guards. She'd kicked his ass at LIFE, beaten him by three million dollars. His hand rested on his thigh, and though I remembered that dark surge when he'd bolted through me, Corpse reached over and grasped it.

He smiled like it hurt. He lasted about three minutes, then tugged his hand from hers, nodding, and rubbed his palm on his suit pants.

Mom sighed, and she looked at Corpse like she was

truly sorry. Corpse couldn't take her eyes off Dad's hand, but I thought how I hadn't liked to be touched either, and I longed to bust through the ceiling and rise to the clouds.

Corpse tried to focus on the pastor's words, tried to hear when Ash's dad stepped to the podium and Ash's mom curved over in shudders, but it was like trying to listen from beneath a pool. They'd asked Corpse to speak, but she'd said no before I'd realized the word had raced through her lips. I mean, we knew it was the right thing to do, but no way could we stand at that podium in front of all these eyes. They'd asked again, yet she'd still said no. Same for the third time.

We hadn't spoken the same language as Ash for so long. "User" was a foreign word to us. Yet if we'd been kinder, she might have still breathed.

"I'm sorry, Ash," Corpse whispered. She concentrated on the amplified words that ringed a halo round Ash's head and glued wings to her back.

# Twenty-Four

From Oona's journal:

*Seashells—whorls—spirals within spirals are the physical manifestations of energy. Energy is primary, the physical form is the secondary effect.*

—Viktor Schauberger

Corpse slid the rhinestone crown from when we were a kid into our coat pocket, alongside that feather.

I pictured her on the operating table. That gray-haired doctor, in green scrubs, mask over his nose, lopped off our fingers with a scalpel and tossed them in the trash. He ripped Ash's crown from our head and shot it like a basketball. It banged into the can and clunked to the bottom, next to our fingers and toes. The nurses clapped and cheered.

Corpse cringed, zipped up our coat, tugged on a hat, and grabbed gloves. As she wriggled her feet into snow boots, she heard clanging in the kitchen and found Sugeidi, changed out of her black dress, easing a baking pan from its cupboard.

"I'm going for a hike." Corpse forced the words through the guilt still clogging her throat.

Sugeidi set the pan on the counter, glanced at the sun beaming through the window, and noticed the feather poking out of Corpse's pocket. "Be strong," she said.

"I don't know what I am," Corpse said. "I've screwed up so many things."

"*Screwed*?"

"Messed up. Ruined." Her voice was impatient.

"Ah, *arruinado*." Sugeidi pulled a face. She waved away Corpse's words. "Things *screwed* without you."

Corpse rolled her eyes. "Not now, Sugeidi. I'm not in the mood."

Sugeidi stamped her foot. "*El mundo es arruinado siempre!* You must." She pressed her hand over her maid dress in the same place where she'd left her soap bubble print, took a deep breath, and changed tack. "*Corazón fuerte.*"

Corpse's own heart felt anything but strong. "Whatever."

She strode out into one of those classic Rocky Mountain March afternoons. The temp was in the mid-forties, and she shoved her hat and gloves in her pockets within the first minutes. She didn't stroll. She marched. Toward that trailhead.

Ahead, at the bus stop, two skiers navigated down from a bus's door in loud ski-boot steps, poles akimbo and swinging. The bus accelerated past us, sounding like a space ship in a movie. Corpse looked away from its driver. When its locomotion grew thin on distance, the skiers' clunking steps grew loud again. Their helmets were cocked back on their heads, their swinging goggles suspended behind from snapped clasps. Their unzipped coats—one purple, one green—were the only way to tell them apart, and their shoulders bumped about every third step.

Corpse arced wide to avoid their poles and their skis, which rode scissored at their hips. I wondered which house they were staying at, since nobody living in our neighborhood would be caught dead looking this dorky. The trailhead arrived on her left, and she started up it.

One of the skiers called, "Excuse me. Is that a hiking trail?" A British accent. Male.

She watched their globe-headed waddling, and laughter bubbled in her. "Yes."

"Where does it lead?" The other one was muttering, so she couldn't tell who asked.

"To the ski mountain eventually."

"Is it difficult?"

"It's not bad," she said.

"Could we hike it in sneakers?" He said it like "snake-uhs."

She thought of our open-toed spike heels, our dress tugging along the trail's snow corridor. She'd been wearing a crown, had one in her pocket right now. Talk about looking dorky. "Sure."

The skiers neared enough that she could see they were both men. Sixties maybe.

"Thanks!" said the one on the left.

"Up that?" the other said and blew out his breath. "Blimey! You're trying to kill me!"

Corpse wrestled against a smile, but a crooked one took over her face. She waved to the guys and started up the trail. She glanced over her shoulder at where I hovered. "'You're trying to kill me,'" she said. "'Blimey!'" She laughed, hard enough to wipe her eyes.

The snow corridor was about the same height along the sides as on the night of the winter formal, and she considered those spike heel prints buried under feet of snow. She held her hands in front like she was lifting a gown and tried to propel herself along using the same trees' trunks, tried to feel that night's Rapunzel sense of release and resolve. Instead, she heard her breaths as she'd climbed the mountain behind the Indian school's dorms, kept seeing red dirt and rock beneath her snow boots.

She passed through the bare aspens' ripples of light and shadow as she traversed toward the spot, and instead of despair, she felt the emergency workers' urgency as they raced along. Today this trail was tranquil.

The rock we'd died on was at shin level now, and Corpse lowered onto it and scooched back. I hovered at her shoulder as she pulled out the crown and slid it onto her head. She pulled her knees close and crossed her arms around them. She rocked forward and back, trying again to summon that night's despair. I concentrated with her, but some noisy, yellow-breasted finches that landed in the branches above distracted her. She unzipped our coat and leaned back, the rock warm beneath her palms. She tilted her altered face to the sun.

"I died here," she said and willed those words to weigh her down, but the sun felt so friendly. She started to say *I'm sorry, Ash*, but "What the hell, Ash?" came out.

I pictured the guy trapped under that burning trunk, the dead one on the stretcher, yet Corpse sat up and considered what had just flown from her mouth. "*What the hell?*" she said again. Each word conjured Ash's mom's fingers against her cheeks. She felt Ash's dad blaming her, felt all the years of Ash's manipulation come to a head.

"Bullshit!" Corpse shouted.

I flinched, and the finches burst into squeaking flight.

She lay on her back. Branches webbed the cloudless sky. After a while, her eyes transformed those branches to roots in the blue.

She sang: "Ah-ah-ah, ah-ah-ah." Tried to make her song more beautiful by adding richness from her chest's depth. I rose to the branch I'd perched on that night and listened. A finch returned to a twig near me and chittered. Another joined it. They craned their heads and peered at me with beady eyes.

"See, Ash," she said. "They came." She listened for her heart's beat. "I'm not a user," she said. She glanced toward me. "Not anymore."

She thought of how easily she could talk to Angel. And William. And Clark. We'd always had to be careful what we said around Ash. If Ash had wanted us to be her roommate at Yale, she'd have been prodding and prodding us. Our friendship had been running on fumes.

Corpse tried to keep thinking about Ash, but Roberta not dancing anymore took over. William going back to Harvard this summer was close behind. Angel wanting to be our roommate came next, which made me nervous because it would take about a month for Angel to grow sick of us. She thought of Gabe loving us. Mom just wanting to be loved. Sugeidi with her hand over her *corazón*. Dad tugging his hand from hers.

Corpse drew out her feather and held it against the sky. After a while she sat up, palming back her hair, and her hand bumped the crown. She traced its outline with her fingers, and smiled softly at how it echoed the jagged peaks' ridgeline.

She turned her face to the sun's rays and closed her eyes. It felt like the touch of God, or whatever it was that watched over this world. "Thanks for letting me live." She drew in the biggest breath she could hold. Let it out and yelled, "Blimey!" She tried not to laugh, but it leaked out as a raspberry.

Laughing felt bizarre when she was navigating grief. She looked down the valley and imagined Crystal High, could see the ski mountain with Crystal Village nestling against its base. She imagined the currents of Crystal Creek as it flowed past the stretch of homes beyond town till the trailer park where Sugeidi spent her weekends, beyond to the airport sheltering Dad's private jet. This landscape had watched us die. Today it seemed to forgive.

"Forgive me," Corpse said to Ash. "*El mundo es arruinado siempre!*" She laughed sadly. "Blimey."

She lay back on the rock, took in the clouds. "I forgive *you*," she said to Ash. She looked at the finches, then focused on me. "And you."

# Twenty-Five

FROM OONA'S JOURNAL:

*In German, the spinal column is known as the spiral*
*column, and vertebrae are known as vertices. All this*
*is related to vertical movement. A mirror of the DNA*
*molecule, which determines the human body.*
*It is the path energy wants to take.*

—Viktor Schauberger

Sugeidi set a sliced brisket on the dining room table, its barbecue sauce in a gravy boat beside it. Mashed potatoes, corn,
salad—comfort food. She rested her knuckles on her hips,
took in the meal and then Corpse, Dad, and Mom. Her eyes
said *Now you all behave*, but only Corpse's seat faced her.

Dad cleared his throat and reached for the brisket.
"Thank you, Sugeidi," he said, but she didn't leave. He
looked over his shoulder at her. So did Mom. Their eyes
had a conversation:

Sugeidi: You two need to straighten up.

Mom: She's right.

Dad: You're the maid.

Sugeidi: I'm not afraid of you.

Dad: There's nothing wrong with me.

Mom: Like hell.

Sugeidi: See what I mean?

Sugeidi's gaze traveled to Corpse, and Dad's and Mom's followed it. "Oona hike today. On the trail she died."

"Thanks, Sugeidi." Corpse sent her a glare but found pride on Sugeidi's face and the trace of a smile. Sugeidi had watched her return, Corpse realized, saw her swinging arms and light step. Sugeidi was showing Dad and Mom that their recently dead daughter was handling things better than they were. I sensed she was also reminding Corpse to be strong on this sad night.

"I thought returning there would suck," Corpse said. "But it was fine."

"Why did you go?" Dad said.

"Because some things you just have to face." She gave him that truth stare.

He concentrated on and reached for the mashed potatoes. Corpse remembered William taking a bite of potatoes. I worried Dad might smash the bowl with his gaze.

Sugeidi snorted and left.

"She's getting bold," he said.

Mom and Corpse looked at each other. Corpse scooped corn onto her plate, the steadiness of her right hand making her smile.

"What made it *fine*?" Mom said.

Corpse shrugged. "I expected to feel out of control or depressed or something. To relapse, you know? But I just couldn't get myself to feel that bad." She laughed. "I really tried. I just couldn't. I mean, it's so awful about Ash. The guilt presses ... " Her hand rose to her chest. "But—"

"I know what you mean." Mom sighed. "It's a strange feeling. Survival, I guess."

Dad stared at his food.

"Poor Ash," Corpse said. "I seriously wanted to kill myself and failed. She just wanted attention and—"

Dad flinched.

"How are you faring, Tony?" Mom said, totally nice. I had to admire her.

He shrugged. "Fine."

"That's great," she said.

"What?" Dad said.

"Nothing." Mom picked up her fork and knife. "I'm glad you're *fine*."

"What's that supposed to mean?"

"Nothing." Mom tucked a bite of brisket into her mouth.

"Nothing?"

"Nothing." She smiled at him as she chewed.

It occurred to me that she'd crossed a boundary, couldn't care less how he was doing, and the same realization took over Dad's face.

"We should have Gabe and Frank to dinner soon," Mom said.

"Frank?" Dad said.

"Gabe's father," Mom said.

Corpse said, "Did you know Gabe's dad fixed our front wall when that car drove into it?"

Mom's eyes twinkled. "Then we really must have him over."

Dad watched her with calculating eyes.

"Sounds great." *User* echoed in Corpse's head. "Do either of you know what happened to the crown I was wearing the night I died?"

"Crown?" Dad said.

Mom pressed her lips and shook her head.

Discomfort stole the room's air. There was only the sound of silverware against plates. The day's weight, the weight of the whole last few months, settled over them.

Corpse assessed Mom and Dad. Bodies braced against one another. "Blimey!" she said.

"What?" Dad and Mom said.

"Sugeidi's right," Corpse said. "You two need to shape up. I mean, look at you."

Mom looked at Dad and down at the fork clenched in her fist. Her head dropped and she laughed. "Thank you, Oona. And Sugeidi," Mom called over her shoulder.

"Come on, Dad. Smile once in a while. It won't kill you."

His eyes widened, turned jittery. He started nodding. He didn't talk after that, just concentrated on his plate. So annoying. Mom and Corpse marveled at the packed memorial service and Crystal Village's support of Ash's family.

"Such a tragic thing. Ash's parents will carry this burden the rest of their lives." As Mom wiped tears with her napkin, her face seemed weighed down with lost things. I heard her blaming herself that day in her Range Rover, and Corpse started crying.

"So much for feeling okay," Mom said.

Dad eyed them like ruins. I turned mad.

"Have you ever cried for anything, Dad?"

His fist banged the table, rattling the plates and silverware. He stood.

"Have you?" Corpse said.

His inky glare swung between them.

"Say something!" Corpse said.

He straightened, inhaled half the room's air through his teeth, and left.

———————

Corpse groped along the windowless wall toward the observatory. Darkness pressed against her. The wall ended, so she stopped, listening for Dad's breaths or the clink of ice in his highball glass. The tiny lights over the built-in bar that usually illuminated the room like a dream were dark, and for once that woman wasn't singing. Corpse waited. After a few minutes she discerned the room's contours in the stars' dim glow.

She entered the observatory, imagining Dad listening, yet she avoided words. She reached the arm of his recliner and stood over him. He slept. We'd rarely seen him sleeping, and her eyes traced his brow's relaxed lines, his parted mouth, his unclenched jaw. Until we'd tried to kill ourself, he'd been like a king. Distant, hard-edged, and unquestioned. Mom had been the evil witch. How had we been so blind?

Dad whimpered. Corpse had never imagined he could whimper. He whimpered again, and though his breath reeked of alcohol, in her eyes he transformed to that boy. She lifted the highball glass from the loose hand on his belly and set it on the end table next to her. I remembered that hand banging the dining room table. He wasn't as big as Gabe, and she considered that maybe each of us was just a kid, playing at being adult.

This made Corpse crawl over the recliner's arm and stretch herself along Dad. I came down close, despite my dark memory of him. He stirred as she nestled in. She put her arm on his arm and matched her breaths to his. She watched the stars till she slept.

———

"Muriel?" Dad said.

I shot to the ceiling.

"Oona," Corpse said, eyes closed, reaching back toward sleep.

"What are you doing?" he said.

"Snuggling."

I warned her, but she yawned.

"Oh." His face assumed its daytime lines.

"Don't, Dad."

"Don't what?"

"Why can't you just snuggle?" Corpse rubbed her drowsy eyes.

"I'm snuggling right now," Dad said.

"Were. You've turned to edges," she said.

She felt him try to relax. He fidgeted his legs, his arms. She finally said, "Why is this so awful for you?"

"It's not awful."

"Today at Ash's memorial, you wiped off the feel of holding my hand on your pants."

"I did not."

"I watched you. So did Mom." She moved her head from Dad's chest to the recliner's edge, making space between their faces so she could see him.

He snorted.

"Don't pick on Mom. She's got it hard."

"Hard? She's richer than—"

"Money doesn't matter, Dad."

He gave her a piercing look. "You have a great life, Oona. You want for nothing."

Corpse shook her head fast. "Right. *Nothing*. Just love."

"Love? Oona, this is—" He started to rise, but she moved faster and sat with all her weight on his belly.

"We can't go on like this! Our family is dying!"

Dad collapsed back. She could feel his breathing's rise and fall beneath her. She braced herself and said, "I'm begging. You're the key."

He went limp, and I felt sick at her words but also felt their truth. He turned his head to the wall. Ash's death pressed down on them like an ultimatum.

"Oona, I ... "

"What, Dad?"

"I'm trying. Really, I am." He ran his pinky and ring finger across his brow. His words rushed out. "I love you. Okay?" Pain ruled his face.

Corpse's mouth dropped open, and then she smiled. "I love you too." Easy, those words. Before I knew it, she said, "Why do you spend every night in this room? Alone? Instead of with Mom? Or me? Or both of us? Like a family?"

"Your mother—"

"Yes, I'm sure she's done things, but Dad, since I died, life's gotten clearer each day. It's like I see my world now through a microscope. All these invisible things that were going on. You're afraid of something. That's what's keeping you from trying."

His eyes flickered, and I saw she was right and he knew it. It scared me even more. "You've never even made pancakes."

Confusion filled his face, but then the kitchen was there in his frown.

"Dad," she said. "I forgive you."

His brows pressed together and he tried to massage them apart. "Forgive?" His breathing turned shallow and fast.

"I want to go on a trip with you for spring break," Corpse said.

"A trip?"

"Yes. To Portugal. I need you to try with this one thing. Can you do this one thing?"

"Yes, but Portugal, Oona." He shook his head, eyes black. Corpse took it for confusion.

She sifted her words. "Those kids from the Indian school, some of them have it so hard. But they have their *people*. Sugeidi has her *people*. Gabe has his *people*. You know? Maybe you just need to return to *your people*."

"No!" He heaved to the side and out of the recliner, tossing Corpse over its arm.

"Okay," she said. "But I'm going. Mom's family is hateful. I want to see where you come from, find your family. I wish you'd come with me."

Dad looked like a cornered animal, but she walked to him. "Be strong," she said. "Right here." She put her hand over her heart like Sugeidi.

He turned away. Corpse moved to the door but looked back. His shoulders had such an odd set. I wished we knew more about his past. Corpse returned, wrapped her arms around his waist, and pressed her cheek against his back. He tensed, but she held on.

"It'll be okay, Dad," she said.

His body seemed poised to cry, yet no tears came. How long ago had Dad become desert? At the bar's tap, Corpse filled a highball glass with water. She carried it to him.

"Here," she said. "Don't worry. You can do this. I'll help you."

# Twenty-Six

FROM OONA'S JOURNAL:

*Water is more than just fluid, it is alive. It is healthiest when it curves and it often needs to spiral. The spiral is essential to water's health. The vortex cools it and the circular motion purifies.*

—Viktor Schauberger

Gabe and Corpse strolled along the bike path. Crystal Creek murmured from between gaps in the March ice. They'd tried holding hands, but the cold bit their skin, so they walked with their hands in their pockets. Their breaths hung over them like dialogue bubbles in a comic strip, forcing me above their fog.

A mom, dad, and two boys came toward them, the two boys yelping and running ahead to pelt each other with snowballs. Corpse reached down and scooped some snow, formed it into a loose ball; its crystals were too cold for good adhesion. She stopped, but Gabe kept walking. She nailed him between the shoulder blades.

"Hey!" He arched his back. He spun, darted to the path's side, scooped snow, and pelted her on the hip.

She bounded for cover over the pile of plowed snow and ducked. Gabe catapulted over the mound. Through me.

He paused, brow furrowed, as his determined goodness filled me.

He lurched forward. Corpse squealed, and he flattened her into the snow. But I'd given him such a sad expression.

Corpse squirmed and laughed. He grinned at that and put his lips on hers. I tried to gather myself. First Corpse, then Roberta. Then Dad. Now this? Each lingering touch a window to understanding I did not want.

"Where'd they go?" one of the boys shouted.

"They're *kissing*," the other said, disappointed.

"Ew!" said the first.

Gabe pulled back and kneeled. Corpse sat up, cheeks flushed, and glanced at the boys. Gabe rose and looked toward the river. He held out his hand and pulled Corpse to her feet. She wiped snow off her jeans.

"This way," he said and started walking toward a bench on the riverbank that sat beneath a giant spruce's skirt of sheltering branches.

Beyond the good, determined thing I'd felt was something else, and it spread through me like a drop of food coloring into a pool, so calming and comforting. I realized it was love.

They post-holed to their knees with each step, but it

237

wasn't far. Corpse was glad her jeans were tucked into her snow boots. Gabe had on just the sneakers we'd given him. Did he even own snow boots? Corpse glanced back. The boys were gone, but their parents' shoulders and heads moved along the bank.

The river grew louder. Gabe and Corpse stepped out of the snow onto pine needles that cracked beneath their feet. The smell of sap and cold enveloped them. Corpse breathed deep, her nostrils freezing together for a second, and she scanned the landscape through the spruce's bows. She thought how Ash would never see beauty like this again. I was basking in love.

"Poor Ash," Corpse said.

"Enough sadness," Gabe said. "Tell me something … " I could tell "happy" didn't seem like the right word. "Not sad," he said. My effect, trapped in the pucker around his eyes, just about killed me.

"Remember that crown I wore at the winter formal?" Corpse said. "When I woke up in the hospital, it was gone. It was Ash's crown. Remember? What do you suppose happened to it? Do you think I could still have been wearing it when I got to the hospital?"

Gabe's eyes dulled. "Something *not sad*."

"Well, I'm on the pill now."

"That's very not sad." He slid his arms around her.

Corpse laughed. "You should have seen Mom. She insisted on driving me to and from her gynecologist, and she couldn't stop smiling. It creeped me out."

Gabe cracked up.

"Mom's a big fan of you," Corpse said, and her face fell. "She's so unhappy, Gabe. I don't know how she's stayed with Dad all these years." She paused, hearing how she'd just blamed Dad. "She's starving for love."

"Yes," he said. "The first time I met her, it showed."

"Really?"

"Really. Guys aren't *that* dumb," he said.

"Some guys," Corpse said. "*I* was that dumb." She kissed his neck. His hair had outgrown its cut, and she liked how it curled at the ends.

"So we could do it? Right here? Right now?" Gabe said.

Corpse surveyed the trail, where the two boys had peered over the bank, and she pulled a face. "Sometime at night, maybe."

"Deal," he said and led her to the bench.

They sat, and he wrapped his arm around her. She leaned her head against his letter jacket. "Here's another not sad thing: Mom's a fan of your dad too."

Gabe laughed softly. "Last night Dad said your mom was nothing like he expected. He said it all reverent."

"*Reverent*," Corpse said.

She craned around to look Gabe full in the face. Their eyes had a conversation:

Corpse: Do you think?
Gabe: No way.

I tried to remember myself ever saying something not sad. Anything.

The rippling water caressed the ice. With each touch, did the liquid become ice or the ice become liquid? The water's sound seemed to be millions of gentle conversions. Corpse let her mind ride that sound, and her consciousness drifted downstream.

"There's no rush." They'd been quiet so long, Gabe's voice seemed foreign.

"It's too cold today for runoff," Corpse said.

"I meant us. To do it."

"Oh."

"I want it to be right. Perfect."

"I'll never be perfect," Corpse said, and her smirk, I knew, was for me.

"Okay. But you know what I mean."

"I'm nervous, Gabe."

"Me too. Maybe it'll turn out all I'm good at is soccer."

Corpse sat back. "Or me at science." Nine months we'd been dating. Roberta's men crowding around that pole with dollar bills lifted in their fists formed in her vision. "Gabe, how have you put up with me all this time?"

"Not sad."

They watched the river again.

"There's one more not sad thing," Corpse said.

"What?"

A blue jay landed on the creek's bank and hopped along the snow, leaving tiny *V*s. It pecked at something Corpse couldn't see. "Dad and I are going to Portugal for spring break."

"Portugal?"

240

"It's where he's from. When he was ten, his parents died, and he was sent here to live with his uncle. Gabe, I think this is what's killing my family. The key to what killed me."

Gabe pursed his lips and stared ahead, seeming to calculate things far down a chain and then back up. "He agreed to this?"

"He didn't say no."

"So you're making him return to the scene of the crime? Face his fears?"

She shrugged.

"How are you going to do that? Take him to where his parents died? Make him stand on the spot and relive the agony?"

"I don't know." She slouched. "I haven't thought that far ahead. Maybe this is a big mistake."

Gabe pulled her closer. "I just don't want you getting hurt any more than you already have been. My mom...for the longest time, I kept thinking she'd come back. Back here to Crystal Village. That her love for me would draw her home."

"Gabe—"

"It's fine now. Maybe your dad can change, but ... "

"But what?"

"That night of your...suicide. His face. It wasn't right."

"I was dead, Gabe."

"I know, but ... " He rubbed his eyes and she could see words crowding to flow out of him. "Never mind. We were all whacked out."

"What, Gabe? What did you see?"

"I'm not sure. He was...well...not *normal*. He started speaking a foreign language. Which is fine, except his face was all weird. He was...having an argument...with himself. He shouted. And his eyes. I don't know, Oona. He lost it, I think."

Corpse eyed the frozen river. She couldn't picture Dad shouting, yet heard his fist rattle the silverware. Saw his strange nodding.

"Sometimes," Gabe said, "I think it couldn't have happened. But when I see him, it's there, between us, and he seems embarrassed. No, not embarrassed. *Confused*."

"Maybe this trip will be a disaster."

Gabe opened his mouth to speak, but Corpse put her finger over it and kissed his dimple.

"He's my dad. He loves me."

"Your mom's not going?"

"Something not sad," she said.

Gabe pulled his arm from around her, took her hand in his warm grip, and slid both their hands into his pocket. The river's muted rush took over the air.

"There's great soccer in Portugal. You should go to a game."

"Okay. Dad watches soccer all the time, you know."

"The man's a mystery."

"That's for sure."

"I love you," Gabe said.

I heard Ash's accusations, but Corpse leaned her head on his shoulder. She glanced at me like *Come along* and said, "Blimey!"

"What?" Gabe said.

"I love you too."

Gabe turned to her. "Really?"

"Really." She spun and took his face in her hands. "I love you. I love you. I love you. I love you. I love you."

"Wow!" His grin was priceless.

Twice, those words. Now, and to Dad. Not the end of the world. In fact, it was nice. Corpse seemed to hear me. She kissed Gabe. "That's for all the times I didn't say it before. And so you'll know it across an ocean."

The river's murmur took over again. He touched her coat in the place where her heart necklace rested against her chest. He put his arm around her, she returned her head to his shoulder, and he rested his cheek against her hat.

"Gabe, I've never really asked you what you want to be. When you graduate, I mean." She hated the gaps in her knowledge of him.

"A doctor maybe. Or a physical therapist, like with a professional soccer team. But professional soccer first, if I'm good enough."

"I can't even think about college till I fix my family."

"Fix?" Gabe said. He pressed his lips, and I felt rotten for the piece of me I saw in his eyes. I'd always considered myself smarter, better than Corpse. Lately, I doubted that.

# Twenty-Seven

FROM OONA'S JOURNAL:

*A healthful daily intake of liquid for men is about
3 liters (13 cups) a day. For women, it's 2.2 liters
(9 cups) a day.*

—Mr. Bonstuber

Tanesha followed Corpse, but this time she was silent. This time she didn't stop in the Student Union. Ahead, Clark stood beside the door to AP Bio. He raised his hand in a wave and went inside.

Tanesha tapped Corpse's shoulder. Corpse turned and Tanesha's fist passed through me and caught Corpse's ear, sent her careening against the wall.

Tanesha's eyes dulled. The hate in her fist scorched me.

She tilted her head, gave Corpse a glazed look, and her eyes turned vicious again. A crowd formed around them. *DEAD GIRL SLUGGED.* Brandy sneered at Corpse from Tanesha's side.

"How many people are you going to fuck up?" Tanesha hissed.

Corpse stepped back. Tanesha cocked her arm, and Corpse lifted hers to block it, but the punch connected with her eye. Pain bloomed in her temple. Stars sprayed across her vision. She slid down a locker to the floor.

Tanesha pulled back her foot to kick. Brandy laughed, but Corpse wheeled out her leg, sweeping Tanesha's standing leg from beneath her. Tanesha hit the floor, her breath billowing out her lips. They were eye-to-eye.

Corpse, palm against the locker, wobbled to her knees.

Sneakers appeared. We knew those sneakers. Loved those sneakers.

Gabe kneeled next to Tanesha and said, low, slow, "Listen, there never was and never will be anything between you and me. I will date who I want, you racist. If your life is screwed up, it's your own fault."

Tanesha's mouth became a slash. One of her front teeth was chipped. Corpse wondered at its history. Faces in the crowd smirked at Tanesha. A couple snickers drifted down. Tanesha glared at Gabe, and her eyes lurched to Corpse. Gabe stepped between them, and Corpse studied his jeans' creases at the backs of the knees.

"Don't even look at her." The flatness of his words scared Corpse more than Tanesha's fist.

Tanesha drew her legs beneath her and rose, never taking her glare off Gabe. I had to admire her moxie. The tardy bell rang. Brandy took a backward step toward the Student Union.

"You shame us," Tanesha said. Brandy nodded.

"Do I?" Gabe said. "Who's shaming who?"

Something clicked behind Tanesha's eyes. Mr. Bonstuber and Mr. Handler arrived. They took Tanesha by the arms and escorted her down the hall.

Mr. Rhoades, the assistant principal, hustled up. His hair was always pushed up in the front, and he looked like he'd just eaten something that didn't agree with him.

"Oh, Oona!" He blew out his breath. "Come on. Let's get to the nurse's office for that eye."

Gabe put his arm around Corpse's waist. She saw Manny watching with narrowed eyes.

"I'm okay," she said, stepping out of Gabe's embrace, and we followed Mr. Rhoades.

In Corpse's throbbing vision, the hallways and the stairs wavered. Mr. Rhoades opened the main office door and led us past Ms. Martinez, the secretary, and down a short hall. Dr. Bell's door was shut, with Tanesha inside. The nurse's office was across the hall, two doors down. The nurse only worked Tuesdays and Thursdays, so Mr. Rhoades sat Corpse on the cot, and Gabe leaned against the doorframe as Mr. Rhoades opened the mini-fridge, pulled out an ice pack, wrapped it in a thin towel from a stack on the fridge's top, and handed it to Corpse. The room smelled like burlap sacks and rubbing alcohol.

A knock sounded. Gabe craned around. Mr. Rhoades leaned into the doorway, partially blocking our view of two police officers waiting outside Dr. Bell's door. Their black gun belts lured Corpse's eyes. Crystal Village's police force was small, and I wondered if Ash had punched one of these officers. If these same officers had been at our suicide. The door opened, they entered, and the door closed behind them. Mr. Rhoades sighed and shook his head.

"If you'll excuse me," he said and walked down the hall. He knocked and entered Dr. Bell's office.

Tanesha was eighteen. Tanesha would be treated as an adult. We were all eighteen: Gabe, Tanesha, Roberta, us. Ash never made it.

"How did you know it was happening?" Corpse said.

"Manny," Gabe said.

"Manny?"

"He saw Tanesha following you and got me." Gabe studied his hands, still in fists. He sprayed out his fingers and blew out his breath. "He doesn't hate you." He closed his eyes and slumped against the wall like he'd walked a thousand miles.

———

Corpse led Mom by the hand into the living room, holding a blue ice pack against her eye. Even though she knew about Mom wanting to be an anthropologist, had knocked the peace pipe down from above the mantel, and had humped with Gabe here, the room still felt like a museum.

Mom sat on the couch, Corpse in the armchair. The last person she'd seen sit in that chair was Ash as she'd played LIFE. Reality seemed to sway, so Corpse closed her eyes.

When she opened them, Mom was looking at her intently. She touched Corpse's blackening eye and bit her lip.

"It's fine," Corpse said, taking Mom's hand. "Mom, you're not going to like this. You're not going to like it at all, but we have to do it."

"We?"

"Dad and me."

"What?"

Corpse took a breath and said, too fast, "I'm making him go back to Portugal for spring break."

Mom seemed to look through Corpse, and one of her eyes squinted.

"Mom?"

Her gaze veered to the window, toward Chateau Antunes's front wall and our trail beyond.

"I think the reason Dad is such a ... is so disconnected ... is because he hasn't gotten over his parents dying. I think he needs to face it somehow. Then maybe he can ... well ... love people."

Mom was a statue.

"Mom?"

She kept staring out the window.

"Mom!" Corpse shook her arm.

Mom collapsed back against the couch and ran her fingers through her hair. "There's that saying: *If you love something, set it free ...*"

"I love you too, Mom."

She smiled, then lifted her chin. "What will you do once you get there?"

"I'm not sure. I just know I need to get him home."

She pursed her lips till they turned a different color. "I tried to get your father to go, years back, just after you were born." She laughed sadly. "He'd always been distant, but after you were born, he withdrew much more, grew defensive and mean-tempered. He was dead-set against kids, was furious when I told him I was pregnant. I couldn't understand it. At work, he's suave, charming. For so long, I thought it was my fault. You wouldn't think a beautiful baby would bring about a change like that. I guess he's just a shrewd business-man. He must be."

She threw up her hand and cast her eyes around the room. "Look at all this." She laughed. Not the good kind of laugh. "It took me three years to figure out he'd married me for my money. The start he needed. I kept thinking there was something wrong with *me*. He's masterful at that."

Their eyes had a conversation:

Mom: I've been lonely so long.
Corpse: I understand. It's almost over.
Mom: You think?
Corpse: I know.
Mom: I'm worried for you.
Corpse: I'll be okay.

I remembered what Gabe had told me the day before. "He wouldn't hurt me, would he?" Corpse said.

Mom sighed. "I don't think so. But he's masterful at damage inflicted with words. Sometimes I wish he'd just hit me." Her eyes traveled to Corpse's swelling one.

"Mom!" Corpse shuddered at the hate I remembered in Tanesha's fist. Heard Dad's fist bang that table.

Mom held up her palm like a traffic cop. "He's too smart for bruises. It might damage his reputation, his career. It's strange, the law. It protects you from bruises, but allows the murder of your spirit."

"Murder? Mom!" That little girl voice. Only this time, I didn't mind it.

"Work is his false front. He prefers the company of strangers and acquaintances. But if you try to get close to him, Oona—"

"I never knew things were so bad."

"No?" Mom said. "You tried to kill yourself."

I shuddered at the thought of Dad down in his office. Could he sense our words?

"Why have you stayed with him?"

Mom looked Corpse straight in the eye. "You."

Corpse studied the ice pack in her hands, scraped a contrail with her thumbnail through its rime of ice. "I won't go if you don't want me to."

"No," she said, "go if that's what your instincts tell you. He's agreed to it. That's something. But I'll be worried the whole time."

"That's pretty much what Gabe said."

Mom's eyes twinkled. "I like that boy more and more. Young man, I should say. Given your doctor visit…"

"Mom!"

She leaned forward and gripped both Corpse's hands. "Oona, I'm happy for you. And a little jealous, honestly."

I remembered how in the recliner with Dad, I'd thought how everyone was just a kid.

"Thanks," Corpse said. "You could come with Dad and me."

Mom shook her head. "I don't think your father or I are ready for that. Even if *he* gets better, it's going to take some time for me. A lot of years will need undoing. It's funny. How a person can try and try for so long, and then one day—"

"You've got to try."

Mom looked like she might throw up.

"Promise?" Corpse said.

Corpse listened to three heartbeats before Mom said, "Promise."

# Twenty-Eight

FROM OONA'S JOURNAL:

*Blood and water fulfill the same function. These abilities are temperature dependent. At 4 degrees, water is able to shift material, remove and transport sediment. Blood must also move waste away. Oxygen is present in both and can promote growth and decay.*

—Viktor Schauberger

Sugeidi set a stack of clean clothes next to the suitcase on our bed. She rested her knuckles on her hips and studied Corpse's black eye. It had swollen shut for two days, which made Brandy smirk. The yellow and purple had long since faded though, and just a faint purple crescent remained on her lid. Tanesha hadn't returned to school.

"It's fine," Corpse said.

Sugeidi continued to stand with her hands on her hips.

"What?" Corpse said. "You told me to heal them."

"*Sí*," she said, "but I no like."

Corpse wished everyone would stop worrying about

this trip. What did they all see that she didn't? She considered how each of us knows a person in our own way. There was Mom's Oona, Sugeidi's Oona, Gabe's Oona, Ash's Oona, Tanesha's Oona, Mr. Handler's Oona, Angel's Oona, Dr. Yazzie's Oona. With literally hundreds of Oonas out there, no wonder we were struggling to understand ourself. Plus, the Tony Antunes we knew was different from Sugeidi's Tony, or Gabe's Tony, or Mom's. Or from the Tony the voice on his phone knew, the voice Corpse had hung up on. Or the one Dad had laughed with. I wondered if he was having an affair, and Corpse swallowed it back. He was returning to Lisbon for her, and she was the only one that could get him there. She thought of those chocolate eyes. He'd said he loved her. That counted for something. Didn't it?

"Sugeidi," she said, "we have to do this."

"You call me?"

Mom had taken our phone to the store, gotten it programmed so it would work in Portugal, and Sugeidi knew this. They must have talked. Planned even.

Corpse grinned. "I call you."

"*Bueno*," she said and trod from the room.

---

"Where are you going to dinner?" Mom said.

"*Le Ménage*," Gabe said.

"That should be yummy," she said. "Think I'll go there soon myself. Do you have a reservation?" In Crystal Village, spring break crowds started the first week in March, moving west across America and then south into Mexico until the mountain closed in mid-April.

Gabe nodded.

"Have fun. And good luck in your tournament. Where is it again?" Mom said.

"San Diego," he said.

"Well, safe travels," she said.

"For all of us," he said.

They looked at Corpse, who rolled her eyes.

Corpse led him through the mudroom into the garage. She got as far as our white Range Rover's back bumper. She still hadn't driven since we'd died. She worried now that if she climbed into its driver's seat, she'd descend toward that suicide self. I worried about that too, but something else had always troubled us about driving, a strange, gnawing uneasiness.

"Could we walk to town?" she said.

"Sure." Gabe closed the passenger door.

"What are you grinning at?"

"Walking's good," he said.

Corpse closed the garage door at the keypad outside. They strolled down the driveway, and as they passed through the opening in the wall, she turned and studied the place Gabe's dad had repaired.

"What's up?" Gabe said.

"Just thinking." She took his hand and laid her head against his arm. "It's funny how the world works, isn't it? If I hadn't forgotten my Chemistry book that day, I wouldn't have been there in the hall. If you hadn't gone to the bathroom, you wouldn't have been there either."

"Fate."

"This wall would be just a wall. Tanesha would still be in school."

"You can't blame yourself for her dropping out."

"And Ash might still be alive."

"Oona. Stop!"

"Don't you ever wonder? What if I'd died?"

He pulled her against him. "I wonder about other things."

His determination and love when he'd passed through me were right there.

They kissed. I drew close. The sound of the bus accelerating from the stop down the road made them pull apart.

"Hey, let's take the bus," Corpse said. She jogged to the stop, tugging Gabe by the hand. The bus pulled up, and the owl-eyed driver assessed them as they climbed on. They found a seat near the back.

"That driver sure finds us interesting," Gabe whispered.

I drifted to the ceiling. A few of the ads had changed since the night we'd killed ourself. That night, I'd felt so vibrant, so ... cocky.

"He's the one who called in my location the night of the suicide."

Gabe studied the back of the driver's thinning hair. "Well, I need to thank him then."

"Me too," she said.

When the bus pulled into the Transportation Center,

Corpse and Gabe waited until all of the passengers disembarked. The driver eyed them in the mirror. He rose and lifted a backpack from behind his seat.

*Hurry!* I said. Corpse strode to him. "Sir?"

His eyes widened.

"Thank you for calling me in that night."

The driver smiled shyly. "You're welcome." His voice sounded like it came from one of those old black-and-white movies.

Corpse didn't know what else to say, so she nodded, and he nodded back. She descended the two stairs off the bus.

"Thanks, man," Gabe said and followed her.

Corpse looked back over her shoulder, and the driver still stood there, smiling.

"What time's our reservation?"

"Seven."

Corpse read the clock tower at Crystal Village's center: only ten minutes. They paused at the heated fountain and watched the shooting arcs of water. I felt like one of those momentary arcs, drawn forever back to Corpse.

"Doesn't that water seem alive?" Corpse said.

"It does," Gabe said.

"Isn't it amazing how it can be separate like that, yet moments later disappear, part of the whole pool?"

"Hmm," Gabe said.

"Did you know water has three phases?" she said.

"Phases?"

"States: solid, liquid, gas. Right now, all three surround us. It's everywhere."

"I knew that, I guess. Doesn't everyone?" Gabe said.

"Yes, but they forget. And water moves between those states and we never notice."

"I didn't know you were so into water."

"Did you know it's healthiest at 4 degrees Celsius?"

"No."

"It's a narrow margin."

Gabe didn't say anything, but he studied her as she watched the fountain.

"Our bodies are 57 percent water."

"Yes."

"Over half." She sighed deeply. "Maybe our spirits are gas while our bodies are liquid. I turned solid when I died."

Gabe looked worried, so she kissed his cheek.

"After dinner could we swing by the hospital?" she said. "There are some other people I need to thank."

———————

At the hospital, Copse started toward the main entrance but stopped. "I want to see where my ambulance arrived," she said. "I want to go in that way."

They followed a sidewalk around the red brick building to a portico that said *Ambulance Entrance* in big letters across the top. One ambulance was parked under it. Corpse paused and imagined paramedics pulling her stretcher from the rectangle of light cast by the ambulance's rear door. She pictured the stretcher rolling across the short patch of asphalt, her head bobbing from the jostling, that crown glinting in the lights.

"I was dead right here," she said.

Pain took over Gabe's face.

She strode to the electronic glass doors and they whooshed open. She strode into the warm air and looked left, right. She approached the reception counter in three strides. Gabe followed a few steps behind, hands in his letter jacket pockets.

"My name is Oona Antunes," Corpse said.

The receptionist behind the desk had spiky purple hair and a diamond stud through one nostril. "Yes, I know," she said.

A nurse in green scrubs stepped to the desk, bent over a list, and ran his finger down it. His ponytail reminded Corpse of Dr. Benson, and she remembered his flute's sustaining notes. Inhaled them.

"I wonder if you could direct me to who was working the night I was here."

"I was." The nurse straightened and stood eye-level with Corpse.

"So was I," the receptionist said.

"Who was the doctor?"

The nurse's eyebrows lifted. "Dr. Hanson. Another nurse was called down from Intensive Care, but he's on vacation."

From the corner of her eye, Corpse saw a white doctor's coat move behind a curtained-off bed. "Could I talk to him?"

"Sure." The nurse walked to the bed and ducked behind

the curtain. After a minute he returned with the doctor, who looked more like a professional basketball player as he assessed Corpse with a glowing grin. His shaved head and stature were so far from what Corpse had expected that the words she'd been rehearsing on the walk over evaporated.

"I know this seems weird. But…I just want to… well…thank you."

The nurse and Dr. Hanson beamed at each other. Dr. Hanson reached out a big hand and put it on her shoulder. "You're welcome," he said. "Moments like this make our job worthwhile."

Corpse looked down and said, "It's so embarrassing."

Dr. Hanson hugged her then. "We all make mistakes."

Before I knew it, I'd joined her in that doctor's arms. That glow I felt: another hue of love.

Corpse stepped back, wiping her eyes. "Was I wearing a crown?"

Gabe tensed at her elbow.

The doctor's eyebrows pressed down, but the nurse's rose. They looked at each other and shook their heads. "No crown," the nurse said.

"Okay. I've been wondering. Are the paramedics from that night here too?"

"They're right outside," the receptionist said, blotting under her eyes with a tissue. She pointed toward the electric doors and blew her nose.

"Thanks again," Corpse said.

Corpse strode to the ambulance parked under the portico, Gabe still trailing. He'd grown pensive. The vehicle's back door stood open now and a guy leaned against its frame, holding a clipboard and talking to someone inside.

"Excuse me," Corpse said.

The guy turned and she could see his partner, seated on a bench within the ambulance. They wore short-sleeved uniform shirts, and she studied the muscles of the arms that had ferried the dead her from that trail.

"My name is Oona Antunes," she said. "A couple months ago, you saved my life."

"Not something I'd forget," said the guy in the ambulance.

The guy outside snorted.

"Thank you," she said.

Both the guys straightened and seemed to take in her live version.

"You're welcome," said the one with the clipboard.

The one inside nodded. "It's what we do. Glad to see you're all right."

She shrugged and glanced at Gabe. "I'm working at it. Anyway, thanks."

"No problem."

"Um, when you found me, was I wearing a crown?"

The paramedics looked at each other. They looked at Corpse and shook their heads. The one outside said, "No crown."

———

Gabe and Corpse walked back to Chateau Antunes on the

recreation path, not talking. But for Crystal Village's distant glow, the moonless night left them in darkness. Gabe put on a headlamp and they followed its beam.

"You're prepared," Corpse said.

"Yep," Gabe said.

I remembered following Angel's flashlight down to the fire.

They neared the place where they'd had the snowball fight. Their path to the spruce was gone, covered by a foot of snow, but someone had made a new one. Gabe took Corpse's hand, led her up the bank, and lowered her by the waist on its far side. He turned off the headlamp and stowed it in his pocket. She followed him down the path.

They came to the river, and it was very dark beneath the spruce. Gabe pulled two blankets down from its branches and spread one on the ground. He sat on the blanket and patted the spot next to him. She joined him, and he wrapped the other blanket around them so their heads were hooded.

"That was intense," he said. "Back there. At the hospital."

"I'm glad I did it."

"You might be the bravest person I know."

"Right." Corpse said, like *you're kidding*.

The river gurgled beneath ice. A little farther down, it rushed softly in a gap.

"That crown?" Gabe said.

"It's hard to explain. I just kept picturing myself being rescued in it and looking so dumb. You know? I just wondered how stuck-up, how stupid, I looked."

"You looked beautiful." Gabe spoke like he was in a

trance. Corpse could barely see his profile. "Your mom called and told me where you were. I sprinted along this path, found your heel marks on that trail. I was the first one to arrive. You lay on your side. It was freezing. You were in that dress with no sleeves. I had on just that tuxedo shirt and was so cold, yet you looked comfortable, content. I was afraid to touch you, but I did. You were like ice. I cried so hard." He looked down, between his knees. "I was sure you were dead." His fingers traced his lips. "So cold. I heard people approaching on the path, so I took that crown. I wanted one thing to remember you. A goodbye, I guess."

"You have the crown?"

"Had. After you lived, after that first time I visited you at your house. Remember?"

She nodded.

"I had it in my coat pocket. I walked back on the path and came out here. I threw it there." He gestured toward the river with his chin.

Corpse shot up, peering at the ice.

"You can't get it now." He drew her back down. "It's long gone." He rewrapped the blanket around them. "Are you pissed at me?"

"I kept going on about it. Why didn't you tell me?"

He sighed. "I don't know. I just … it's embarrassing. I mean, you're not even the crown type. Don't be pissed."

"Pissed? No. I should thank you, I guess. Nobody else saw me in it. Oh, Gabe, how awful. I just left you at the dance. Finding me must have been so—"

"Don't."

"I've hurt so many people."

"Don't do that to yourself."

Silence settled between them.

"What kind of girl am I? I can't seem to figure it out," Corpse said.

He held up a little velvet box. "My kind."

Corpse took it and opened it. Gabe turned on the headlamp, set it in his lap. She tilted the box and saw a heart pendant that matched the one on her necklace.

"That one heart was mine," Gabe said. "Now that you've said you love me, well, I thought our hearts should be together." He felt around the back of her neck and unclasped her necklace. She lifted the tiny heart from its box and slid it onto the chain as Gabe held it open. He returned it to her neck.

I lurked outside that blanket. It hung down so only their illuminated cheeks and chins showed.

"There," he said, turning off the headlamp and stowing it in his pocket. "Now we're together." He pressed his forehead to hers. Corpse took his hands, ran her thumbs over his fingernails, and imagined their pink crescents. She kissed him.

He unzipped her parka. She unsnapped his leather jacket and unzipped his jeans. The blanked writhed, and I imagined he toed off his sneakers and pulled off her snow boots. They wriggled out of their pants and looked at one another.

Corpse could barely discern Gabe's face, yet she understood him clearly, knew he understood her too. They slid off their underwear. I remembered Gabe's love. It wasn't fair. I funneled into that blanket and layered myself over her skin.

Darkness ruled. There was only touch and sound and taste. Corpse lay back, pulling Gabe's furnace-warmth onto her, onto me. Gabe's breaths turned heavy. Corpse pressed her mouth to his so she breathed his air. Their chests pressed against one another, and I felt their skin's introductions. He pulled back, put his mouth on her nipple, his lips through me. He moved to the other as his hand traced down. His saliva on her vacant nipple turned cool as it evaporated. She gasped when his fingers arrived where only ours had ever been.

"Prince Charming," Corpse said against his cheek and felt her breath eddy back onto her. He laughed and she pulled him down, felt him slide between her legs and into her. It hurt. She caught her breath.

Gabe stopped, but her legs wrapped around his and pulled him deeper within while her hips pushed down. She owned a knowledge I didn't. Reasoning, doubting, judging were foreign language here. Gabe stilled, a sheen of sweat gluing them. Corpse rested her hands on the swale where his back turned to butt. I luxuriated there as she fanned her missing fingers across this intimate skin.

# Part Three

*Upon A Foreign Shore*

# Twenty-Nine

FROM OONA'S JOURNAL:

*In Nature all life is a question of the minutest,
but extremely precisely graduated differences in
the particular thermal motion within every single
body... The slightest disturbance of this harmony
can lead to the most disastrous consequences for the
major life forms.*

—Viktor Schauberger

Out the egg-shaped window of Dad's plane, clouds illuminated by the plane's lights smeared past. In the dark below rolled the Atlantic. How many thousands of breaths, how many evaporations of different places did each cloud contain? Corpse leaned back, ran her fingers over the tan leather of the chair arm. Were her and Gabe's breaths from last night in these clouds? Was Ash? When we died, were our spirits lifted on the sighs of the living? Or was Ash up higher at the pearly gates?

Dad emerged from the cockpit. Corpse could see Dan

and Carol's headphone-topped crew cut and ponytail. Our husband-and-wife pilots glowed excitement for their coming week in Portugal. Corpse glanced at Dad and thought how different their stay was going to be from ours.

Dad settled into the chair across from her and nodded without seeming to notice. In the week leading to this trip, his eyes had grown even sharper, but there was a jitter behind the sharpness. As if he was being sucked down into himself. Conversation had grown treacherous.

"It's going to be okay, Dad," Corpse said. I wasn't sure about that.

After a while Dad eyed Corpse's pajamas, checked his watch. "It's late. You should sleep."

"I guess."

Across the back of the plane were two couches that folded down to comfy beds. Corpse had prepared one with sheets, blankets, and two pillows. The other was still a couch.

"Want help making the other bed?" she said.

Dad forced a smile. "I won't sleep. I'll just sit here. Maybe doze off."

"Why can't you ever sleep?"

He shrugged.

"Could you sleep when you were a kid?"

He walked behind Corpse's chair to the bar. She listened to the fridge open and close, to ice clink into a glass, to liquid pour, to a short burst of water from the sink. He strolled to the control panel behind the cockpit and dimmed the cabin lights. He sat back down and set a highball glass holding amber liquid on his thigh. He stirred it with his finger, licked it, and sipped.

I pictured him sitting just like this in the observatory. Same man, same drink, just a different chair. Except now we were *in* that sky. Dad spent so much time crossing the sky, or gazing at it.

They didn't talk for a while, just stared out that oval window at hypnotizing scraps of glowing clouds.

"What are you really hoping to achieve with this trip, Oona?" Dad's voice pulled Corpse back from near sleep. She blinked.

A shrug rode her shoulders, but she contained it. I mean, wasn't it obvious? What could she say? *For you to get over your parents' deaths. Work out whatever makes you unable to love. Grow up and stop acting like a kid. Learn to love Mom. Become a normal dad. DEAD GIRL FIXES FATHER.* Corpse cocked her head. If she looked at him, her eyes would say those things, so she focused on the clouds. "I want you to get better."

"I'm not well?"

Corpse shrugged.

"Look at me," he said.

Corpse shut her eyes. She touched the heart charms at her neck.

"Look at me!"

I thought of the easy bond in that Angel-Kenny gaze. She looked.

Dad snorted and took a sip of his drink. "Sometimes it's better to leave things. Alone."

"Sure. Things are rolling along just fine," Corpse said. "Things were rolling along for me too."

"I must love you." His words were flat.

"What about Mom?"

Dad scraped his bottom lip with his fingernail, dropped his hand to the chair arm, and looked at Corpse like she'd asked the world's dumbest question.

"Okay. How did your parents die?"

"They drowned."

"How?"

Dad scrutinized his glass.

"Dad?"

"Let's not talk about it."

"You never want to talk. You need to," she said.

"I'm not sure this is going to turn out how you planned, Oona. There's not going to be some big happy reunion."

"Don't you have an aunt left?"

"We lost touch."

"Why?"

Dad shrugged.

"Was she your dad's sister? Their brother was the uncle you came to live with in America, right?"

"After he died, she and I drifted apart."

"Drifted?"

"Look, I'm going back. For you. Isn't that enough?"

"But you need to face things."

"Face what?"

"Dad, can you honestly say that you have a loving, happy family? Something's stopping you. Maybe facing

where ... well, seeing where you were as a kid ... will help."
I couldn't get over Corpse's courage. "Maybe something
happened there. Maybe facing it will help us all."

His gaze made her push back in her chair.

# Thirty

FROM OONA'S JOURNAL:

*I years had been from home,*
*And now, before the door,*
*I dared not open, lest a face*
*I never saw before*

*Stare vacant into mine*
*And ask my business there.*

—Emily Dickinson, "Returning," lines 1-6

Corpse stepped through the French doors of their elegant hotel room and onto a narrow, metal-railed balcony. Dad had reserved two rooms, but she'd insisted on one, didn't want him escaping.

Below stretched a soccer-field-sized plaza with a humongous tiered fountain at each end. In the middle, atop a marble pillar, an iron statue of a guy in a cape faced her. On the twenty-minute cab ride from the airport, we'd seen more four-story statues than we'd seen in our entire well-traveled life.

"What is this place?" Corpse called over her shoulder to Dad inside.

"It's named Rossio Square. That's all I remember," he called back.

"Thanks for nothing," she muttered. She'd heard that much in his conversation with the cab driver. After Dan and Carol had landed the plane, they'd taxied it to where it would stay while we were here and let Corpse sleep there until seven a.m. U.S. time. We'd been awake two hours now, but it was four o'clock Lisbon time.

Corpse took in the hills sloping down toward the plaza, covered with orangey-red tiled roofs atop mostly white or yellow stucco walls, occasionally blue or purple or green stucco.

Corpse googled "Rossio Square" on her phone. She pulled up its map and description. She read loudly, so Dad could hear: "In ancient times, Romans held chariot races here. That wavy pattern in the cobblestones originated with them."

No response.

Corpse looked to a castle that loomed on the right. "That's St. George's castle on the hill. Built by the Moors. And those—" She turned left and peered at stone arches resembling a whale's ribs that poked above buildings on the opposite hill. "Those are the ruins of Carmo Convent."

No response.

"Dad, won't you even come look?"

Dad stepped onto the balcony. He sighed. Not the

happy-to-be-home kind of sigh. The don't-panic kind. He'd changed into jeans and a polo shirt. He scanned everything.

"That statue in the middle is Dom Pedro. King in the early 1800s," Corpse read.

"*Dom*," Dad murmured.

"Back there"—Corpse pointed to the far end of the square, toward a building fronted by six pillared steps like a Greek temple—"is the National Theater. In its place used to be a palace where the royal family entertained guests. During the Inquisition, its back rooms were used to force confessions from heretics."

"*Force confessions.*" Dad shot Corpse a look.

She blushed.

"I used to stand on those steps. Dream of seeing a performance," he said.

"Really?" Corpse said.

"A guard would shoo me away."

She read, "The palace was destroyed in the earthquake. Earthquake?"

Dad ran his fingers over his brow, looking at it all in a cringing way. His phone rang. "Excuse me." He disappeared inside.

Corpse listened to him talking business and observed the teeming square. Tourists paused to take pictures. Cars, taxis, and busses rolled along the three-lane road that circled it. On the square's right side, people formed a line as a bus pulled to a stop. A distant trumpet blasted as businessmen and women walked about briskly. From every fourth or fifth storefront stretched the tables of an outdoor café.

"Yes. Four hundred. Yes. Thank you. Goodbye," Dad said.

He didn't return.

"Dad, won't you come back out?"

He joined her, crossed his arms, and leaned against the hotel's purple stucco.

"How many calls do you get a day?" Corpse said.

He shrugged.

Corpse googled "Lisbon Earthquake." She read, "In 1755 a huge earthquake leveled most of this." She swept her hand across the panorama. "What didn't fall was ruined by the tidal wave it caused or by fire."

"People always talked as if it happened yesterday."

"Really?"

"History dogs people here."

"Everything looks so old," Corpse said.

"It is. Even the new things are 250 years old. Old and run-down."

"I think it's cool."

Lisbon's light was like looking through fine gauze that blurred the edges of things. The ocean's humidity, no doubt.

"That area"—Dad gestured toward St. George's castle—"survived. The rest of this was rebuilt." He seemed to catch himself, eyed the roofs below the castle, swallowed like sand blocked his throat, and turned away. A church bell clanged, and his head jerked back toward the hill. Shock filled his face, and for one moment he looked vulnerable. With each of the bell's four echoing tolls, the muscle at Dad's jaw tightened.

Corpse gripped the balcony and sipped a calming breath. "It's so hilly." The air felt balmy compared to home. She checked her phone: 62°F. She would put on shorts in a minute. She glanced at Dad and leaned on the rail to seem relaxed.

"So, wow! Romans were here?" she said.

"Egyptians, Romans, Moors, French, Spaniards. Portuguese endure."

A group of boys, maybe eleven years old and dressed in matching Boy Scouty uniforms and wearing packs with sleeping bags strapped on, filed across the square. I thought of the kids at the Indian school, of Ash, of Gabe, even Tanesha, and Corpse longed to say, *We all endure, Dad. That's life.* This constant suffering was a poison. Why couldn't she and Dad just have fun on this trip?

Accordion music from a street performer rose to them. Corpse watched the closest fountain's water arc inward from the smaller statues around its perimeter. She remembered watching that Denver fountain when she'd ditched the leadership conference. Remembered acting just like Dad was now. It seemed like reaching back into a nightmare.

"What should we do today?" She forced cheerfulness into her voice.

"You're calling the shots, kiddo," he said, like *whatever.*

———

Dad had always stood out for the tint of his skin, the set of his mouth, the proud way he carried his head and shoulders.

In Lisbon, he looked like everyone else. So did Corpse. Everywhere were women with her chocolate eyes, her lush dark hair, that way her waist connected to her hips that drove guys crazy.

Their talk, though, was nothing she recognized. She could hear some Spanish behind the slushy French-sounding accent, but there were tons of words she'd never heard, and she couldn't grasp any patterns. Yet Dad spoke it. As he asked the waiter about something on the menu, she watched a language she did not know flow from his mouth. A chill crept up her spine as she remembered Gabe's description of him on her suicide night.

"Oona?" Dad said.

"The cod," she said.

The waiter nodded and wrote on a little pad. He looked sixty. Trim, with a neat moustache, and serious about his job. Dad ordered. The waiter slipped his pad of paper into the pocket of a red apron.

Dad's phone rang. He answered it.

They'd wandered to this first café on the pedestrian street that stretched adjacent their hotel. Corpse scooted her chair from the umbrella's shade into the direct sun and shrugged off her sweater. She looked down at her flip-flops' worn spots where her pinkie toes had once been. She rested her hand on the white tablecloth and studied its scars. She peered down the street: café after café, ending in what looked like an arch.

She heard music. The music Dad played nights in his observatory. Its source was a storefront two doors down.

In its window hung a poster of a woman with fifties-style short hair, cradling a guitar as she plucked its strings. Her face seemed lost to the song flowing from her mouth.

On the sidewalk, below the poster, sat a woman with her legs curled to her side beneath a tattered green skirt. A yellow scarf was knotted under her chin. Threads hung from her sweater's red arm as she held up a dented saucepan to people walking past. Her mouth pleaded in words Corpse couldn't hear. For a moment no one passed, and the woman looked directly at Corpse with piercing eyes. Corpse looked away. Dad hung up.

"That woman on the poster." She nodded toward the storefront. "She's the one you listen to back home?"

Dad didn't look at the poster. "Amália."

"Who is she?"

The waiter set two bottles of water and two glasses on the table.

Dad didn't answer.

Corpse googled "Amália." "When she died in 1999, her state funeral lasted three days. All of Portugal mourned."

"No one sings *fado* like Amália."

"Fado?"

"Portugal's music."

Corpse googled "fado." "It says the way to see fado is in local clubs. Fado helped people endure the dictatorship. What dictatorship? When?" Corpse scanned the bustling street, looking for signs of such history.

"It ended two years after I left." Dad sat back and

inhaled. I thought how he breathed in that beggar woman's exhalations.

"She sounds beautiful, but so ... depressing," Corpse said.

The beggar woman held up her pan to a passing man who clasped the hand of a little girl. The man gave the little girl some change, and she dropped it in the pan.

"It's *so-dawge*," Dad said.

"So *what*?"

"*So-dawge*."

Corpse pulled up Google Translate. "How do you spell it?"

Dad snorted. "S-A-U-D-A-D-E."

The waiter delivered their food.

"There's no translation. What's *saudade*?" She savored this first Portuguese word on her tongue.

The waiter made a knowing half-smile.

"*Obrigado*," Dad said to him. *Thank you*, I realized.

The waiter made a little bow and left.

"How do you remember Portuguese?" Corpse said.

"My uncle," Dad said. "He insisted I speak it at home. It's a little rusty, but embedded."

A memory of that uncle's funeral flooded me: Mom and Dad dressed in black. Mom watching Dad's every move. An expression on his face that hinted at the one he wore now. To settle herself, Corpse took a bite of the cod. It was the best fish she'd ever tasted.

"Well?" she said. "What's *saudade*?"

Dad took a bite and looked around, mulling. "Longing. Nostalgia."

"Like missing things?"

"Sort of. But also things you haven't lost yet. It's hard to explain."

"No. I think I get it. Longing's what made me kill myself."

"Oona—"

"What? It's true!"

Dad sat back. "But *saudade* is about enduring. It's in Portuguese blood." He raised his hand into the woman's singing.

"Blimey!" Corpse said.

"You keep saying that."

"Life's hard all over, Dad."

He scanned her, nodding in that unknowing way, and his eyes turned chocolate for a second. "Maybe I should have helped you understand it."

"Yes, well. That would require communicating."

His stare became glare. They both looked away.

They ate and listened to Amália. I thought how her music drifted over the head of the beggar woman, was carried on all their breaths. Corpse worked not to inhale those dreary notes, but I thought how this music had lived in the basement of Chateau Antunes all along. How many other hidden things pulsed in our veins?

Corpse leaned forward. "Can we hear fado music tonight?"

Dad slouched back.

"You love it, right?" she said.

He poured more bottled water into his glass, sipped it, and watched her over the rim.

I thought, Seriously? Grow up and answer her. But Corpse said, "Please?"

Dad's phone rang. His face washed with relief. He held up his finger, rose, and strolled down the street, phone to his ear, movements stiff. He passed the beggar woman and she didn't hold up the pan, just watched him, and then looked at Corpse like she knew all our secrets.

---

Dad, usually a big tipper, left the waiter only two euro.

"They get insulted if you leave too much," he said to Corpse's puzzled expression.

They strolled down the pedestrian street. That arch grew to eight stories. Corpse read *Rua Augusta* on a sign, pulled her phone from her shorts pocket, and googled the street.

"This is Rua Augusta Arch, the old gate into the city," she said as they passed under it. They waited for an old yellow trolley to clank past, then a red bus, and crossed a street into another wide plaza. On its far side teemed another busy street. Then water. Corpse peered across its glinting, mile-wide span, surprised to see an opposite bank with buildings on hilltops.

"I thought Lisbon was on the ocean."

Dad looked at her like she was crazy. "That's the Tagus River. The Atlantic is ten miles that way." He pointed right with his thumb.

Corpse shielded her eyes and looked back up at the arch. At its top a woman in a toga held halos over the heads of seated angels, one a guy, one a girl. Below them stretched Latin words. Below that, a huge crest. Then more statues, all of guys, some dressed like Ben Franklin, some like ancient Romans.

"Wow!" Corpse felt Dad's eyes. "You really don't remember this stuff?"

He shrugged. The words "dad" and "daughter" seemed all that connected us.

They strolled toward the river, past a statue of a guy riding a prancing horse. Corpse was sick of googling. Why wouldn't Dad just share what he remembered instead of making her pry it out?

"How could there be a tidal wave?" Corpse said, more to herself.

"Thousands fled to this square from the earthquake's fires and destruction. They thought they'd be safe here."

Corpse smiled, careful not to overwhelm Dad by looking at him. She kept walking, watching the river. "That wave must have been humongous to make it this far up from the ocean."

"Never underestimate water."

Corpse halted, looked at him now. He paused and looked back at her, puzzled. She caught her breath and turned away.

*They thought they'd be safe.* What happened to all those screams? Those final breaths? Corpse looked from the river back to the square, so idyllic. She looked at the sky's puffy clouds. Might those clouds contain the Indian school fire? Could they harbor the hungry breaths of those men who'd watched Roberta dance? Ash's final exhalation? All the world's sighs pressed around Corpse, and she didn't want to breathe.

"Dad?" she said. "Do you think the air gets cleaned?"

"Pardon?"

"Like, washed from the people that used it before?" She needed him to say yes.

"Well, I guess…maybe it…" He looked toward the Atlantic and his face turned hard. "I don't know, Oona. What a question."

———

When they got back to the hotel, Dad made some calls, so Corpse settled in a metal chair on the balcony, feet propped on the railing, and opened her journal. Her feather from Angel marked the page she was on. She ran her finger up one side of it and down the other. For a while, she sketched the closest fountain. Under that she wrote:

*Never underestimate water.*

*—Dad*

# Thirty-One

*I fumbled at my nerve,*
*I scanned the windows near;*
*The silence like an ocean rolled,*
*And broke against my ear.*

    —Emily Dickinson, "Returning," lines 9-12

At nine o'clock, we left for fado. Corpse was wide awake since it was only two p.m. back home. She wondered what Mom was doing. It was Saturday, so Sugeidi was with her son, and Corpse worried Mom would be lonely, but when she'd called earlier, Mom had sounded happy. In fact, her words were airy, like she was thinking of something else.

"What are you doing tonight?" she'd said.

"I'm making Dad go to a fado club. That's Portuguese music."

"I'm impressed."

"So what are you doing?" Corpse said.

"I'm going to *Le Ménage* for dinner later. With a friend."

"Who?"

"How's your father?" Mom said.

As Corpse and Dad skirted the hill toward the castle, I wished Corpse had told Mom more. They walked through an area that seemed less touristy. Corpse counted six more Amália posters. All of the shops were closed for the night, but the restaurants were brimming.

They ascended a hill, and Dad stopped an old man ambling down to ask him something. Directions to a fado club, Corpse guessed. The man wore a red vest and a black cap, like a tugboat driver, and he pointed up the hill and gestured right.

"*Obrigado*," Dad said.

Corpse gaped at the decorative flags or strings of lights or laundry that hung over the narrow streets. I drifted up and weaved between them. After a while I got tired of that and just followed.

Finally they came to an open door with music and people spilling out. As Dad peered in, Corpse watched two smokers blow rings that rose against the dark. Why was smoke white at night and gray during the day?

The music stopped. "Oona." Dad gestured for Corpse to follow him.

The club was tiny but packed with people sitting shoulder -to-shoulder at long benches on either side of ten tables along a wall that ended at a bar. Against the opposite wall stood two men in their thirties. Between them sat two guys with guitars. Dad and Corpse squeezed onto the end of a bench.

Dad leaned to her. "Drinking age for beer and wine is sixteen. Eighteen for spirits. You're eighteen now. I'm ordering you sangria."

Corpse started to protest, but *sangria* sounded like *sangre*, "blood" in Spanish. Besides, she'd forced him to come, so she could do this in return.

Moments later a portly, balding guy Corpse guessed was the owner banged down a glass and a carafe before her, a little of the red liquid sluicing over its rim. He set two highball glasses with amber liquid in front of Dad. Dad chugged one, then poured the sangria for Corpse. The carafe's orange slices and grapes kept the same relative position though their container tilted. Dad's eyes, a slanting glint, clashed against the carafe's glass. A discord that creeped me out. It was too crowded down there anyway, so I rose to the smoke-clogged ceiling.

The last time we'd drunk alcohol, we'd tried to kill ourself.

As Dad watched, Corpse blushed and took a sip. It was fizzy and sweet and fruity. The lights dimmed and the guitars sounded. Dad turned toward the music. One of the men stepped forward, put his hand on his stomach, and sang a word that sank to the floor. His words stayed low. Then they rose to bench height and filled with such longing and honesty they yanked up goose bumps on Corpse's arms though the room was steamy.

She couldn't take her eyes off that singer, wondered what he'd been through, because sadness poured out his mouth. His voice turned high and shot to the ceiling with grief. Corpse hunched forward to shield her listening heart. Dad looked at her with glassy eyes.

This was nothing like she'd planned. This music was like a conversation with every wrong thing she'd ever done. She'd thought they'd appreciate fado like looking at a painting, not be thrown into its spin cycle. She gulped sangria to handle it.

In the third song, Corpse poured another glass. The second guy joined in a call-and-response that made her skin crawl. She fingered the two hearts on her necklace and squinted up at me.

At the break, Dad ordered two more glasses of amber liquid, and during the next set his body began to sag, sagged more with each song. At the next break, he put his arm around Corpse, mouth near her ear.

"I thought I'd made a new start." His words, spilled against her cheek, made her flinch. "I guess I'm just no good at family. I wanted things to be so much better for you than they were for me." Eyes like melted chocolate, he shuddered, reminding me of the hospital, except this time it was like a goodbye. Then Dad gazed ahead, toward the bar, ghosts all over his face.

Corpse and I saw, at exactly the same moment, that forcing Dad to come to fado, to his people, to Lisbon at all, was destroying him. She covered her mouth, rocked to keep from cracking, and watched him. Dad, yet not Dad. She tugged his sleeve. "Let's go."

He just stared ahead, jaw slack. She tugged harder. He turned his head slowly and looked at her from a vast distance. She felt that if she moved, his eyes would skid off her to the wall.

"Dad, I'm tired."

Her words registered in his face. He wobbled to his feet and lunged through the door.

Even though it was almost midnight, people still milled around outside. Two guys gawked at Dad and stepped back. His wide-eyed gaze seemed to behold things no one else saw.

Corpse sensed touching him wasn't safe. She kept two-step's distance between them, even though he weaved on his feet.

They came to the restaurants they'd passed on the walk over, still brimming with diners. Dad didn't seem to notice. Back in the hotel room, he crumpled into his chair and conked out. Corpse watched him for a long time. When she finally lay down, her bed spun.

Late that night she woke to Dad whimpering. It was louder than when she'd heard it in the observatory. She sat up and watched his head lash side-to-side.

On the bedside table lay our journal. Corpse pulled her feather from it and drew her knees to her chest. She fingered her heart necklace as I blanketed her shoulders and tried to emit the good determination Gabe had left in me.

"Courage," she whispered.

She'd never be able to wake in time to greet the sun. It would be awkward with Dad there anyway, so she opened her journal and found this page:

*You're a good person. You're going to be okay.*

*—Dr. Yazzie's rock*

# Thirty-Two

"Dad," Corpse said, "honestly. We don't need to do this."

He kept striding across Rossio Square, through its border of scraggy trees, across the busy street, and past two shoe-shine boys. Corpse hustled along at his elbow. Dad's chinos and short-sleeved Oxford shirt were a lot like what other men wore, yet the fineness and cut of Dad's clothes oozed wealth. He ignored street traders holding out sunglasses and a woman selling cherries and peaches from a cart. The woman stood below a red umbrella that blocked the late-morning sun.

That sun felt wrong. Like it was shining in the night. Which it was, in Crystal Village. Corpse rubbed her pulsing forehead and tried to look past the outstretched male hand of a beggar. Dark crescents hung beneath Dad's eyes. Like he'd gone a few rounds with Tanesha. Corpse knew he'd slept more than she had, though, because she'd watched him till dawn. His sharp edges had returned, and that, at least, was comforting.

"Dad," she said, "Listen, I was wrong. Let's just go to the beach, or sightseeing or something."

Dad shook his head.

Corpse wanted to reach out, take his arm, make him stop. But he seemed on the margins of sanity. What damage had we done, making him come here?

Dad turned right and stopped. His mouth sagged open, cocked a little left. He stared at a church.

Like most of the buildings in Lisbon, this church was part of a block-long structure. Its front was Roman columns and regal doors. Somewhere back in history, other buildings had been built right against it. On the ground level next door was a shoe store.

"Did you used to go to that church?" Corpse's words seemed to skitter on ice.

Dad took a few zombie steps. He craned up at the iron cross atop the church's white front. Corpse studied his rigid shoulders. His phone rang.

"Aren't you going to answer your phone?" she said.

He walked past the church, not even looking at it now, and started up a steep road. Toward the castle. The sidewalk's cobbles had been worn to a sheen, and Corpse's flip-flops slipped a bit with each step. A breeze lifted her skirt. She gathered it into a knot in her hand.

Laundry snapped above them. They passed narrow streets, narrower walkways.

After fifteen minutes Dad stopped at a door the color of twilight. On it was a knocker: a blue-painted fist holding a big ring. Below, a mail slot read *Cartas* on its top edge. Dad ran his fingers over the fist's knuckles.

"Was this your house?" Corpse stepped back, shielded her eyes from the sun, and peered at two open second-story windows. Lemon yellow curtains billowed out. "Do you want to knock?"

Dad stepped back and looked up. "Our curtains were white." He seemed to be talking to himself. "Out back was a garden. An orange tree. I'd climb that tree. And escape."

His gaze fell on a red door on the right. He leaned toward it, peering. He straightened. He turned on his heel and strode off down the street. His phone rang. He didn't answer it.

Corpse stepped to that door. Beside it, a bronze plaque read *Antunes.* Her heart slammed against her chest. She jogged in careful steps to catch up with Dad.

He turned left into an alley marked with a wall plaque: *Beco da Rosas.* The alley traversed the hillside and came out on another narrow street. Dad stopped again, just as Corpse reached him, and she almost plowed into his back.

Ahead, three tables filled a spit of sidewalk where two rising streets met in a triangle like a ship's prow, the building filling it with a matching shape. Diners sat at two of the tables: a young couple at one, three reclining, smoking men at the other. Dad strode toward the restaurant like he was being reeled in. He pulled out a plastic chair at the empty table and sat down.

"Lunch?" The other chair screeched against the cobbles as Corpse pulled it back.

"This was my parents' restaurant." The flatness of Dad's words made her heart bang harder. He took it all in, nodding.

A waiter came out carrying a tray. Dad froze. The waiter set a plate of cheeses and rolls and two glasses of red wine on the table between the couple.

"You will like this port." The waiter's accent was thick, and he looked about Dad's age.

One side of Dad's mouth went up like he'd heard a joke.

The waiter turned to our table and set one menu in its center. "Olá."

"Two glasses of port. Any kind. Surprise us." Dad spoke in precise English.

Corpse wondered why he hadn't spoken Portuguese. I wondered why he kept buying her liquor.

The waiter left, and Dad took his phone from his breast pocket, eyed it, and put it back. His face seemed to unravel. "I'm going to wash my hands." He disappeared through the door at the apex of the restaurant's triangle.

Corpse read the menu and decided on halibut and potatoes. The waiter brought out two tumblers half-full of brownish liquid. She lifted the glass and sniffed. She hated wine, but this smelled sweet. She took a sip. Sweet, yes, but the alcohol stung her tongue. Maybe, she reasoned, alcohol anchored Dad in his adult self. She considered how crazy that sounded and banished it. It stuck with me though. Liquor might relieve the press of that inky yawn.

One building across the street had doorways and windows lined with yellow and green Moorish tiles. This part of the city had survived the earthquake, Dad said. Might those tiles date back to actual Moors? She peeked over her shoulder at the young couple. They held hands and half their cheese plate was gone. She took out her phone and texted Gabe: Miss you. She rubbed the two hearts on her necklace and remembered the sense of his calming arms. She rose and entered the restaurant.

Five tables: two on each side of the triangular room, and one in the middle. Diners sat at the tables on the sides. A kitchen filled the back. On the left was a door with the word *Banheiro* painted above. Corpse knocked on the door.

"Dad?"

The waiter glanced at her as he hurried past with two plates of fish. It took Dad a while to open the door. When he did, pout ruled his features, and she stepped back.

"Are you all right?" she said.

"Fine." He started back outside.

"I'm going to wash my hands."

In the bathroom, Corpse kept her elbows close to her sides to keep from hitting the walls. I squished next to a bare light bulb on the ceiling. What had Dad been doing in here?

When we returned to the table, he was holding his port

to the sun, eyeing it. The waiter showed up. Dad was careful not to look at him.

"Oona?" he said.

"The halibut."

"I'll have the *linguiça*."

I found it on the menu: sausage. He'd seemed to purposely stumble over the word.

The waiter nodded, took the menu. Dad watched him walk through the door. His eyes shot to the cobbles at our feet.

"The hours I spent scrubbing this sidewalk," he said. "This sidewalk and that bathroom."

"At least that bathroom's little," Corpse said.

"So was I!"

Dad's words were so sharp, she leaned back in her chair.

Over his shoulder, from up the street, came a stout woman with swaying steps that reminded Corpse of Sugeidi. The woman's hair was grayer, though, and chin-length, but pushed back as if by a hand accompanying years of sighs. She had on a black dress and a pink smock with white polka dots and two front pockets.

An apron, Corpse decided. Was this the uniform of the Portuguese maid? Longing for Sugeidi filled Corpse. The woman wore a permanent smile that dimpled her cheeks and flashed a yellow front tooth. Each hand carried a laden bag that moved up on each side as she stepped. Like scales in the balance. She walked straight toward Corpse, looking at her all the while.

She said something ending in *bonita* as she passed.

Corpse smiled, recognizing "pretty," and watched the woman enter the restaurant. When she turned back, Dad was standing, eyes on the door. He yanked out his wallet, set fifty euro on the table, and bolted down the street.

"But—" Corpse said.

He didn't even look back.

Corpse stood and peered into the restaurant. The old woman lifted rolls from her bags and set them on the counter of the kitchen. A cook clunked a plate of halibut on the counter next to the rolls. Corpse's stomach grumbled. She considered sitting right back down. I seconded that, but she took off after Dad, forgetting the cobbles' slickness and practically killing herself on the first sloping step.

At the bottom of the hill, Corpse still hadn't caught up with Dad. He took a ninety-degree right turn and marched into that church.

Corpse eyed the cracked pillars on either side of the door. I thought of the last church we'd been in, at Ash's memorial service. Crystal Village Community Church was built a year ago. We'd never actually been in a Catholic church. Hadn't even realized how, on family vacations in the past, Dad had avoided churches, even the famous ones.

Inside, people were scattered in pews down the immense, high-ceilinged space. Many kneeled, heads bowed, clasped hands resting on the backs of the wooden pews before them. The front of the church was painted blood red, and there were statues in a gothic Biblical scene. Down the middle and side aisles, tourists strolled, whispered, and took photos. Near the front branched perpendicular areas, also filled with pews. I rose halfway to the ceiling and saw that the inside was shaped like a big cross. Tourists milled around and took pictures of whatever was at the end of each arm.

I drifted up, up, toward that ceiling, but the higher I went, the closer the air became. It felt crowded, though I couldn't see anything. I shot down to Corpse.

She'd found Dad.

He kneeled in the sixth pew from the back, forehead pressed against his clasped hands, his body shaking. When she touched his shoulder, he looked up with flinching eyes. His sagging face was a labyrinth of tears.

"Dad?"

Something seeped from between his brow and chin that did not belong in a church. His phone rang. He put his forehead back on his hands and shuddered.

Corpse retreated three steps. The church smelled faintly of smoke. And ruin. She felt she was choking. We fled to the sun.

Tilting her face to its rays, she held out her open palms. I was right there with her.

# Thirty-Three

FROM OONA'S JOURNAL:

*I breathe water, smell water, hear water, walk with its
rushing companionship. My body: a sea. Water the key.*

—Oona

"Dad?" Corpse rubbed her eyes and squinted into the shaft-
ing sunlight. It felt like the middle of the night again. She
knew that wasn't true, though, because last night, she'd seen
the digital clock announce 12:00, 1:00, 2:00, and finally 3:00.
She'd pretended to sleep but watched Dad as he sat in his
chair and stared out the window, that eerie expression ruling
his face.

Corpse threw back the covers and walked to the bathroom. "Dad?" She opened the balcony door and stepped
into morning. At eight o'clock, Rossio Square was already
bustling. She didn't see Dad anywhere below, so she washed
her face and tugged on shorts and a blouse, scuffed on her
flip-flops.

Dad wasn't in the hotel restaurant either. Corpse returned to the room, cursing herself. Yesterday afternoon, we'd been scared enough to consider getting a room of our own. Yet we'd been afraid of what Dad might do to himself, so we'd stayed. Now he'd snuck off, right under our nose. Who knew what he might be doing? Corpse realized her phone was still off from the night. She turned it on and texted him: Where r u?

It beeped with a new text.

"Yes," she said. But it was Gabe: Third in the tourney. Love u. Sent two hours earlier. Before he'd gone to bed, probably. Now that he was home and didn't need to focus on soccer, she wanted to spill her guts to him the way she had to Mom last night, but he'd flip out.

As she'd told Mom about their day and Dad's steady decline, Mom had turned quieter and quieter. "Oona, be careful," she'd said and hung up. Now Corpse found another text that must have arrived in the night. Mom: I'm in Newark. B there soon. It was followed by a text from Carol, our pilot: How r things? Carol's text sounded casual, but Mom must have called her, because Carol would never have our phone number.

I suddenly felt sorry for Dad, for the humiliation of this situation we'd caused. Corpse texted Carol: Fine.

Though she was standing, Corpse rocked back and forth, rubbing her thumbs over the phone. Our world seemed about to implode. I thought of Sugeidi. Mom would have told her everything. Sugeidi would be sick with worry. Corpse lunged onto the bed, sat cross-legged, started to dial home. I realized it was one thirty in the morning there. Sugeidi would still be at her son's trailer, lying awake with concern. Corpse buried her face in her hands.

All those texts from Ash. If we'd just answered them, would Ash be alive today? We couldn't let Dad do anything stupid. Corpse remembered him saying, *I love you. Okay?* He'd been the first—not her, not Mom—to say it. We wished she could call Sugeidi. Sugeidi would know what to do.

Yesterday's old woman rose in Corpse's memory. I remembered how the woman appeared from Beco da Rosas, the alley Corpse and Dad had walked down after leaving his house. I remembered the unanswered ring of his phone. I thought how Dad had freaked when he saw the woman. Suddenly, we knew where he was.

At the shiny desk, Corpse found a little pad of paper. On it, in case she was wrong, she wrote *Gone for a walk*. She tore off the note and set it on the table next to Dad's chair.

————

Corpse stared at the twilight door with the blue-fist knocker. She ran her fingers over its knuckles. What had gone on behind this door? What had Dad hidden for so long?

She marched to the neighboring door, the red one, and traced the letters on the bronze plaque beside it. *Antunes*. She tried to sense family.

On the door's left edge were three different locks and a gold handle like from a kitchen drawer. In the top half, a raised rectangle framed a curtained window. A click sounded from inside, and the window swung inward. Corpse flinched back. So did yesterday's old woman, hand over her heart like Sugeidi.

"I'm sorry," Corpse said. "Do you speak English?"

The woman seemed to recognize her. "A little." Her voice moved slowly.

"Is your name Antunes?"

"Yes," she said suspiciously.

"Are you the aunt of Tony Antunes?"

The woman peered at her.

"He is my father."

The woman's hand flew to her heart, and she said something ending with a word sounding like *dios*. I realized she'd said "Dear God!" The woman's eyes shot left, then right. "He is here?"

She said "is" so like Sugeidi it almost made Corpse cry. She took a deep breath. "He's not with you?"

"No!"

Their eyes had a conversation:

The woman: You're afraid.

Corpse: Yes!

Corpse smelled baking bread. "Can you tell me about him?" she said slowly.

The old woman wore the same black dress with the pink apron. As she leaned on the window's opening, the skin of her thick arms folded over the edge like fabric. On her left hand glinted a silver wedding band. That hand reached out and rubbed a lock of Oona's hair between two fingers.

She smiled and said something ending in *bonita*. She stepped back, closed the window, and opened the door. "Come." She gestured inside.

---

A plate with a roll, hot from the oven, and some cherries sat before Corpse on the square white table in Dad's aunt's kitchen. It was a spare kitchen, without even a microwave, and dazzlingly clean, but I could tell it produced tons of food. Corpse wondered what this woman would think of Chateau Antunes's kitchen.

Out a back window, an orange tree spilled over the fence from the yard next door. I tried to picture the kid-Dad in its top branches, peering down, but I kept seeing his grown self there, in his Oxford shirt and chinos. Corpse inhaled the yeasty air. Dad's aunt. His people. His home.

The woman sat down across from Corpse and smiled. "You resemble he."

Corpse nodded.

"You have brother? Sister?"

Corpse shook her head.

"You live in America?"

"Crystal Village, Colorado."

"Ah, Colorado." She said a word sounding like *montañas*.

"Mountains, yes. It's very pretty." Corpse tasted home-sickness for Crystal Village's ridgelines, its rushing creek, its pines and aspens. She longed to plant her butt on that suicide rock and let it anchor her world.

Instead she felt Dad's shallow breaths as she'd sat with all her weight on his belly, forcing him to return home. *I love you. Okay?* She took a bite of the roll. It was airy and delicious. A fat silence settled on the table. Corpse chewed, touched her heart necklace, and gathered courage.

"Dad's family. What happened?" she finally said, flicking a bread crumb from her shorts.

The woman's eyes snagged on Corpse's missing fingers.

"It's nothing." Corpse dropped that hand to her lap.

*Nothing?* I couldn't believe she'd said that. Yet it was true. *No-thing. No-where. No* words meant everything lately.

The woman put her palms on the table and studied the backs of her own age-spotted hands. "You no know?"

Corpse straightened.

The woman looked at Corpse through a face hung with such sadness that Corpse turned shivery.

"Ah," the woman said, like a thing had been confirmed. "My brother, he die. His wife, she die. And his son."

Through numb lips, Corpse said, "Son? But Dad lived."

"No. What word ... he ... Ana."

"Dad had a sister? A sister?"

The woman's head tilted. "He no tell?"

*No tell. No know.*

The woman eyed Corpse. "You have trouble?"

"What happened to his family?"

The woman sat back and studied her lap. "We never ...

how you say?" She took a huge breath. "I know he kill them."

The woman's mouth moved, but Corpse strained to hear through the blood rushing in her ears. The woman struggled, gave up on English, and spilled words. I heard something like "*accidente de carro*." Corpse felt like she was drowning, but I heard "*cayu no mar*." Did that mean "no more?" Wait! *Mar* in Spanish meant "sea."

"I don't understand," Corpse said. "A car accident? Dad said they drowned."

The woman nodded, but as her mouth parted to speak again, our phone chimed with a text. Dad: At hotel. Rented a car.

Corpse stood so fast, her chair back clapped the floor behind her. She looked from our phone to the woman. "How did the crash happen?"

The woman pressed her lips. "I speak too much."

"Please."

She pressed her lips harder and shook her head.

"Please! I have to go now!"

Dad's aunt smiled, that dark tooth showing. "What is you name?"

Corpse blew out her breath. "Oona." She gathered herself. "What's your name?"

"Call me *Tia Célia*. You come again?"

Corpse forced herself to speak slowly. "What was Dad's family like?"

His aunt smiled sadly, and her eyes blurred with tears. "You resemble Ana. They call he *princesa*."

Corpse stepped back, bumping the wall. "They called Ana *princess*?"

Dad's aunt nodded.

Corpse realized her hand was pressing her heart and straightened. "I have to go. Dad's waiting." She spoke through numb lips.

From her red doorway, Tia Célia waved, and Corpse waved back. As soon as she'd walked down the hill, far enough that she was out of sight, Corpse paused and pulled up Google Translate on her phone. She typed in "cayu no mar."

It responded: *Did you mean caiu no mar?*

She clicked on that.

The translation read: *Fell into the sea.*

# Thirty-Four

FROM OONA'S JOURNAL:

*Because I could not stop for Death,*
*He kindly stopped for me;*
*The carriage held but just ourselves*
*And Immortality.*

—Emily Dickinson, "The Chariot," lines 1-4

"Where have you been?" Dad said.

The whole way down the hill from his aunt's home, Corpse had said, "Dad loves me. Dad loves me. Dad loves me." Tia Célia's words couldn't be true. But I'd felt that inky surge, and now the skewed way his mouth lined up with his eyes made sense.

Corpse worked to steady her voice. "Breakfast."

Dad studied her like he knew everything.

She swallowed, and it was loud in her ears. "You rented a car?"

"We're going to Cascais. To the beach. Pack your things."

Corpse saw his phone, resting atop her note on the table next to his chair. It looked turned off.

"The beach?" she said.

"Isn't that what you wanted?"

"Yes, but—"

"But what?"

"Is it far?" Mom would be so worried.

"Half an hour."

Corpse couldn't hold Dad's gaze. Its flicker terrified us. I thought how he'd meekly played LIFE with Corpse in his office, the way she'd talked to him that day. She'd been toying with fire. Now only his silhouette was familiar.

Corpse stepped back and focused on his outlines against the light streaming through the balcony doors. Our whole life we'd had only one arms-length day a week with him, and we'd resented it. But maybe his absence wasn't selfishness after all. Maybe he'd been protecting us. And Mom. Corpse almost choked on tears. What had we done? She turned to pack her things.

She put her bikini, sunscreen, Kindle, journal with Angel's feather, a pencil, and a hotel towel into a beach bag. Just three days ago, she'd set that bag in her suitcase so naively. Dad sat in his chair, nodding as he watched her every move.

She went into the bathroom, shut the door, and pulled her phone from her shorts pocket. Mom was still an hour from landing, but Corpse texted: Gone to Cascais. Dad rented car. She texted Gabe: Decided on Yale. Love you big. She needed to make that promise, to believe in the future. To give him at least that. Then I realized that attending

Yale actually was our decision, finally made at such a ridiculous time. A sad laugh bubbled out of Corpse. She rose and gazed at her reflection in the mirror over the sink.

She pressed her five-fingered hand over her heart and traced her reflection with her three-fingered one. "Courage," she whispered.

"Let's go, princess." Without seeing his face, she thought Dad's voice was a boy's. As Corpse stepped out of the bathroom, Dad moved to the door. His phone remained on her note.

———————

The hotel's valet pulled up in a midnight blue convertible, top down. Dad gave him two euro and climbed in behind the wheel. Our phone vibrated in our pocket. Mom, I was sure. But Corpse didn't dare take it out. She knew what it would say: Don't go! But we had to go. A third suicide would kill us: *DEAD GIRL MURDERS FATHER.*

"Well?" Dad said.

Corpse squinted to transform him to outlines. She tossed her bag in the backseat and climbed into the passenger one. Dad turned onto a street heading toward the river, the convertible's tires thunking along the cobbles. Traffic clogged the road, and they stopped three times. Corpse had to force herself not to bolt to the sidewalk.

Finally he turned onto the busy asphalt road that ribboned along the Tagus. As the wind whipped back her hair, she took in the wide river dotted with sailboats, and

I thought how Dad drove the direction the water flowed. Corpse saw many fishing boats in docks. Across the river, container ships.

Dad took it all in with flinching eyes. He chuckled at a docked cruise ship. "How things change."

They came to a humongous concrete monument on the river's bank. It resembled the prow of a ship, with statues of people dressed like Christopher Columbus standing along its edges. Across from it, on the road's other side, were beautiful gardens and what looked like a huge church. They drove past a castle tower in the river. To enter it would be to stroll through hundreds of years. After all the happiness and tragedy its stones must have witnessed, our life was just a blip on its timeline.

Corpse studied Dad's white knuckles on the steering wheel. I thought of the blood pumping through them. Mom's hands had gripped her Range Rover steering wheel like that, snow all around us as surface tension corralled her tears.

Corpse blinked back the vision of Dad in that church. She sprayed out her hand on her shorts and studied her missing fingers, then her toes. Had her blood felt these digits' absence? Had it panicked when her freezing heart stopped? Dad glanced at her with flickering eyes. She found her reflection in the side mirror.

They drove beyond Lisbon into Portugal's version of suburbs. White walls mostly. Red roofs, but more spread out. A beach lined with green umbrellas appeared on their left and the Tagus's banks scrolled back, away from each other.

Now the water was constant on that side. Corpse peered across it and thought how the fresh water must bash the salty waves. I considered their churning battle, how neither could ever win.

Dad exited the road. He negotiated a roundabout, drove toward the sea, and there was another Moorish castle on a promontory. He steered onto a side street and parallel parked. Corpse finger-combed her hair. Maybe they really were just going to the beach.

———————

What had we been thinking? That in thirty minutes the climate would evolve to the tropics? It was only 60 degrees. Of course she wasn't putting on a bikini, even though the sky was cloudless. The beach was coarse golden sand. The water beyond, steely blue. This was the Atlantic, not the Caribbean. Dad must have known this as he'd watched her pack. It seemed a cruelty.

Corpse walked barefoot down the hundred yards to where gentle waves rolled up the shore. She dipped her toe in the icy water. She turned.

Dad leaned, arms and legs crossed, against the rock retaining wall below the cobbled sidewalk. Above him, cars and busses flowed past and people moved along, some strolling, some striding. An impressive six-story hotel stood at the street's far side.

From here, tall as her thumb, Dad seemed normal. A businessman in a yellow shirt and chinos. Maybe the hotel's manager, contemplating a problem over his lunch hour. Corpse sighed. Yet as she got closer, his body's rigidity indicated it would have had to be a really bad problem.

She reached Dad, saw him looking intently at things on the beach. She looked where he looked. Nothing was there. She looked back at him, and he seemed an exile from even the air.

She could bolt up the stairs leading to this beach, hop on a train to Lisbon, find Mom, and be safe. I pictured her settling into the train seat, leaning her head against the window as it pulled from the station. And then what? What might Dad do to himself?

Seagulls took to squawking flight and hovered above. *Birds do not fly, they are flown.* Did the air really fly them? Corpse took a long sip of air, realized she now stood where he'd gazed all those years ago from that Bahamas beach.

"Remember when I was nine, and we were on that beach in the Bahamas?" She braced for his biting response.

Nothing.

"You told me how the sky was like one big ocean? How the air moved in waves that transferred the sun's energy to the oceans? How that energy ended on beaches in waves? Remember?"

Nothing.

"Dad, what's going on? We didn't come here to swim."

He blinked. "We had a picnic here."

"We?"

"We drove Tia Célia's truck. It was so loud, and the gears scraped every time Pai shifted. He was a pathetic driver. *Dom,* Mãe called him. *Dom?* He was no king. Mãe spread a worn blanket on that sand. My life was a prison of worn things. I refused to sit on it. My old pants, cut off at the knees, infuriated me." His hands formed fists.

"The water was frigid, even in July. I refused to swim. Mãe, Pai, and Ana splashed and laughed. Mãe laid out cod sandwiches on rolls, the same old sandwiches from our restaurant where I worked every single day, even after school. Couldn't she have brought something different on this rare day? I wanted to spit at her, at Pai, at the patheticness of it all. Ana watched me. Sweet Ana, always adoring. She took my hand and said, 'Smile, Tony.'"

Dad wiped his right hand on his pants without seeming to notice, and Corpse's mouth went dry.

"She was always saying that. I turned, and there was that hotel: so grand and elegant. I wanted to escape with her there, order lunch. Just another thing I could only dream of. Portuguese families have a way of trapping you. Did you know? Forever. I looked from that hotel to my parents and realized I'd never, ever, be free."

Corpse felt the rock wall at her back. Finally, the truth was pouring out.

Dad barked a laugh. "I never did get free of them." He looked at her with those puddle eyes.

Corpse reached out and took his hand. "Dad? Everything's okay."

His head cocked right as if she'd slapped him. He pulled his hand loose and wiped it on his chinos. He nodded for a minute and rolled his head to crack his neck. He stared at that beach and said, "I'm going to drive up the coast. I'll be back in an hour."

"I'm going with you." Corpse scuffed on her flip-flops.

He wouldn't look at her. "Stay here!"

"No!"

"Go to that hotel." He gestured behind us with his chin and chuckled. "Use your credit card. Book a room so you can lounge by the pool. Spend *a lot* of money."

"No!"

———————

"Maybe I should drive. You could enjoy the scenery," Corpse said as they approached the convertible.

"Stay here!" Dad climbed in.

Corpse strapped on her seat belt, listening for the buckle's click. She hugged her beach bag in her lap.

"Oona, stay!" He would not look at her.

"So this would have been where the tidal wave started up the river?" she said.

His chin dropped.

"Dad, what's going on?"

He slumped. Didn't move. Finally, he nodded in that unknowing way. He whimpered. Corpse reached toward his hand on his thigh, but stopped. He straightened, cracked his neck, and rubbed it like it ached.

"Dad?"

He looked directly at Corpse. A stranger. He started the convertible, pulled out, and turned onto the main road.

Two lanes. The road curved along the coast, past the town, that castle, and a botanical park. He drove out of Cascais proper, along neighborhoods stretching up a gradual hill. On the left, the steely sea rolled against volcanic cliffs.

Corpse was thankful for the traffic. Other cars might keep them safe. Tourists strolled or rode bikes along a paved path between the road and the cliffs. Dad cracked his neck again.

He started spewing Portuguese. I couldn't get his meaning, but I heard *Pai* and *Mãe*. And *Ana*. His voice turned high and trailed off. And then he said, "*Princesa.*" He shuddered. His eyes darted all over, but they didn't seem to see Corpse. I pressed against her, felt her terror as she realized that the flicker in his eyes was suffocating grief.

"Dad?" Corpse said. "You're grown up now. You're rich. You have me."

Nothing.

"Tell me. What happened?"

Nothing.

"Dad, remember your promise? Things would be different?"

His face softened. "*Promesa.*"

"Yes! Yes! Remember? You love me!"

He gazed down the road. "Love." He moaned like a hurt animal. Then he pointed with his chin. "Just up there, I yelled, 'I hate you! I wish you were dead!' I hit Pai."

Dad lifted his right hand and studied its palm. "Pai's eyes seemed to bleed when he looked at me. Those words killed him. And then we were flying." Dad's body sagged. "I killed them all!"

"No! No, you didn't! I was the same way with you and Mom. We all make mistakes!"

He shook his head. "I'm evil."

A strange pile of lava rock on the roadside snagged his eye. His head swiveled, watched till he was looking over his shoulder, and the car swerved. His head snapped back. He straightened and flung Corpse a grin. "*Princesa.*" A single tear, pushed by the wind, traversed his temple.

Corpse could not look away from that tear. It disappeared into his hair. She knew that expression ruling his face. He was no longer in the same place as her.

Dad floored the gas. Corpse was flung against the seat. They approached a curve, and I sensed what he was planning. Corpse unbuckled her seat belt.

"Dad, don't! Please! Don't!"

He jerked the steering wheel left. She lunged and grabbed it. A woman screamed, an arm's length away, as the convertible zoomed across the recreation path.

It soared across air. Flew far out over the sea. *Flown.* Corpse noticed that a crescent moon and the sun inhabited opposite horizons. She seemed halfway to heaven.

The convertible dove, tossing Corpse above it. She floated for an instant, watching the car plummet, and remembered those gossamer fruit fly wings. She became mass, and gravity grabbed her. The air's velocity pressed her skin.

"Dad!" she screamed. But he stared ahead as the convertible's nose hit the water and his hands steered toward its depths. *Caiu no mar.* Dad was driving to his people. Reunion after all.

Corpse's fingertips touched the surface. Her body splashed, and she remembered that video's drop of water: coalescence cascade. Then bone-numbing wet erased thought. Darkness consumed her.

———————

Arms out, palms up, hair fanned, she undulated on waves. She looked like she did sleeping on that suicide rock in that silly crown. Fifty yards away, Dad surfaced on a circle of steam and bubbles. Limp, eyes closed. His forehead pink shreds. Drowsiness seeped through me.

*Wake up!* I yelled. *Wake up! You'll die!*

Corpse was two hundred yards from the lava rocks lining the cliff's base.

*Wake up!*

She slept.

Could I survive if she died? Alone? A ghost? And Dad. He could be alive.

As Corpse rocked on the waves' rise and fall, she resembled a mermaid offering. One foot had lost its flip-flop. I slunk close and tried to hear her breaths. Heard instead the frothy water churning Dad.

She'd taught me that touching was more than skin. I now liked touching people. Even loving them. I even loved her.

And then there it was. The answer. The key: me. I was

what drove us to suicide. I was the bullshit. Not Ash. Not Mom. Not Dad. Me. Reasoning, doubting, judging me.

I longed to evaporate. To rise to the clouds. Become indiscernible, even to myself. But then Corpse would die. Dad too. I had to wake her. To return. But not to exist as two selves. I wished for one Oona, only. Now or never. I funneled between her parted lips.

Her cough rolled me through her echo-y body. Her eyes shot open. My world grew confined to her vision. She remembered cold's deadliness.

"No!" she said.

I coursed into her limbs as she rolled onto her belly. Ahead, waves foamed over the black rocks at the cliff's base. She swam toward shore.

*Dad!* I yelled.

She paused, turned, and trod water hard so she bobbed up and saw the yellow and tan blur of his body. She swam toward him, furiously at first, but the current wore her out. He was inching toward her, but it was so cold.

She started again, ignoring her numb fingers. She neared him and tasted his blood on the water. She shook him. He didn't wake. She tried to shout, but her numb lips wouldn't form words. A distant siren wailed.

*Hurry!* I said, weak with dilution.

She wrapped her arm across his chest, his head lolled back against her shoulder, and she swam with one arm, kicking hard. Her strokes turned clumsy. Sleep was like a drug, but she forced it back and found efficiency if she floated right at the water's surface.

*Fish do not swim, they are swum.* Sugeidi's image, hand over her heart, rose before Corpse. She sobbed, but found strength. She listened to her heart, blew out stronger breaths to its rhythm.

She neared the rocks, but could not feel her body. Her eyelids weighed a thousand pounds. She lay her cheek on the water.

*Swim!* I shouted.

She closed her eyes.

*DEAD GIRL DROWNS!*

She started a dim crawl, kept it up. Lava rock rose beneath her, ripping her numb skin. The waves rolled them, like driftwood, till they flopped on their backs.

Shouts fell from the cliff top. Corpse squinted at their tiny figures. Within her, our confluence. No feeling now. No pain. She groped for Dad's hand. Gripped it.

A thwapping consumed the air. A shadow passed across her. A rectangular silhouette lowered down. It got close and became an orange stretcher with a man astride, dangling from a cable to a helicopter. Just as he knelt beside us, Dad squeezed her hand.

"Dad!" she croaked through wet hair wrapping her face.

"*Pai?*" the man said.

She barely nodded.

Like a comet across that sleepy veil, I realize *this* had been our life's map. Now, dwindling, our entire journey has played out before me. That suicide, one swaying step. *We* and *she* become *I*.

# Epilogue

FROM OONA'S JOURNAL:

*The majority believes that everything hard to comprehend must be very profound. This is incorrect. What is hard to understand is what is immature, unclear and often false. The highest wisdom is simple and passes through the brain directly to the heart.*

—Viktor Schauberger

What do you suppose evil is? Does it exist? Or is it just the way some people juggle terror, or guilt? I've thought about that a lot since Portugal. Especially when Ash's ghost whispers *User.*

I have to believe Dad was trying to kill only himself. No doubt I pushed him there. I've also thought a lot about love. How before we can expect it from others, we have to be willing to give it to ourselves. We are all so fragile. Such precarious concoctions.

One thing's for sure: the ability to live when our spirits are dead runs in both Dad's and my veins. He stayed in

Portugal to heal, Tia Célia nursing him. He had broken limbs, a broken heart, all resistance gone. Yet he'd held my gaze with a new, ragged hope. I'll visit him this summer, but I miss him with an ache cradled in that suffering voice of Amália. I have a word for it: *saudade*. *Saudade* is about enduring.

Dad's absence yawns at Mom, Sugeidi, and me. Even after moving into this condo. A *For Sale* sign stands in front of Chateau Antunes now. It's a hard property to sell. No local wants a house so laden with tragedy. A rich tourist will probably own it someday.

Sugeidi, after being so busy during and after the move, mills about now. "You no need me," she said one day.

"We'll always need you, Sugeidi," Mom said through a sad smile. "You're part of our family." Her eyes shot to mine, because our family's new definition includes divorce.

"Besides," I said, taking a huge breath, "Mom needs someone to keep track of her next year, with me gone and her starting college herself. Someone has to make sure she does her homework."

Sugeidi still wears that maid dress. I've come to love it. Today, though, she wears a belted dress the color of sky. I don't have the heart to tell her it's the exact color I soared through in that convertible.

Mom wears a clingy designer dress, but she hasn't gotten the pearl buttons near the top right. "Here," I say, and I fix them for her.

I step back. Her eyes travel over my lavender dress, the shiny new scars on my arms and shins. She studies my face, swathed and saved by all that hair. She smiles and shakes her head.

"Survivors," she says.

We three look at each other, Dad in our gaze.

"Let's survive our way to graduation," Mom says. She grabs her purse, and Sugeidi grabs her purse, and we head out the condo's front door.

Graduation is at the town's amphitheater, so we walk. This late-May afternoon whispers summer. We follow the bike path Gabe and I first strolled along, tentatively holding hands, almost exactly a year ago. Crystal Creek churns with runoff. Always when I look at rivers now, I see the Tagus, and they all seem the linked veins of one omniscient body.

We don't walk fast. They know I'm dreading all those eyes. When we turn off the bike path, I look down it and wish I could escape with Gabe to our spot beneath the spruce.

Our car crash made the newspaper: *DEAD GIRL SURVIVES AGAIN*. Flowers from Dad's financial world laced Chateau Antunes with a melancholy perfume that suspended that crash in present tense. I tried to imagine those suited, groomed strangers, wondering if any of them really knew one another. All the while, Crystal Village's eyes watched me. I'm looking forward to Yale. I'll be anonymous there. Just a girl with four missing digits and a constellation of scars. No, not a girl. A woman.

The river is so loud, I can't hear the music in the amphitheater till we enter its gates. Gabe and his father stand just inside, each holding a program. Gabe holds out my cap and gown. Mr. Handler has arranged for my late arrival. Like I said, he's smart as a fox. I can feel Mom and Gabe's dad looking at each other, then working not to look at each other.

Mom admitted that while I was in Portugal, it was Mr. Hernandez she'd dined with. After what happened to Dad, they haven't gone out again, but I hear Mom talking with Gabe's dad on the phone sometimes. Her voice sounds younger, lighter, brighter, when he's on the line. It makes me miss Dad so much I choke. Standing between these two, here, feels like standing between the north and the south halves of a magnet.

Gabe and I glance at each other and he raises his eyebrows. I kid Gabe that maybe Hernandez men love twice, yet we've talked about how our parents seemed destined for each other. We've decided this attraction's in our genes, but still, it's weird.

Sugeidi turns me to her. She hands Mom her purse, takes bobby pins from her breast pocket, and secures my mortar board. She straightens its gold tassel and pulls a lock of my hair forward over each shoulder. She kisses my forehead. "*Querida*."

My eyes brim, and I'm thankful for surface tension. *Querida*. That's what Tia Célia called me in that Lisbon hospital. She has my address. She said she'll write.

Gabe takes my hand and we walk behind the stage to where the other 113 seniors are milling around. Brandy, with Tanesha gone, only frowns at us.

We find our alphabetical places in line, me near the front, like always. The processional starts and we file onto the stage. I follow Todd Adams, Brian Alonzo, and Norma Alvarez down the aisle between two banks of chairs to the far side of the first row on our right. Following me is Nick Bowlton, who's suffered a crush on me since second grade. Not anymore.

I sit and look up at the audience, half in the sheltered seating, the rest on blankets patchworking the bowled lawn. I picture the worn blanket Dad hated so much, see him refusing to sit down, and I blink.

I do the math and figure that easily eight hundred eyes are on me. I take a long sip of air and find Mom, Sugeidi, and Mr. Hernandez in the seats halfway back. Mom and Sugeidi dab their eyes with tissues. I have to look away but mentally thank Mom again for telling her bullying parents not to come. It's the first time she's ever stood up to them.

My eyes meet Norma Alvarez's beside me. She's one of the immigrant girls I passed each morning on the entry steps. When she smiles, I smile back. She waves to a man and woman on the lawn. They sit amid maybe forty friends and family. On the woman's lap is a little girl in a frilly white dress.

I notice the police officers who entered Dr. Bell's office after Tanesha attacked me. They stand, uniformed, to the side on the wide sidewalk between the seats and the lawn. Today must be a reprieve from deportations.

Dr. Bell strolls down the aisle between our rows to a podium at the front. He lowers the microphone, mugging a face, and the audience laughs. "Welcome," he says, "to the graduation of the class of 2014."

Whoops rise behind me. I turn, knowing from rehearsal where to find Gabe. His grin is so big and his eyes shine so brightly, I can't help but grin back. I hold that image, spread my hand on my black-robed thigh, and study my missing fingers.

Dr. Bell's words are murky from where we sit behind him. The audience bursts into applause, and a woman I recognize as the famous ski racer giving the address to our class steps to the podium. I try to hear her words too, but they slip from my grasp. My mind has such a hard time focusing on anything lately. I couldn't take my AP exams, barely made it through the rest of the school year. Mr. Handler says that's normal. That I'll heal.

My brow sears from the eight hundred eyes. They see my suicide. They see Ash's and deem me responsible. That verdict spreads to Dad's crash. Even Tanesha dropping out seems my fault. Their judgment is like a downpour that drenches every part of me.

I search for Ash's parents but don't find them, realize they have no child. No reason to be here. I wonder what they're doing at this moment to keep from breaking down. My parents came so close to just that. I hunch forward in shame. The ski racer stops talking, and applause rises like the waves on those Portuguese rocks that cut me like glass.

Clark steps to the podium. He's valedictorian, and I'm glad. "Thanks for pulling out of the race," he said on the last day of Bio, but his closest competition had turned out to be Tony Rodriguez, who moved through each day in such silence that people forgot he was there. Clark's going to CU, like Mom, and plans to study astrophysics. His voice soothes me, and I straighten. The audience laughs once, twice, three times. I smile for Clark and wish I could understand his words.

Two students approach the podium next and introduce Mr. Bonstuber as Teacher of the Year. He wears a navy blazer that flaps out from his narrow frame as he approaches them. "I'm not sure if this is an honor or a curse," he says. His German accent fills the amphitheater. "Though I speak in front of your children every day, public speaking is my greatest terror." The audience laughs politely.

What is a person's greatest terror when they've twice shaken hands with death? I look out furtively and realize, for me, it's always been the same. Having no home. No people to make me strong.

My eyes travel to Mom and Sugeidi. I sigh. Perhaps they are enough. There's Gabe too. And now I have Tia Célia. I say a prayer for Dad. Mom gives a little wave, leans to the side with a sly smile, and there, in the row behind her, are Angel and William.

William wears that short-sleeved Oxford shirt and tie. Angel waves, and her face transforms in that way I love as she smiles. We've texted, but I didn't expect this. I find Mr. Handler at the end of the row behind me. He gives a thumbs-up to Angel and William. William chuckles, his whole body shaking.

Dr. Bell is at the podium again. "Todd Adams," he says. Todd, at the end of my row, walks to the podium, and there's polite applause as Dr. Bell hands him his diploma. I remember sitting next to Todd in kindergarten, how he'd hold his pencil all wrong and Ms. Miller would correct him. His face would look pulled tight with a string. I've hardly talked to Todd since, yet I hold this intimate scrap of his history.

"Brian Alonzo," Dr. Bell says. Brian plays soccer with Gabe, but that's all I know about him. A rowdy contingent, spilling off one of the closest blankets, hoots and whistles. A stout, gray-haired woman, his grandma probably, pumps her fist.

"Norma Alvarez," Dr. Bell says, and her people applaud timidly. The little girl in the white dress stands and yells, "Norma!" Norma looks embarrassed as she approaches the podium, wiping her cheeks.

Her empty chair beside me is a chasm. Those eight hundred eyes are eight hundred pounds pressing me down. My chest is tight. I glance back at Gabe, and he nods. My eyes skid over Manny in the same row, watching us.

"Oona Antunes," Dr. Bell says like a verdict. There's silence, and my legs will not lift me. Guilt's weight and all those eyes paralyze them. Though Crystal Creek shouts, this audience's silence roars in my ears.

Gabe appears, helping me stand. I take two wobbling steps. Applause takes over the amphitheater. Though I work against it, there's that bob in my step. Dr. Bell hands me my diploma, and the cheering grows louder, almost wild.

I look out and see all the people in the auditorium rising to their feet. I look from Gabe to Dr. Bell, who nods. I realize there's clapping behind me and see my fellow graduates standing. Even Manny. Even Brandy, though her claps are slow. The immigrant girls bawl. Mom bawls and Sugeidi glows. Angel and William wear amazed expressions. I see the doctor and nurse who I thanked. I see the two paramedics. I see the owl-eyed bus driver. All those cheers rise beyond a spiraling bird, and I hope Dad and Ash can hear. My eyes trace the valley's ridges, ending in its jagged line of peaks: my pulse. I hear the creek's rush join this cheering sea of people who know my history, and care.

"Home," I say, and though I cannot hear myself, my heart listens.

## End Note: Viktor Schauberger

Viktor Schauberger (1885–1958) was an Austrian forest warden, naturalist, philosopher, and inventor. Descended from a long line of foresters from the northern Alps, he was fascinated by creek and river flow and the patterns of nature. An eco-technology pioneer, Schauberger controversially asserted that humanity must study nature and learn from it rather than try to correct it, hoping to liberate people from dependence on centralized power resources that were inefficient or polluting. His theories contradicted established scientific theory, which he felt viewed nature as something to be exploited for the imagined benefit of humanity. He was often ridiculed, even after his theories were proved successful. Thanks to Gill & Macmillan Publishers for permission to quote from Callum Coats's *Living Energies*, the source of all Oona's journal entries in this novel attributed to Schauberger.

# Acknowledgments

Many hands helped shape this book. First, I must thank my princesses: Sue Staats, Loranne Brown, and Nancy Stebbins for always ensuring my words toe the line. Ditto to Rick Attig, especially for calling me on the realities of the male experience. Thanks to all the folks who helped me with details of culture, medicine, language, and law. Each day, I thank my writing family at Pacific University. Thanks to Bri Johnson for her fabulous insight and representation, and Brian Farrey-Latz and Sandy Sullivan at Flux for honing Oona's story into its final shape. Thanks to the Mr. Bonstubers, the Ms. Summers, and the Mr. Handlers of the world who dedicate so much time to teens. Most of all, thanks to Ross and Sydney for their patience and support on this long journey.

Katherine M. Schmidt

## About the Author

A Colorado native, Heather Sappenfield lives in Vail and is passionate about three things: her state, especially its mountains; science, physics in particular; and the ways people attain a sense of belonging in this mobile-techno world. She left a perfectly stable job as a high school English teacher to pursue a writing career. After earning an MFA from Pacific University, her fiction started getting published and winning awards. In her spare time, she can be found in Vail's back bowls, teaching people to ski in winter, or on her mountain bike in summer. She has mad love for trees.